THE VIRGIN PROVOKED

A MEDIEVAL MYSTERY

E A. RIVIÈRE

wordcarver
WC
books

Again for

*Lovely, laughing
Eleanor,*

honorable Henry,

and wise Chelsea.

All of you inspire me.

CHAPTER I.

*L**ittle sisters are more precious than rubies*, Bertwoin thought as he put on his big-brother smile and stepped into the shadow-filled bedroom.

Maud lay on a straw-filled mattress, her spidery legs and arms sticking out of her sweat-soaked undergarment. Though the room was chilly, her woolen blanket lay in a pile beside her bed with her tunic and cloak on top. The house kitty, Jolie, lay against her side, soaking heat from her feverish body.

"Am I going to die?" Maud asked, clutching her poppet as if it might save her.

Keeping his face impassive, Bertwoin waved away her concern. "It'll take more than a bellyache and a middling fever to carry you off to heaven, Little Bug."

She held her doll up for him to see. "Poppet is worried."

Poppet was nothing more than a wooden head with a cross for a body and a scrap of brown hemp for its tunic, but Maud treated it as if it was a living part of herself. Bertwoin felt a jolt in his stomach. Why had he never noticed before now that the crude eyes and down-turned mouth scratched on the doll's wooden face made Poppet look worried?

He squatted and felt Maud's forehead, which was damp and hot. Jolie opened her green eyes and pricked up her furry ears.

Bertwoin stepped over to the other bed in the room and sat down on its pine-straw mattress, making the bed's wooden frame creak. Maud still thought he, as her older brother, was wise and could answer all her questions. Not wanting to disappoint her and Poppet, he pretended to know all of the answers.

Maud coughed. The smell of burning wood from the kitchen's hearth fire wafted through the bedroom's doorway. Did the smoke bother her lungs? "You want me to open the shutter wider?"

"But what if I have leprosy?"

"Leprosy?" So that was foremost in her mind. A few days earlier, their Uncle Laurence had told them a story about two buffoonish lepers who begged for coins on the Toulouse Road.

Bertwoin leaned across the narrow space between the two beds and patted her bony shoulder. "Nah. You're not speckled with rash. And there's not a white patch anywhere on your skin."

"I itch sometimes."

"We all do that."

"I don't mean with lice," she whined. "This is a deep down itch. I got ants under my skin."

"Don't worry, Little Bug. Someday, you'll dance at my wedding, and you won't need a crutch." He tapped her nose with his forefinger. "And leprosy won't have rotted away your snout."

She stuck out her bottom lip. "How do *you* know I don't have it?"

"That's easy. I've seen neither front nor back of the leprosy imp."

"The what?" With a satisfied smile, Maud curled on her side, which disturbed Jolie, who peevishly resettled herself.

Maud cuddled her poppet and waited. A big-brother story was coming.

At least, he had distracted her. "Well, you've been good, right? You haven't been dipping into the honey jug when *maman's* back was turned, have you?"

"Does that make the imp come?" she asked, dodging his question.

"Ah-h," he said, waving away her childish thievery, "stealing a taste of honey isn't enough to catch the imp's attention."

"I gave the sow some bread when nobody was looking."

"That's okay. None of us went hungry because of it." He leaned forward and tapped the poppet's wooden head.

She pulled her doll away from him. "Don't hurt her."

He reared back as if shocked. "I wouldn't do that. I was just thanking the Lord for our not being hungry. If you weren't sick, I'd have tapped your noggin. It's the same as wood."

He held his hands up as if he had claws and growled, "So, the leprosy imp sneaks into bedrooms when the moon rules over the night and poisons naughty girls and boys with its rotting disease. But good girls like you have a halo around them that only the imp can see. Your halo will cause the imp to burst into flame if it comes too close."

"So all the people with leprosy are bad?"

Sometimes, little Maud was smarter than she needed to be. "It's more complicated than that. There are other reasons people get leprosy."

"Like what?"

"Well, God gives some people the disease to test them. Others get it on purpose so they can sacrifice themselves, like nuns who minister to lepers. Their helping the sick pleases God."

"But she's a Moor!" they heard their uncle shout in the kitchen beyond the bedroom door.

"She's a bit dark," their maman admitted, "but no one knows her ancestry, and what her parents were is no fault of hers. She was raised Christian, and she cured Maud's last sickness."

Bertwoin felt weary. Would his uncle never stop accusing Flowia of being a Saracen?

"If I'm bad, will it pour poison down my throat?"

"Down your throat? No. The leprosy imp sneaks into your bedroom while you're asleep and changes into a snake. Then guess what she does?"

Maud rolled over onto her back, again displeasing Jolie. "She? Imps aren't *girls*."

"Not all imps are boys."

"*Maman* says they are," Maud argued with the smug assurance of someone quoting the Bible.

"Clanoud," their uncle shouted in the kitchen, "Are you going to put Maud at the mercy of a heathen after what they did to you in the Holy Land?"

"I'm fine," his father said.

"Fine? You're a limping, one-eared tomcat. You cry out in the night and stare off in the daytime like a deaf and blind rock. It takes you five nights to get one night's worth of sleep. You call that fine?"

Bertwoin felt trapped in the cold, narrow bedroom. Maud lay on the rough bed in her white undergarment as if wearing a shroud. He made the sign of the cross.

"So," he said to distract himself as much as her, "the imp creeps into your bedroom while you're asleep, changes into a slimy snake, and then slithers up your nose."

"Eewu." Maud pinched her nostrils together. After a moment, she smirked at her big brother. "My nose is too little."

"Maud is sick and needs more than our prayers," their maman said.

"The virgin's no better than a witch," his uncle yelled. "The apothecary in Montredon can give you the medicine you need."

"Your apothecary is well enough for men, but he knows little about the needs of womenfolk."

"Bah," Laurence said. "What's good for men is good enough for women too."

"The leprosy imp," Bertwoin told Maud, "can make itself smaller than a baby maggot. It can crawl up a mouse's nose. Then once it's inside you, it curls around your heart and goes to work."

"What does it do?"

He paused and scratched the linen coif on his head as if she had asked a question needing serious thought. "Nobody knows for sure, not even trained doctors. Probably it sinks its fangs into your heart and poisons you like a snake does."

"That hellcat," their uncle shouted, "has already cast a spell over Bertwoin."

Their father said, "We'll do whatever we have to, to take care of our children. I'll not let another one die on me."

"I'll plug up my nose with mud," Maud told Bertwoin.

"That'll make it hard for you to breathe." He again patted her overly warm shoulder. "First, we need to find out if you have leprosy. We'll put ashes around your bed and check them in the morning. No tiny footprints or snake's trail in the ashes means the imp didn't come, and you don't have the disease." He held up a finger and smiled. "And tomorrow I'll go ask Flowia to come heal you."

"Uncle Laurence says she'll sell my soul to the Devil?"

"She didn't do that when she cured your diarrhea."

"We can get a potion from Montredon," his uncle insisted.

"Flowia did alright last time," their father said. "But she doesn't need to come into our *ostal*. She can just send us what medicine we need."

After a few moments of quiet, Bertwoin heard the front door slam shut. His uncle was probably stomping his way to The Noble Head to cool his anger with a tankard of ale, or maybe he had just gone outside to walk around and sulk.

Bertwoin told Maud. "Now let me fetch some ashes to put around your bed. Flowia will want to know if you have leprosy or not."

"You just want to go visit her."

Bertwoin shrugged. Maud, like Flowia, had the habit of getting in the last word.

Jolie raised her head and stared at the doorway. Was someone there?

When he stepped into the smoky main room, he almost bumped into their *maman*, who stood near the ladder that led up to the *solier* where his parents slept.

"Your voice carried all the way to the kitchen," she whispered. "A snake that crawls up her nose? Did you want her to get *any* sleep tonight?"

He moved farther into the main room, away from the bedroom's dark doorway. His *maman* followed him. "And we heard you," he said. "I'll go fetch the medicine from Flowia."

His *maman* slapped his chest. "No, you won't. We've got enough bad weather in this household already." She raised a hand to forestall his argument. "Rachel will go. Laurence has no sway over this. Healing Maud is women's work."

"I can go while you and Rachel tend to her. I'm faster."

"Hah. You'd not come back until sunset. You'll stay here and braid me a new rope for the water bucket."

He glanced at the end of the long room into their kitchen, which was built of stone to safeguard it from fire. Two hams dangled from a beam running under the shingle roof to keep the meat beyond the reach of cat claws and rat paws. His father sat on a bench at the oak table with his back to the hearth fire, weaving a reed basket. His sister, Rachel, also sat at the table, cleaning a squirrel she had killed with a rock.

"*Maman!*" Maud screamed. Jolie darted out of the bedroom with her ears laid flat.

They leaped into the bedroom and saw Maud clawing at her face. *Maman* pulled Maud's hands away. Bertwoin saw the wriggling, tapered end of a tiny white worm push itself out of the corner of his sister's eye.

"It's the leper imp," she cried. "It didn't wait for night."

Bertwoin knelt and patted his sister's head. "It's just a maw worm, Little Bug."

Their father stood in the doorway a moment, grim-faced, before he sighed and strolled toward the front door.

Their mother also sighed. "Well, now we know what the problem is. Flowia needs to prepare wormwood for me."

"I can run right now and get it."

"Rachel will go."

Maud whined, "Will the medicine taste bad?"

"Probably no worse than pig piss," Bertwoin said before he could stop himself.

"Pig piss," Maud squalled.

His *maman* punched his shoulder and told Maud, "He's just teasing."

"But medicine always makes me gag," Maud whined.

"Don't worry, Little Bug, it'll be no worse than snail slime."

His *maman* pushed him toward the doorway. "Bring me a dish of wine."

Rachel smiled at him as he fetched the wine and shook her head to show there was no hope for him.

When he came back, his *maman* took the dish from him, dipped her thumb into the sour red wine, and wet the sign of the cross on Maud's forehead. "Now you're under God's protection." She patted her daughter. "And if the medicine proves too foul, I'll sweeten it with a dollop of honey. How's that?"

CHAPTER II

Bertwoin sat on a three-legged stool in their barn, spinning fibers into thick threads he would later braid into a rope for their water bucket. The rickety hand reel squeaked woodenly, its sound causing all three of their mules to lay their ears back.

The barn cat, Belle, jumped into the warmth of his lap and snagged the wriggling strand with her claws. He stroked her rough fur and tapped the six toes on one of her front paws—the sign of a good mouser.

Her mother had been a champion mouser until a falcon had swooped down on her. That was the reason his father allowed Belle to live in their barn. He assumed she had inherited her mother's skill in hunting mice. Bertwoin sighed. His father judged all things by their pedigrees.

Belle sat up, suddenly alert, and stared at the barn's front door.

Outside, his Uncle Laurence shouted, "What are *you* doing here?"

Bertwoin set the cat aside on the hard-packed dirt floor and glanced at a nearby hayfork. Was somebody threatening his uncle?

He heard Flowia say, "The alchemist sent me to fetch Bertwoin. The master has need of him."

Warmth spread through Bertwoin's chest like water soaking into thirsty dirt. He gazed upward at the underside of their barn's shingle roof and thanked God for this miracle. Flowia was needed, and she had appeared, even before Rachel had gone to get medicine from her. Now he would get to see her.

Then a dark thought swept away his joy like a cold, night wind. It was evil luck that Flowia should meet the one man in their *ostal* who hated her more than the plague. Why had she come? Had there been another murder?

"He's busy here," his uncle said. "And what does an alchemist need from a plowman now? The winter crops are already asleep in the ground."

There was a pause, then he heard Flowia chant:

"I doubt if it's just a whim,

I doubt if it's only for show,

why not go and ask him

if you really want to know?"

Bertwoin dropped his forehead onto the palm of his calloused hand. Why did she have to do this now?

Sometimes, especially when she was angry, Flowia began flyting. Her ability to make up these rough rhymes in an instant delighted him, except of course, when her barbs were aimed at him. But Laurence would judge her words as an insult against his dignity.

Bertwoin ran to the barn's doorway. Laurence stood in the early morning sunlight with his fists on his hips, his rigid back toward the barn. Flowia scowled up at him, her face tight with hate. She had pulled her blue cloak close around her and looked besieged but also determined not to yield to her enemy.

Behind his uncle, Bertwoin smiled to show her he would take care of Laurence. He saw her relax a bit.

Another wave of warmth—half ache and half elation—flooded through him. Hers was the only face in the crowded marketplace or at mass that mattered, the one that lifted his spirit into sunlit clouds.

"Get gone, witch," his uncle said. "We don't need your insolence here." He raised a fist and shook it in front of his chest. "In this *ostal*, we don't take orders from a whore's brat."

She adjusted her wimple with deliberate calm.

Laurence hacked and spat near her feet. "Why does the old fraud send *you*, anyway? We'd rather see a turd floating in our soup." He waved her away, then hissed and put a hand against the small of his injured back.

"The master sent *me* because he knows *I* enjoy talking to you."

Bertwoin gave Flowia a pleading look. Making fun of Laurence was like pricking him with her knife. He stepped forward to stand shoulder-to-shoulder beside his lanky uncle, who flinched and eyed him as if a viper had slithered close to him.

Flowia said to Bertwoin, "The master has need of you. *Now*."

Laurence said, "My brother will decide if my nephew goes or not. Bertwoin has honest work to do here."

She fluttered her hand with swanlike grace. How could his family not admire her slender fingers and her delicate ways? Why could they not accept her? Why did he have to stand here and prevent his uncle from smacking her?

"Let me get my boots and cloak," he said to her.

His uncle snarled at him. "You'll go when my brother tells you to go."

"But he's not here, is he? And he'll not stop me from helping the master."

"So you say."

"My *father* has wit enough not to anger the alchemist." He stared hard into his uncle's eyes.

Laurence hesitated, and Bertwoin knew he had made his point. Laurence didn't believe the rumors that the alchemist had learned dark spells from the Jews and Moors while in the Holy Land or that the master could turn common metals into gold or raise his enemies' images on a polished black stone and punish them, but he did believe the alchemist was dangerous. The wily old man had the ear of the *visconte.* Only a careless fool would dare oppose him.

And though the master was usually a peaceful man, his manner would change in a single breath if anyone offered violence to his virgin. He loved Flowia like a daughter. Slapping her was certain to bring down "eye for eye, tooth for tooth" punishment on their family.

Of course, there was also the possibility that if smacked, Flowia might snick out her knife and stab Laurence. She hadn't survived a vagabond life on the road by being meek.

Bertwoin added, "And my *father* brags that my helping the master brings us honor."

"Well, we all wish the alchemist had wit enough not to send a whore's bastard for you." He waved at Flowia. "Always smartens herself up and wears dresses like a merchant's wife, doesn't she? Always uses fancy words when common ones are wanted." Laurence ridiculed her with a mean laugh. "Putting lace on a toad and teaching it to stand on its hind legs doesn't change its nature. Deep down, it'll still want to hop and croak. It'll still be nothing more than a witch's pet."

Flowia smiled sweetly at Laurence.

 "Why is it you now revile
an innocent girl for the sin
of her absent father while
holding blameless the masculine?"

Laurence measured Flowia from crown to toe with gleeful disgust. "Bertwoin will never marry you, whore's daughter. You can bury that thought deep as Hell's cellar. Even your alchemist can't make that magic happen."

Flowia stiffened, and a veil of hatred seemed to drop over her face. Laurence smirked, pleased as a fed pig that he had wounded her. She put a hand on her hip and looked at Bertwoin.

What did she expect him to do? He would marry her this afternoon if given the chance, but his father was more likely to wed him to a hangman's daughter than to her. Besides, arguing with his uncle would delay their leaving.

Laurence made rude kissing sounds at her. "No one but a crippled beggar would have you."

She scorned his insult with a pitying smile. "I have turned down offers, unlike you, whose offer was rejected."

Bertwoin felt Belle rub against his ankle. Glad of the diversion, he bent down to scratch her head.

"Well," Laurence told her, "you won't ever get an offer from here."

Flowia hissed and said,
"Why do you believe, bachelor,
that I desire to marry
and bind myself to a cur
whose reticence makes me wary?"

Bertwoin jerked up in surprise. Startled, Belle slunk away from him. What did Flowia expect from him?

His uncle shook a finger at Flowia's nose. "Well, the cur, as you call him, is gold to your tin."

Bertwoin needed to stop this now. But first, he had to change into his traveling cloak and boots, which were in the back corner of the barn where he slept. He dared not leave these two alone together. "Come with me," he told Flowia. "I need to get my things."

She shook her head. "I'll wait for you out here."

Laurence sneered. "Queenie doesn't want to muck up the soles of her goat-skin shoes." He turned and swaggered away, keeping his hurt back as straight as a spear shaft to show his contempt for her.

Bertwoin patted her arm, and she jerked away. Avoiding his eyes, she gazed at the mountains along the southern horizon, their snow-covered peaks glowing in the sunlight.

What was he supposed to do now? He felt like a soldier who had disgraced himself by throwing down his axe and running away from a battle. Had she expected him to fight his uncle? Did she think that would win them anything?

He had looked forward to their time alone together and their walk to wherever the master alchemist waited for him. No doubt, now their trek would be a silent, grim-faced march.

He slipped into their musty barn and put on his gray, woolen cloak and boots without waking his younger brother, Wilfraed. When he came outside, Flowia had her arms crossed under her breasts. Not a good sign.

She turned without a word and glided toward their east field. He caught up and kept pace beside her. He knew not to touch her, though his body thrummed like a plucked lute string with a desire to do so.

"Another murder?" he asked, hoping to talk the anger out of her. Flowia wasn't usually unreasonable.

"You'll know when we get there." She continued to stare straight ahead, clearly only enduring his company because it was her duty to bring him to the master.

"I don't know why you're so vexed at me."

She stalked along the forest path that led to the Aude River in tight-lipped silence. He watched the braided end of her dark hair bounce against the small of her back. When they reached the river, she turned onto the road that followed its bank and chanted,

"Am I annoyed?
Why do you think this?
I quite enjoyed
your lowly cowardice."

Cowardice? Didn't she realize that arguing against Laurence meant his uncle would abuse her even more? Had she expected him to bloody his uncle's nose?

"I don't deserve this," he muttered. "There's no profit in shouting back and forth with Laurence. He's as rooted in his hate as an old tree. Don't listen to him. He only wins if you let him scrape you the wrong way."

Stomping along, Flowia punched the air in front of her. "Why should I stay silent and let him have his way? He's just a preening peacock. He. . . ." She huffed and shook her head.

"He what?"

She whirled to face him and stabbed his chest with a forefinger. "Forget your uncle. You don't argue to change *his* mind. You argue to show what *you* think of me." She slapped her chest. "Me!"

He threw up his hands. "Why argue with a mule-headed fool? You can't make a river flow backward. And my fighting Laurence would make my father ban you from coming to our farm."

"But it defends *me*. It shows you choose my side, not his."

"My coming out of the barn to protect you showed whose side I was on. And my being with you here and now argues that I'm on your side."

She marched on, her expression that of a martyr. "Your uncle won't think that. He'll believe you just obeyed the master's summons. He needed to hear you defend me. *I* needed to hear you defend me."

"Oh, come on, Flo. You know I'm always on your side."

"So, your uncle is wrong?"

"What do you think?"

He put a hand on her shoulder, stopped her, and turned her toward him. She gazed up into his eyes as if searching for something that she couldn't find. When he tried to pull her closer, she put a hand flat against his chest and shoved herself away.

"I know your family will never protect me," she said, "but I always believed *you* would." She strode away, her mouth a tight line of anger.

Bertwoin blew out his breath and followed her. He felt like a mule forced to carry a load that was too heavy for him. How would he ever appease his unmovable family and this unmovable woman at the same time?

CHAPTER III.

Flowia stayed tight-lipped, her face leather hard, as she led him through a forest made glum by early winter. There was nothing he could do to appease her at this moment, so he relaxed and enjoyed the quiet morning. It was the season for repairing tools and storing food after the winter plowing was done. He could almost smell crisp Christmas in the brisk breeze. It enlivened his blood.

She led him to Hebert's tidy *ostal*, a farm close enough to the Aude River for Hebert's wife and two daughters to lug their household water from it. But the river giveth and the river taketh away. Hebert's young son had drowned some years ago, leaving him bereft of a male heir.

Raimunda, the eldest daughter, stood rigid and unsmiling in the poultry yard behind the wattle fence. She frowned in anger at Bertwoin, then pointed toward a copse of chestnut trees. She had reason to loathe him, but he saw more than hate for him on her grim face. She seemed panicked.

People considered surly Hebert a successful farmer, but he had an army of enemies. Had someone knifed him because he hadn't paid a debt? If so, he had failed to follow his usual practice of doing business only with people weaker than himself.

Bertwoin heard the hum of the alchemist's voice before he saw the white-haired master lying flat on his back in his red cloak. He stared up at the wind-swept heavens while Bertwoin's stout Aunt Guillema stood over him.

Bertwoin realized his mouth was open and closed it to hide his surprise. When Flowia glanced at him to see if he could explain the master's odd behavior, he shook his head. If she didn't know, no one did. She knew the alchemist better than anyone.

Bertwoin studied his aunt, who had her arms crossed resolutely over the front of her blue woolen cloak. Her red-eyed stare didn't welcome him. Had she been crying? Her shedding tears surprised him, and beyond that, astonished him if she had done so over Hebert's death.

Bertwoin straightened his spine and strode toward her. "Aunt Guillema, what are you doing here?"

"Trying to make certain I don't lose a daughter-in-law," she snapped. "The real question, nephew, is why Flowia brought *you* here?"

He hoped she didn't order him to leave. He would have no choice but to do so. Even his stern and unruly father obeyed his older sister.

The alchemist sat up. "Greetings, plowman."

Bertwoin dipped his head to show respect. "I hope you are well, master."

"I'm still above ground." The alchemist rubbed his bony hands together as if this miracle pleased him.

"You look to be more *on* the ground than *above* it."

His aunt made a disapproving noise in her throat.

"No offense meant," Bertwoin added.

The alchemist waved away his apology. "None taken, though your aunt is correct. Levity at this time may not be welcome." Still sitting on the ground, the master looked up at

Guillema. "Your nephew is here because I find his common sense and his powers of observation valuable. He is also sprier than I am. And who cannot want the company of a young man who unseated two squires from their horses with a simple hoe."

Guillema continued to stand over the master, looking as solid as a fieldstone wall. "You know, of course, that he is no more welcome here than a sheep-killing dog."

"I am aware of the canceled wedding, but I decided it was more important for me to have a dog with a keen nose for sniffing out clues." The alchemist grunted his way to standing. Flowia slipped behind him and brushed leaves and twigs off his woolen cloak.

The alchemist pointed at dark splotches on the fallen leaves where he had lain. "Ermessen was found here. Someone murdered her as she gathered firewood."

"Murdered?" Bertwoin again closed his open mouth. So the victim was Hebert's wife, not him. How could this be? "I never heard tell of *her* having any enemies."

"That's because she had none," his aunt said, her tone waspish.

She was angry with him for the insult of daring to think her best friend might have an enemy. He scanned a copse of chestnut trees. "Why would Ermessen collect firewood? She has two daughters."

The alchemist threw his hands apart. "*That* is a question we must answer. Had she used gathering firewood as an excuse for a rendezvous? If so, did her secret visitor attack her?"

Bertwoin looked down at the few dry leaves spotted with blood. "So, maybe we're looking for a deadly enemy who pretended to be a friend?"

"Pshaw," his aunt said.

The master raised a forefinger. "If Na Guillema is correct, there will only be one or two people to consider. We also need to learn why her daughter, Armendis, wallowed in blood."

"Blood?" Bertwoin bleated. "Was she wounded too?"

The alchemist's face turned gravestone solemn. "Hebert assumes the blood on her is her mother's. The *bayle,* when he comes, will be like-minded."

"Those fools believe nonsense," Guillema muttered. "They think that if someone eats pear seeds, pears will grow in their stomachs?"

"But Armendis would never turn her hand against anyone," Bertwoin protested. "Especially not against her own *maman.* She's as gentle as a puppy."

"Then we must prove her innocent," the alchemist said. He looked at the surrounding woods. "Come," he said to Bertwoin, "help me search the area. We'll gather what evidence we can before the *bayle* comes and officially runs us off."

Guillema patted Flowia's shoulder. "Mendy lies bewildered inside the house. We're wanted there."

Flowia glanced at the master, who nodded. Bertwoin watched her glide away, following stiffed-backed Guillema, who had already begun marching toward the house. His aunt didn't bother to see if Flowia obeyed her. People always did.

CHAPTER IV

Bertwoin watched the master start at one corner of the copse and pace off the length of its front edge, hunched over as he examined the ground. He then moved inward three paces and rustled through the dead leaves in the opposite direction. Bertwoin joined him and followed the same pattern four strides away, hoping to find something dropped or disturbed by the killer.

"Is the lawman coming?" he asked.

"He is being summoned. Raimunda fetched me before she went to the blacksmith's forge in Montredon to tell her father to come home. I came straight here. Flowia went to find a boy and sent him to notify the lawman of the killing. Fortune favored me. I had just enough time to examine the corpse before Hebert arrived." He clapped his hands, the sharp sound echoing through the quiet grove. "By now, the boy must have located the *bayle*."

Bertwoin hummed in praise of his aunt's cleverness. Had Raimunda told her father first, Hebert might have stopped her from bringing the master.

"And Armendis is in the house?"

"Yes. Guillema told Raimunda to wash the blood off her and keep her in a bedroom. Cleaning her mind, unfortunately, will not be as easy as cleaning her body. We can only hope she becomes coherent enough to remember what happened to her before the *bayle* arrives."

"How did she get bloody? And why? Do you think she saw the murder?"

"Let's hope not. The killer stabbed Ermessen eight times. He also slit her throat."

"He?"

"It is men who usually commit this type of brutal murder, though an enraged woman doing so is possible."

"Were her forearms slashed?"

"No. She didn't try to protect herself. It seems she was caught unawares by a killer she trusted, a person who stripped her and left a child's doll lying between her breasts. One wonders what she did to provoke such savage rage?"

A powerful gust shoved through the copse, scurrying a few dry leaves across the ground. Bertwoin glanced at the skeletal chestnut trees around him and pulled the cowl of his woolen cloak tighter around his head. He felt the lingering presence of death.

The master continued, "There isn't much blood where Ermessen was found. It's probable the killer murdered her inside the grove, then dragged her out. If so, he covered the trail well. The wind may also have helped him."

"Would a man not carry her out? It's quicker."

"Maybe. Some men have the strength for it. You perhaps. But corpses are awkward to handle."

"So the killer brought her body to where it would be found right away?"

"It would seem so. It would behoove us to learn why he did this."

Bertwoin stopped when he saw a small pile of limbs and twigs, as if someone had dropped them while gathering firewood. The leaves nearby looked wrong—too loose and unnatural. He squatted, his knees popping, and brushed aside the top leaves. A thick layer of dried blood lay under them, and the dirt was gouged and disturbed. "Here, master. This is where he killed her."

"Well done, plowman." The alchemist walked a circle around him, looking for further clues. He glanced back at where Ermessen was found. "He didn't drag her far."

"Was it Raimunda or Armendis who found her?"

"Neither. That misfortune fell to your aunt. Raimunda had discovered her younger sister lying near their dung heap, so addled that she knew not her own name nor why her tunic was crusted with blood. A dagger smeared with blood lay beside her. Scratches marred her cheeks. Raimunda panicked. She abandoned her sister and fled to your aunt for help."

"Why my aunt?"

The master began searching the copse again. "Think you not that Guillema would be a reassuring presence if evil beset you?"

"Yes, if my aunt likes you. If she despises you, you're more likely to get a lecture on your faults than her help." He smiled down at the droppings of a fox and stepped around them. "It also carries weight if the person asking for her help doesn't pee standing up."

The alchemist chuckled. "Yes, there is that. She seems to believe that men have more faults than virtues."

Bertwoin glanced back at the quiet spot on the edge of the copse where his aunt had found Ermessen. "Guillema has sympathy for the women here. My aunt chose Armendis to wed her son, Jehan. She chose Armendis to be her daughter-in-law. She chose a marriage that would make Ermessen her sister. So if called, she would outrun a pony to help them."

The alchemist studied Bertwoin for a moment. "And you? Finding yourself in dire need of aid, might you not run to her?"

"It was you I ran to when the *bayle* came to arrest me for the murder of Emeline."

"Yes, but if I am not available?"

"I might, but my father deals with most threats against us." Bertwoin's lips curled into a tight smile. "Except those coming from my aunt. He's never dared slap her. Not that I know of, anyway." He snickered. "My Uncle Laurence sometimes stutters when he argues against her."

"You just justified my argument. Your aunt is a wall of strength. You have luck in that your staunch father keeps you safe and sees to your comfort?"

Bertwoin glanced sideways to see if the master was serious. He was. Yes, his father was a wall of strength, but he didn't bring anyone, not even his wife, warm comfort.

"So, master, you're saying Raimunda didn't know her mother was dead when she fetched my aunt?"

"She ran off, knowing only that her sister was distracted and needed help. It was Na Guillema's fate to discover Ermessen's body." The alchemist stopped as if he expected a small elm growing among the chestnut trees to move out of his way. He grunted and slapped its supple limbs as he stomped around it.

"Raimunda, then, wasn't with my aunt when she found Ermessen?"

"Correct. And probably for the best." He gazed at Bertwoin, his eyes full of thought, and said, "When trouble comes to you, Na Guillema is the one you want beside you. This situation did not overpower her."

"Though it must've been brutal for her," Bertwoin said. "She and Ermessen have been like loving sisters since girlhood."

"I saw you notice that she had cried. Na Guillema is not hard-hearted, just strong-willed. I think if she caught the killer, she would give him like for like. Anyway, when your aunt arrived, she and Raimunda carried Armendis into the house and tended to her. Then, while Raimunda washed her sister, Na Guillema searched for Ermessen. She wanted to tell her about Armendis's condition. She assumed the blood came from a gander or a rooster."

Bertwoin saw a large patch of ground gouged by foraging pigs. Why hadn't the killer buried Ermessen in the grove? Why strip the body and leave a doll on it? Who was he sending a message to?

"So," he asked, "Hebert was at the blacksmith's forge in Montredon when his wife was killed? Other men saw him there?"

"It seems so. He brought the blacksmith an iron hinge for repair. We may assume Raimunda would have run to him or to her mother had they been home. Still, her mother was closer. Why run all the way to your aunt's house in St. Vincent?"

Bertwoin scanned the bleak grove. "She had just found her dazed sister covered with blood. Maybe she thought she was also in danger. So instead of searching the woods alone, she ran to where she knew she would be safe."

The master tipped his head sideways in agreement. "Of course." He stopped and turned in a complete circle, surveying the copse from its center. "You are right. It was a simple choice." He held up a bony finger. "You asked about Hebert. It is still possible that he murdered his wife before going to the blacksmith."

Bertwoin hummed, not sure he agreed. Hebert might overdo it and kill his wife while beating her, but would he stab her eight times? "He could have beaten her more than he meant to," he said in a doubtful tone, "then tried to make her death look like a stranger had done it?"

The master held his palm up in disagreement. "Her body isn't covered in bruises, not fresh ones anyway. I do not accuse Hebert. His doing so is improbable, but we dare not slam the door in the face of any possibility."

Bertwoin said, "Could Armendis have been demon-possessed and not known what she was doing? She's the one covered with her mother's blood."

"Yes, and with a bloody dagger lying on the ground beside her. And you are correct. What lies before our eyes may be the simple truth. Anyway, guilty or not, her mother's blood marks her for the gallows in Bourg, or more likely, hanging at the Devil's Doorstep. Guillema's arguing that Armendis is innocent will not carry even a feather's weight on the *visconte's* scales of justice. But if the girl did savage her mother, we must at least find out why she did so."

"Could she have been demon-possessed?"

"It's possible. There are countless kinds of demons. Many of them live in herbs." The alchemist balled his fists in frustration. "We need evidence. All fingers point boldly at Armendis. The lawman is tenacious and more often right than not, but in this case, he might hang an innocent young woman if he doesn't take care."

Bertwoin bent down to examine an indentation in the ground, decided it was an eroded deer print, shook his head, and walked on. "So you don't think it's as simple as it looks? A fox print in the poultry yard doesn't always mean a fox stole the missing hen. A neighbor might put down a false print to cover his theft."

"Exactly so. One or two details disturb me. Mayhap a cunning killer *has* lain a false trail for the *bayle*. Or did Armendis do this, and I am trying to make clues out of sunlight to prove the girl innocent?"

When the wily master had doubts, they usually proved to be more than just sunshine. But the *bayle* would demand solid evidence. An opinion was as useless as a dropped egg. "I'm surprised the lawman hasn't already arrested Armendis."

"Ah well, our boy may still be looking for him, or the *bayle* may think there is no need to hurry. He will blunder in here ere long."

Bertwoin murmured, "This murder will leave unseen scars on Raimunda and Armendis."

"And Hebert," the master said.

Bertwoin doubted Hebert would grieve for long. "His scar will scab over quickly once he remarries. My *maman* says Hebert is a cockroach that sees himself in a puddle and likes the look of himself. He uses his wife and daughters like cart ponies and shows little liking for them. Still, he will miss Ermessen's labor." Bertwoin made a sympathetic sound in his throat. "Raimunda is the only slave Hebert has left now. No woman will envy her."

"No," the alchemist agreed. "He was a demon to live with even before these troubles fell upon him. The loss of his wife and daughter will disgruntle his temper even more?"

The bleak trees in the brown woods weighed on Bertwoin's mood. They had found no clues other than the exact place where Ermessen had died. But how could it be otherwise? Windblown leaves covered most bare places where mud might have captured a stray footprint. Even the murder spot had shown no blood until they had uncovered it.

"You were lying on the ground when I came."

"Yes, I wanted to know if my body would sense why the murderer dragged Ermessen to that precise spot. I found none."

Bertwoin stopped, ready to end their search, and again surveyed the skeletal trees. "When you examined the corpse, master, did you find anything else?"

The alchemist waggled his head. "Two more things of interest. First, Ermessen had this in her death grip." He flapped open a leather bag that hung from his shoulder and pulled out a small wooden heart on a brass chain. "The chain is broken. She may have grabbed it during the attack or as she lay dying?"

Did the master believe he had the authority to thwart the *bayle*? "You're keeping the heart aside?"

The alchemist listened a moment to a nearby crow squawk angrily at something, maybe them, before he answered. "Does the *bayle* need to see it? I doubt he will give it much attention. We must learn if Hebert gave this token to her, and if he didn't, who did? We need to show it to people." The master slipped the heart back into his bag.

The alchemist lowered his eyebrows, and sorrow deepened the lines on his face. "A crude doll lay between Ermessen's breasts."

"A poppet," Bertwoin muttered. It seemed shameful for a killer to use a doll in this way. Like babies, they were meant to be loved.

"Yes, another puzzle for us. It seems the killer is challenging the *bayle* to a duel of wits."

Again, he opened his shoulder bag and pulled out a roughly carved wooden figure with two legs, no arms, and a blank face. "I doubt Ermessen would carry a doll while she gathered firewood. So why did the killer bring it and leave it on her? What is he telling us?"

Bertwoin realized that, like the heart, the alchemist was also not going to give the poppet to the *bayle*. He needed to show it to people. "Whose doll is it?"

"Exactly. We must determine that and see if the killer is taunting Hebert or the *bayle*."

The master put the poppet away, paused, and stared at the trunk of a chestnut tree as if he could see deep inside it. "There are also a number of small puzzles that might be negative clues, and there is the fact that your aunt's faith in the girl's innocence knows no doubt. Guillema is a shrewd judge of character." The master smiled, a change in demeanor that startled Bertwoin, and said, "Hebert nearly came to blows with your aunt."

Bertwoin snorted. "He might not have won that fight. She was reared among reckless brothers. She's not the type to scratch his cheeks. She'll stab his piggy eyes with her fingernails and blind him."

Looking ill-pleased with the chilly wind, the alchemist adjusted his red cloak tighter around himself. "So, where do we stand now? Na Guillema has Armendis in a bedroom and stands guard over her like a mother dragon while Hebert curses his daughter and wants her hung. In the meantime, we await the arrival of the *bayle* who will, no doubt, arrest her."

"Hebert has no faith at all in his daughter?"

"The fervor of his belief in her guilt matches that of your aunt's belief in her innocence. The *bayle* will escort her to the citadel before the sun sets on this day with Hebert's blessing. Only a fool would bet against her hanging."

"Negative clues?" Bertwoin asked.

The master pointed at him as if to say he knew Bertwoin would insist on discussing these clues. "I found one thing missing that causes me to question the girl's guilt. We will speak of it later."

On the backside of the copse, the master took a deep breath, as if to gather his strength. "Come," he said, "we are better placed in the house. Hebert and your aunt should not remain long in each other's company without our presence."

Bertwoin hesitated. "Hebert will never allow me to step into his house."

"Ah, yes. I recall hearing that you and Raimunda were to be married, but your father abruptly canceled the wedding." The alchemist waited, clearly expecting an explanation.

Bertwoin stared up into the cold sky as if he were looking into his past. "One of Hebert's sisters was starving, and though he had plenty of food to spare, he refused to help her. Also, she had a baby girl. And when Ermessen disobeyed him and gave the sister food under the table, he beat her. My father can't abide a man who turns his back on his family. And Hebert might do the same to us. My father also doubted that Ermessen would support Raimunda."

"Yes, I have heard that she favored her youngest daughter over her eldest."

"She blamed Raimunda for the death of her little son, Jacme."

"I have not heard this."

"When Raimunda was young, she went with her mother and her little brother to the Aude to wash clothes. Raimunda and Jacme wandered away. When Ermessen looked around for her children, she saw Raimunda standing alone on the bank, an arrow's shot from her. Ermessen later told Guillema that a mother's dread fell over her like a shroud."

Bertwoin remembered his two small sisters and the brother who had died and paused. Each death had been a knife-slash to the heart.

"Anyway, Raimunda said she didn't know where Jacme was. He had wandered off. Ermessen ran up and down the riverbank, screaming his name. The other women, of course, helped her search the woods. But she knew the horrible truth in the well of her heart. She knew she would never see her dearest boy again this side of Heaven.

"One of the women was afraid Ermessen would drown Raimunda, so she took the girl home with her. Distraught with grief, Ermessen slept on the riverbank for two nights, hoping for a miracle. Hebert, too, was beside himself with sorrow. When he fetched his wife from the river bank, he beat her almost to death. Someone who saw the beating said Ermessen never raised her arms to protect herself. Besides blaming Raimunda for Jacme's death, she also blamed herself. Guillema says Ermessen sometimes kept away from Raimunda, so she wouldn't hurt her."

The alchemist sighed. "Some tragedies cause wounds that never heal. Ah well, let us now go see if I can persuade Hebert that you don't despise his family, and that you have come to help him, even if he would never help you."

CHAPTER V.

They strode through the poultry yard where eight peeved geese stretched out their necks, flicked their tail feathers, and complained. Bertwoin hissed back at them. When the alchemist frowned at him, he realized his playfulness might not be well-timed. Ermessen's body lay inside the cottage.

They entered a narrow front room that became a stone-walled kitchen at its far end and stood a moment to let their eyes adjust to the dim light. The bundled rushes under their feet stopped at the kitchen's bare dirt floor around the hearth fire. The quiet, chilly house reminded Bertwoin of a church with its congregation waiting for a funeral. Only this one stank of blood and feces.

On the floor to their right lay Ermessen's corpse covered by a woolen blanket, her white feet sticking out.

Bertwoin made the sign of the cross. "Why is she lying here like a dead dog?"

"It's Hebert's will that this be so," the alchemist said. "Neither I nor Na Guillema could convince him otherwise."

Bertwoin had hoped he wouldn't come face-to-face with Hebert, but now he wanted to confront the bastard. "Dishonoring his dead wife like this is a sin."

Flowia was alone in the kitchen, her wooden spoon clacking inside a wooden bowl as she mixed something on a waist-high cask. Where was everyone? The long wall on their left had three open doorways, and women's voices murmured inside one of them. Guillema must be soothing Armendis. A ladder leaned against the wall, leading to a second-story *solier*, the family room. Was Hebert up there, feeling sorry for himself?

Flowia waved them forward into the kitchen, where the master seated himself on a bench at the long table. The faint smells of cabbage and sweet ale hung thick in the chilly room. Bertwoin stayed standing. Someone had scratched a fresh cross on the cellar's oak door. Hebert? Raimunda?

The master gazed at the hearth built into the stone wall. It had a few glowing coals in its belly, but no flame. "I fear the heart of this household has turned forever cold."

Flowia poured two mugs of brown ale from a clay pitcher. "We used up nearly all of the firewood heating water for Armendis's bath. She thumped Bertwoin's mug on the table near him, her face as grim and distant as an executioner's. Would she ever forgive him?

"Where is everybody?" he asked.

Flowia twitched her head toward a doorway in the long room. "Na Guillema and Raimunda tend to Armendis in the second bedroom."

"And Hebert?"

"He has gone off to see to his sheep," she accused.

Bertwoin waved at an overhead kitchen beam with a dead rabbit hanging head down from it. "The man gives more thought to that dead rabbit than he does to his own dead wife."

The alchemist grunted. "Perhaps he hopes to find a modicum of solace in the company of his sheep. What's more, the needs of his animals cannot be denied. It may also be to our advantage if he keeps himself distant. When together, he and Guillema eye each other like two rams in a tiny pasture. One wonders how they ever agreed to let their children marry."

He looked at Bertwoin for an explanation and got only a shrug for an answer.

"Another mystery, then," the master said. "Ah well, let us not criticize Hebert for leaving his wife unattended. She feels it not. And we know not what his true feelings are."

Flowia muttered,

"No need. We know he's the type

who enjoys drowning puppies.

We know he's ever ready to gripe

and prefers his women on their knees."

"You judge harshly today, daughter," the alchemist said.

She aimed her eyes at Bertwoin. "I expect more from men than they do from themselves." Then she asked the alchemist, "Raimunda told me Na Guillema wanted to lay Ermessen's body out on a table in the spare room, but her father wouldn't allow it?"

"True. He also won't allow women to come in to wash Ermessen's body. Says Raimunda will do what's needed for the burial."

"Then the cur doesn't care what people think of him," she growled.

"He's been shamed," Bertwoin said.

"If so," the master said, "then the farmer does care about his reputation." He patted the tabletop as if that laid the matter to rest. "Hebert has been found wanting. He didn't protect his wife. So now, he wants to hide the body by burying it quickly."

"And Armendis shames him too," Bertwoin added.

"Yes." The master nodded at the bedroom with the women inside it. "Guillema said Armendis had owl eyes when she first saw the girl. Said they were filled with the darkness of a cave."

"Armendis is still as weak as milk," Flowia said, "and has no memory of what happened to her. She is, however, now aware of her situation. She grieves for her mother and also fears the *bayle's* coming."

The master brushed a bread crumb off the table. "We—"

The front door heaved open, and Hebert shoved inside. He eyed them, clearly angry at seeing intruders inside his home. His mouth dropped open when he saw Bertwoin. "You dare—" He shook his head, choking on rage.

"I came to—" Bertwoin said, but the master said louder, "I brought him here to help us solve this murder."

"Solve?" Hebert stared at the alchemist as if the old man was addled. "Solve? We know who did it. And no snotty Teisseire need ever step through my door. Get out," he shouted at Bertwoin, then looked at all of them. "That goes for all of you. Get out." He muttered to himself, "I come back to see that Raimunda is doing what needs to be done and what do I find? Vermin has overrun my household."

Bertwoin pointed at Ermessen's body. "We're doing this for her."

Not bothering to look at where Bertwoin was pointing, Hebert marched toward them. Guillema stepped into a doorway to prevent him from entering the bedroom. He glanced at her with contempt as he swaggered past her into the kitchen. He stopped in front of Bertwoin and put his hand on his dagger.

"If you pull that knife," Bertwoin said, "there'll be two bodies to bury, and mine won't be one of them."

"You've no right to be here." Hebert shook his head in disgust. "Ah, you're not worth the trouble. Why should I tussle with something I'd find at the bottom of my latrine? Your family is a blight to us all."

Bertwoin relaxed. The farmer had sense enough not to start a fight he couldn't win.

"Stealing my ale, huh?" Hebert accused. "I'm honored that it suits your royal stomach. I never thought anything in my *ostal* would be good enough for Clanoud or his son. My daughter wasn't."

So he was blaming Raimunda instead of himself for the canceled marriage. "It wasn't because of her," he told the farmer.

Hebert glanced at the pitcher of ale on the wall shelf, then looked expectantly at Flowia.

Rather than serve him, she moved from the cask to the kitchen table and stood beside the master. Bertwoin saw his aunt in the bedroom doorway smile and nod to Flowia.

The master watched the farmer with sympathy. "We lament your loss."

Hebert snarled at Flowia and mumbled, "Slut," as he grabbed the clay pitcher off the shelf. He looked inside it to measure how much they had drunk and frowned, then poured himself a mug of ale. He drank half of the contents before saying, "Where the hell is the *bayle*? I'll not let that murderous bitch remain in my house. No honest man would."

"She's your daughter," Guillema argued from the bedroom doorway.

He turned, his lips cocked to one side in contempt. "Rai is the only daughter I claim now."

Guillema told him, "Armendis didn't do this. I know she didn't."

"Oh," he scoffed, "did you divine this from your black mirror, hellcat?"

The alchemist cleared his throat. "I wondered about the wooden heart your wife held in her death grip. Did you carve it for her?"

Hebert passed his palm over the ale remaining in his mug and intoned, "I see Armendis hung from the Gallows Oak, her heels kicking in the air. I see her buried at the Devil's Doorstep in an unmarked grave." He smirked at Guillema.

"The heart?" the alchemist insisted.

"Ah, she came to our wedding wearing it on a chain around her neck. Silly woman deemed it precious, though it wouldn't have fetched a single denier at the Sunday market."

"She wasn't silly," Guillema snapped.

Hebert smiled, pleased that he had angered her. "You and she were two goose eggs from the same clutch. Silly people don't recognize how foolish they are."

"Did Ermessen usually gather firewood?" Bertwoin asked.

When Hebert laughed and ignored him, the alchemist repeated the question.

Sounding weary, Hebert said, "Armendis usually took care of that."

So Ermessen had used the need for firewood as an excuse to go into the woods and meet someone. Either that person had killed her, or Hebert had seen them together and killed her.

The farmer gulped down the rest of his ale, then scanned the room. "Where's Rai?"

His daughter appeared behind Guillema and pushed her way into the main room. Hebert swaggered toward her, and she shrank back, the whites of her eyes showing. He smiled a moment, seeming to enjoy her fear before he shouted into Raimunda's face, "What are you doing in there? Hiding?"

Flowia put her hand on the hilt of her knife. Bertwoin considered stepping forward but was afraid that doing so would provoke Hebert into hitting Raimunda just to spite him. As her father, Hebert had the right to punish her as he wished. However, Bertwoin also didn't want to repeat his earlier mistake by not defending two women in one day.

Raimunda cowered with her forearms up to protect her face. Hebert raised a hand, then sniffed in disgust and dropped it.

"We need you to gather firewood," Guillema told Raimunda, who fled to the front door.

"Hey!" Hebert yelled, but Raimunda flung the door open and slammed it behind her before he could stop her.

"She's got to come back," he said with satisfaction. He pointed a finger at Guillema's nose. "You don't hold sway over my daughter, bitch. She belongs to me."

"Na Guillema is correct," the master said. "A cold hearth comforts no one. Even in times of misfortune, a fire is most welcome."

"Unlike people," Hebert said. "Few of them are welcome here." He sneered at Bertwoin, "and one of them being here is an insult a saint wouldn't accept." He glanced behind him at the far end of the room, where Ermessen's corpse lay near the front door. "My wife got killed collecting firewood?" he said, as if the thought surprised him. He jerked his chin at Flowia. "Maybe somebody ought to run out and find Rai. Make sure she keeps safe. They might even help her gather up a few sticks."

Flowia snorted.

"Is it not a father's solemn duty
to protect his own daughter?
To be ever en garde and ready
To keep her safe from slaughter?"

"I don't need some mouthy whore's daughter thinking she can teach me my duties." He turned to the alchemist. "I've got to get back to my sheep. Got a ewe in trouble with a backward birth." He stared a moment at the flameless hearth. "It's just the two of us now, and the farm won't run itself. So if you're done here, all of you can get out." He flicked a hand at Guillema. "The sooner you and your simpleminded nephew get out of here, the better. You can also take that murdering bitch with you. The *bayle* can just as well arrest her at your place as he can here." He glanced around. "There's no telling what she'll do if left alone in this house. Might even set fire to it."

"If Armendis did this," the alchemist said, his voice low and gentle, "we need to know her reason for doing so. Did she and Ermessen get along well?"

"What difference does it make now? Get out."

The master let out a slow breath. "You can answer my questions now," he said, his voice still low but no longer gentle, "and I can pass the information on to the seneschal. Or you can answer my questions at the citadel. Talking to me now saves you time and keeps you near your sheep."

Hebert licked his lips. "Even a halfwit can see Armendis did this."

"Bah," Guillema jeered. "Why would she kill her mother? They were devoted to each other."

"She was bewitched, wasn't she?"

"Bewitched?"

"Didn't a witch come by before dawn and bother Armendis? And didn't I run her off? So to punish me, the hag laid a curse on my *ostal*."

"If that's the reason she *was* bewitched," Guillema said, her face tight with contempt, "you caused all of this."

"Me?" Hebert pointed at his chest. He swaggered over to Guillema and stood nose-to-nose with her. "You interfering old shrew. I've had enough of your lip. Calling you silly gives you more dignity than you merit."

Bertwoin ran over to prevent a fight. Guillema and Hebert glared at each other, neither one of them willing to take a step backward.

"Well," Hebert muttered, "at least now I won't ever have to call you family. That was all Ermessen's doing anyhow."

Sudden tears glittered in his eyes, and his face twisted in a spasm of grief. Guillema's eyebrows raised in surprise.

"They'll hang Armendis for this," he blubbered. "Then who'll take care of our house now that my wife is dead? Only Rai is left to me. Only Rai."

"Armendis needs to leave now," the alchemist announced.

Everyone stared at him. He jerked his chin at Guillema. "Before the *bayle* comes."

She nodded emphatically. "Well said. I'll take her with me. We have to take control of this if she is to get justice. Somebody," she gazed at the alchemist, "needs to find the witch and force her to take this curse off Armendis."

Bertwoin made a disapproving sound in his throat. "How do you find a single leaf hidden in a forest?"

Ignoring him, Guillema shifted her eyes back to Hebert, who still stood huffing in her face. "Who was the witch?"

A cunning look stole into his expression. "A heretic. One of your kind. You know her well. Mayhap my wife was a sacrifice to your god."

Bertwoin glanced at his aunt. So the witch was one of those who, like her, called themselves Good or True Christians. His father and uncle often scolded their older sister for her wayward choice of religion. This usually brought forth a sermon from her on how the Church manipulated its flock for its own benefit, and how both her brothers lacked even a mustard seed's worth of godliness.

Guillema waited, but Hebert refused to tell her the witch's name. So she told Flowia, "Help me get Armendis ready," and disappeared into the bedroom. Flowia shoved past Hebert into the room.

Bertwoin wondered if the master could force Hebert to give them the witch's name. Maybe he couldn't. And bringing it up at the citadel in the *visconte's* Great Hall might start a witch hunt, something the alchemist would want to avoid.

Crying without a sound, Hebert slouched into the front room and dropped to his knees beside his wife's corpse. "Look at her, look at her," he lamented. "Killed by a heretic." He rose and went out the front door.

Guillema slipped from the bedroom back into the kitchen and told the alchemist, "Na Thea will know who the witch is and where she lives."

The master nodded. "She will know other things about this as well."

Guillema aimed her attention at Bertwoin. "You can help me bring Armendis to my house."

Bertwoin asked her, "Why does Ermessen still lie by the front door?"

She looked him up and down, not liking his tone. "Hebert prevented us from moving her body."

"Well, he's not here now."

Her face softened. "I agree," she said.

The third doorway led into a huge storeroom where animals were sometimes kept during winter. Bertwoin had seen a table top leaning against one of its walls. He set up a trestle table in the main room—where it should be. Let Hebert move it back into the storeroom if he wanted to hide the body until it was buried.

Guillema brought him a blanket. He wrapped it around Ermessen and picked her up. Guillema held her friend's head, so it didn't hang down, and helped him move the body to the table. Crying, she then began arranging the corpse.

The master told Bertwoin, "Tomorrow morning, plowman, return to your aunt's house and check on the girl's condition. Then report to me. Flowia and I will now visit Na Thea, a wise woman it seems, who is also an expert on our local witches."

CHAPTER VI

Bertwoin dug the stubby toe of his felt boot into the kitchen floor, each stab shivering up his leg. He made a dimple in the hard-packed dirt, then smoothed it over with his boot's wooden sole. The *bayle* might throw the door open at any moment and arrest Armendis, yet his aunt dawdled in the bedroom. Why? Was Armendis still dazed? Was she even strong enough to hike the entire way to his aunt's house in St. Vincent?

He needed to go to Na Thea's shop in the high citadel and hear her talk with the master and Flowia. Not knowing what she said might hinder his ability to help find the murderer.

Guillema finally stepped through the bedroom's doorway with Armendis coming out behind her like a gosling following its mother. He had expected to see a disheveled fifteen-year-old woman tottering about like a child just learning to walk. Instead, she walked with a firm step of confidence.

She wore a hoodless blue cloak over a long tunic and goat-leather shoes, the usual clothes of a successful farmer's daughter. Stingy Hebert may have treated his women like slaves, but he didn't dress them in rags. He wanted people to mark his success as a farmer. He wanted them to envy the clothes his women wore. He seemed blind to the fact that most women would rather go naked than agree to live in his household.

Had Ermessen worn the same type of cloak and tunic when she was murdered? Why had the killer stripped her and carried off her clothes?

Armendis also wore a straw hat as if she were going to harvest barley under a hot sun instead of walk down forest paths in early winter's light. Bertwoin was pleased to see the hat's cloth strap tied under her chin. Though the wind wouldn't come to full strength until after nightfall, small gusts already swept through the woods and across the fields. He didn't want to waste time chasing her hat.

Bertwoin felt her eyes watching him from the shadow thrown by the hat's wide brim over her face. People on the paths—and he hoped they met only a few—might not recognize her. It was difficult even for him, close as he was, to see the scratch marks on her cheeks. She stood as quiet as a well-trained dog and waited to be told what to do.

Guillema handed him a large horsehide bag with a drawstring mouth. "You can carry her things." She glanced around the room. "Where can Raimunda be? It doesn't take all afternoon to collect a few sticks of firewood. She slapped a hand over her mouth. "I hope *she* too. . . ."

"Do you want me to look for her?" After finding Raimunda, he might visit Na Thea's shop on his way to his aunt's house.

"No. We don't have time now. The *bayle's* on his way, and Hebert might come swaggering home again. Raimunda is sure to be on her guard after her mother's killing."

Armendis sobbed.

Guillema grimaced, clearly angry at herself for mentioning the murder. She patted the young woman's back and whispered, "Come, dear, we must be away now."

Armendis stumbled once passing through the doorway and again at a dip in the uneven path just beyond the poultry yard, but she had little trouble after that keeping pace with his aunt. Bertwoin admired her toughness and judged her to be more than worthy of marrying his cousin, Jehan. Did her toughness come from being Hebert's daughter? If he didn't break you, he might make you scrappier than a forest rat. Was Jehan marrying a younger version of his mother?

Guillema didn't lead them down half-hidden forest pathways as he had expected. Instead, she boldly used the main road along the Aude River, the fastest route. It seemed foolhardy. Did she think the *bayle* wouldn't recognize Armendis with her face half hidden?

None of them had anything to say. They hadn't traveled far, just out of sight of Hebert's tidy farm, when Jehan came bouncing into sight on his four-wheeled cart pulled by a brown mule. The worry creases around his aunt's eyes and mouth relaxed into laugh lines.

Jehan stopped beside them and jumped down. "I heard the news." He patted and stroked Armendis's shoulders and back as if soothing a skittish cat. "Are you well, Mendy?"

"I'm better now. Your mother has been ever so kind. And Bertwoin too."

Her movements were livelier now. Jehan put his arm across her slumped shoulders and led her to the cart. His mother watched with an approving smile as her son moved behind his fiancée, put his hands on her waist, and helped lift her onto the cart's box seat. Armendis scooted to the middle of the seat's rough boards so she could sit close to Jehan when he climbed onto the cart.

He turned to his mother. She waved for him to go on without them. Bertwoin slung the leather bag into the back of the cart as it moved away.

His aunt tarried on the rutted road until the lovers had driven well beyond hearing. Then she said, "Keep me company." She began to stroll toward St. Vincent.

His muscles jittered with frustrated energy, but he put a halter on his longing to run to Na Thea's shop. At least they were moving in the right direction.

"So, Chubby," she said, "you still seem to have a fondness for Flowia."

Most people called him Ox, but she had this personal nickname for him, which she only used on cozy, private occasions.. Of course, he knew better than to return the favor and call her Aunt Ema.

He sucked in his breath. The subject was personal, but he had no one else to talk to, and even his aunt's enemies admitted, however grudgingly, that besides being willful, she was also clever. If she were to argue in his defense, his family wouldn't spurn her words without giving them due thought. "Is it so apparent?"

"A goose would recognize your prancing and preening as courtship, and a blind sow would smell the male musk on you." She clasped her hands together in delight. "Why, nephew, I believe I spy sunrise on your cheeks."

"I thought we had hidden it well."

"We? So, she returns your affection?"

"She does."

"Does or did?"

He glanced at her, afraid she might know something he didn't.

"I'd have to be as blind as stump not to notice Flowia's temper against you. But that might mean she still has warm feelings for you. She cares enough to feel peeved at whatever sin you've committed."

"You put all the blame on me? We might just be on opposite sides of an argument."

"Hah!" His aunt slapped his shoulder. "Flowia sees the world as it is. And if it were a trifling matter, she wouldn't bother to pout over it. And I'm here to tell you, nephew, she sees whatever you did as a serious."

Bertwoin kicked a small rock off the road. "Jehan was lucky to have you to champion his cause and change Hebert's mind."

"He was," his aunt said without a hint of modesty.

"And only Hebert opposed you. With me, it's my uncle, father, and my mother who are against my marrying Flowia.

"But Hebert was an army all by himself."

True, and his changing his opinion was a miracle. But things always just seemed to come out easy for Jehan. When he was a mere boy, he bragged to everyone that he would grow up to be a carter like his *papa*. So his doting parents built a small dog cart for him. They assumed he would enjoy playing with it, and he did. But Jehan had inherited his mother's shrewd flair for business. He adopted a sturdy dog and tamed it to pull his cart. He then set himself up as a little carter. He delivered small loads to wives, who laughed and pinched his cheeks and fed him honey on bread. They made sure he had trade and earned small coins or barter. Other boys began to beg their fathers for a cart and dog of their own.

Now Jehan was preparing to make the girl he loved his wife, something that had seemed impossible because Hebert openly despised Guillema and her "spoiled" whelp.

Bertwoin tilted his head toward his aunt. "It may be meddling in your business, but I have a question. How did you manage it? I mean, it's no secret that Hebert and you both show your fangs whenever you come within sight of each other."

"Money," she said.

"Ah, the pagan gold coins." He had heard that one of these coins had bought the mule and cart that Jehan used now.

So, even after dying, Uncle Josse's luck had given his aunt the means to buy her way into this wedding. His uncle had found a sealed clay jar hidden in an abandoned mine, a jar full of thick gold coins left by the pagans who had ruled over their area before the Romans conquered it. No one knew how many coins Uncle Josse had or where he kept them or why the *visconte's* stern seneschal hadn't filched them away from him.

His father and Uncle Laurence often bragged about what they would do with gold coins if *they* found any. Their brother-in-law's luck had inspired them to go treasure hunting in the mountains. Of course, they came home empty-handed.

"So the gold softened Hebert's hatred toward you?"

"I doubt that. But it made him put aside his meanness for one moment."

"I'm surprised people don't spy on you and try to find out where you hide the gold."

"What gold? That's just a rumor." She elbowed his arm when he stared at her in disbelief. "Only Hebert, one goldsmith, and close family know the rumor is true. I was born with a brain, nephew. Having gold brings enemies, not friends. A goldsmith handles the coins for us, and he believed Josse represented a rich client. He thinks I now represent that client.

"After all, how can the widow of a simple carter own gold, the metal of kings? This goldsmith turns my coins into common money, taking a hefty fee for himself. I promised Hebert the value of one gold coin if he agreed to the marriage."

Bertwoin whistled. "That's a high price to pay."

"Not for love," she said in a tone that locked the door against any further argument from him.

Ermessen and Guillema had been childhood playmates, so naturally, they wanted their children to marry. Ermessen had ended up in a loveless marriage. But it was apparent from the way Guillema and Josse had looked at each other and touched each other that their spirits had danced together with joy. Jehan and Armendis hoped to follow in their footsteps. Bertwoin, too, hoped to follow them.

He grunted. "Well, as I said, Jehan is lucky."

"There's more to it than just luck, nephew. He had the good sense to fall in love with Armendis." She wobbled her head, smiling. "Then again, maybe there is some good fortune in the solid fact that she loves him. What about your situation?"

"The alchemist doesn't seem to object to me courting Flowia. And she likes me well enough."

"Only well enough?"

"Ah, a little better than that." When she stared at him and waited for more detail, he shrugged. "Okay, much better than that."

"Good."

"It *would* be good if anyone in my family, other than our barn cat, would welcome her into our *ostal*. Well, actually, Wilfraed and Rachel don't oppose her, and Maud is still too small to care. Uncle Laurence especially rants against her. They'll accept Eudes, who is a cook, for Rachel's husband, but not Flowia for my wife."

"Many families wouldn't accept her."

"Would you?"

"It matters not what I think."

Bertwoin blew out his breath. "That's a courtier's way of not answering."

"Watch your tongue, Chubby." She playfully pulled his beard. "But your anger does you credit. And maybe my opinion does matter. I have some sway with my brothers, even if they'd cut off their right hands before they'd admit it. So, yes, I would willingly accept her as my daughter-in-law. My only doubt would be to wonder why she chose you. Of course, she may not have any other suitors."

"She says she has rejected offers."

"*She* rejected them?"

"Yes, the master means to let her make her own choice, though I'm sure she asks for his advice." He hummed. "But like you, her choosing me makes me scratch my head. She can read and write. She knows plants and can cure diseases. She—"

His aunt raised a hand. "I know well what she can do, nephew. Like many, I too am in her debt. While Na Thea was away, Flowia cured Jehan of a cough that had me on my knees night after night, praying to the Good God."

Bertwoin glanced toward the northwest horizon, the direction of the coming wind. Guillema believed that an inferior male god, not her Good God, had created their world. That was why so many sinless babies died, soldiers bloodied each other for land and religion, lepers festered and limped along the roads, and so on. He shook away these thoughts like a dog shaking off water.

"Still," he said with downcast eyes, "I doubt you'll have any say in whether I marry the alchemist's virgin. My father might overlook Flowia's background, especially if I somehow prove she never had a Moorish sire, but he'll not abide her frank manner. And my uncle would rather marry me off to a leper bride than to her."

He smacked his fists together, making his knuckles sting. "What does *he* know about having a wife? Laurence has never loved anyone but himself. No woman would ever have him."

"Not so, nephew." She looked down the road as if staring into the past, her face sagging with sudden pity. "Laurence is bitter because he suffers from a lack of love. Oh, how he loved a girl once, and how she loved him. Just the mention of her name made him as giddy as a colt kicking up its heels."

"Did she die?"

"Worse than that. Her father gave her to another man, a man who beats her and whose soiled reputation leaves her friendless."

"Do I know her?"

"I'll not name her."

So he did know her. "Wouldn't you think, then, that Laurence might show sympathy for my plight?"

"He could do so, but he chose instead to be as bitter as mugwort. He already felt singled out by misfortune by having a girl's name."

Bertwoin shrugged. "We can't always choose how we feel."

"Our feelings are one thing. How we behave is another. We can't dodge life's sorrows, but we can choose how we answer them. Laurence wallows in misery, and so, has no friends to ease his way."

Bertwoin blew out his breath. "Now, I pity him. If he never married another woman, then he must still love her."

He thought of the wooden heart clasped in Ermessen's dead hand. "Did Ermessen love someone before Hebert took her as his wife?"

"She was like the woman Laurence loved. Full of hope but fated to live a life of sorrow. She was always so spry, even as a girl, and excellent at the loom. She hoped to marry a weaver and help him with his trade. Her dream was to live in town. She doted on company. Keeping her prisoner on a farm as Hebert did was like shutting a dove away in a cage so small it can't spread its wings.

"I doubt anyone except me and her daughters gave her any attention. Hear me well, nephew, Hebert may not have killed her, but he's the reason she's dead. When her parents married her off to him, they condemned her to this death." She huffed in anger. "May they die in torment because of it."

She tapped his shoulder with a forefinger. "Well, enough of that. The alchemist told you to come by my house tomorrow and learn how Armendis is faring. You need not do so."

"You oppose my following the alchemist's order?"

"I do. Armendis will not spend this night at my house." She raised a hand to stifle his protest. "The *bayle* has ears and eyes everywhere. He'll know to come to my house for her. So I'll hide my future daughter-in-law in a burrow where she'll be safe from the wolf. Now go visit Na Thea."

He stopped. "How did you know I wanted to go there?"

She turned to face him. "Bertwoin, you're like a little boy trying to hide the fact that he wants to go out and play instead of doing his chores. A mother knows his thoughts. If you love her, go now and beg for forgiveness for whatever you did to make her angry. And remember to tell me everything that Na Thea says."

Because his aunt was no nonsense and sometimes brusque, he sometimes forgot she could also be kind.

Na Thea lived in the shadow of the Basilica of Saints Nazarius and Celsus, a convenient location for her trade in sacred relics. Her house was a tiny fortress made of rough-cut limestone blocks with timbers adorning the edges. The ground floor was her shop. Bertwoin waited in the narrow lane beside her door, which was painted bright red to ward off evil. Strangers who mistook her red door as the sign of a bawdy house quickly learned they had erred.

When the alchemist saw Bertwoin, he glanced at Flowia, his eyes glowing with amusement, and called out, "Well met, plowman. You have tended to Armendis?"

"My aunt hides her elsewhere. I thought I'd be of more use here than staying there and getting in her way."

Flowia quipped,

"The plowman flees his aunt,

and his duties he does shirk,

for like a hive's queen ant

she's sure to put him to work."

"There's that too," he said and gave her his naughty boy look.

Ignoring his attempt to make her smile, Flowia squinted up at the third story of Na Thea's house, which jutted out over the two lower floors. "It's reputed to be haunted by a Roman nobleman who gives her advice."

"One wonders how that is accomplished," the master said. "I assume the Roman doesn't speak the local language, and I know Na Thea knows only a few words of Latin, which she learned while attending mass. Or she thinks they are Latin."

Seeing that he didn't understand, Flowia explained to Bertwoin, "Her priest uses the wrong words, and not only that, he mispronounces them. A Roman ghost might only recognize every fifth word of the priest's Latin."

Bertwoin pointed at the bunch of gray-green leaves in Flowia's hands. "Wormwood?"

"Correct," the alchemist said.

"Does Na Thea not already have this?"

The alchemist nodded as if he had said something wise. Bertwoin knew from Flowia's expression that he hadn't.

"I asked the same question," the master said. "And yes, she already possesses this remedy. But Flowia insisted we stop at our cottage to harvest something that will bring Na Thea a profit. It will honey our visit."

Bertwoin hummed his approval. Na Thea was known to be moody, and a guest gift might loosen her reluctant tongue. He smiled at Flowia. "Wormwood. I know it's used to treat maw worms."

Flowia held the bundle up to her nose and drew in a deep breath, its scent turning her face blissful. "We also use it for stomach ailments. And when people come to Na Thea complaining that they glut like boars on autumn's acorns yet grow ever thinner, she knows to purge them with wormwood. She is famed as the scourge of tapeworms. Anyway, it's as costly as a merchant's dinner. She'll welcome it more than us."

The alchemist patted her shoulder. "Well then, let us see if our giving of it causes her to tolerate us."

Both the alchemist and Bertwoin had to duck to enter the shop's low door. The alchemist studied the heavy beams supporting the ceiling, which had symbols carved on them. One side of his mouth twisted upward in amusement.

"Healing words?" Bertwoin whispered.

"Symbols for herbs and plants that might poison or produce sickness." He raised a cautionary finger. "However, if one studies these plants, one might find that given in small doses, they also cure diseases."

To their right, a fireplace was built into the wall, its blaze heating the room. In the middle stood a long table with benches of rowan, a wood that repelled witches. On the left wall hung three shelves lined with clay medicine jars. Bertwoin scanned the long room for the saints' knuckles and charms written on scraps of parchment that Na Thea sold. He saw none. Maybe she kept them safely hidden in her cellar.

Na Thea sat at the table with the bottom of her linen tunic pulled up to her knees. She was dicing what looked like a length of dried vine or a snake's skin. Her movements were deliberate, almost ritualistic, and after making each precise cut, she glanced at them—her expression guarded but not hostile.

When Flowia laid the dried wormwood on a corner of the table, Na Thea picked it up and sniffed it. She raised her eyebrows. "You grow this yourself?"

"There's a sunny spot near our *ostal* where they thrive. I harvested these under a full moon."

Na Thea kissed the wormwood. "You brought me leaves from the base of the bush, those full of vigor. You honor me, and I thank you for it. But I think you didn't come to trade herbs." When Flowia wiggled her head in agreement, the older woman smiled. "Information then."

"You are correct, as usual," the alchemist said. He listened a moment before asking, "Is your servant not here?"

"No, he carries a sleeping draught to Artal. It will calm Armendis. I'm told she can't catch her thoughts. Mayhap a deep sleep will restore her mind."

Bertwoin thought it interesting that she would use dreams to bring Armendis out of her dreamy state.

The alchemist asked, "So you already know that someone killed Ermessen?"

"Oh, was it to be kept a secret?"

"You misunderstand me." The alchemist walked to the shelves on the left wall and peeked into an open medicine jar. He picked out a green leaf and sniffed it, his expression softening as he savored its smell. "I am merely surprised everyone knows of this tragedy so soon."

"Are you, master alchemist?" She watched him, smug as a duchess. "Didn't Raimunda run to Na Guillema for help? And didn't the women who gathered at Guillema's *ostal* to pick up their warm loaves of bread hear Raimunda say that her sister was muddled and smeared with blood? Didn't Guillema go and find this to be true? And didn't Guillema discover her friend's corpse? Didn't she then send Raimunda running to you and to the blacksmith's forge in Montredon to fetch Hebert? I learned of the murder from one having a key made at the forge. So I thought it my duty to send medicine for Armendis."

The alchemist watched Na Thea's face with care. "But you sent the sleeping draught to Artal's house?"

"Yes, he will carry it on to Na Guillema for the girl. I might have sent it straight to Guillema, but Artal will want to judge Armendis's condition himself. He will want to care for her."

"How did you know Armendis would go to Guillema's house?"

Na Thea seemed more amused than insulted by his questioning her. "Saint's bones. Do you think *I* killed Ermessen, drugged her daughter, and then ran back here? If so, you restore me to the body of the girl I once was. And if that were true, old man, I would now pretend I knew naught of this murder." When the alchemist was about to interrupt, Na Thea raised a hand for silence. "As to Armendis, she left Hebert's *ostal* with Na Guillema. Where else would she go? Na Guillema is used to hiding people. Besides, Armendis was seen riding toward St. Vincent's on Jehan's cart."

She smirked at Bertwoin, as if she meant to poke him in the ribs, "People saw the plowman on the road with his aunt. I'm surprised he's here now."

Bertwoin told her, "So am I."

The alchemist studied Na Thea. "I admire the speed and efficiency of the gossip web you've woven. You ride at the gallop while we walk."

She acknowledged his praise with a nod. "Na Guillema is often the center of this web, as you call it. Like Flowia and you, I need to know what is happening out there," she waved at the door, "if I am to help those who suffer."

"So you believe Armendis is with Guillema at her house?"

Na Thea paused. "I did until you asked." She stroked her chin. "Probably moved to Artal's house then. So he'll not need to take the medicine to Guillema. It will please Melisende to host Armendis." She smiled at Bertwoin. "It seems you and some of your kinfolk intend to protect Armendis. That's Christian of you. Clanoud wasn't so kind to Raimunda."

Bertwoin knew not to try to defend his father.

The master came to his rescue. "What has Artal and Melisende to do with Armendis?"

"They will welcome and comfort her like a daughter. They will tell her we don't believe she murdered her mother." She gave the alchemist a challenging look, as if daring him to argue with her. "Ermessen and her youngest daughter were two fingers on the same hand. Neither would harm the other." Na Thea nodded at the rightness of her words. She put what she had cut up into a mortar and began powdering it with a limestone pestle.

Flowia blew out her breath. "Armendis was out of her head when her sister found her. Drug-addled, she might not have recognized her mother. She might have seen a devil in her place."

Bertwoin was surprised that Flowia would argue with Na Thea, the woman who had taught her most of what she knew about turning herbs into medicine.

Na Thea stopped grinding, and there was a moment of silence as she considered Flowia's words. "There *are* plants that cause waking nightmares. If poisoned with such, she might see her mother as a dragon, one she must kill to save herself. But more likely, she'd piss on herself in fear and flee or faint."

The alchemist said, "Hebert told us a witch laid a curse on the girl. Would you know who this woman is?"

Na Thea rolled her eyes. "Hebert is a walking pustule of hate. I can guess the name of the woman. The cur carries a mighty grudge against her. She's no more a witch than I am." When the alchemist raised his eyebrows, she laughed. "I know. I know. Some call me a witch, and if truth be told, I don't discourage the rumors." She gave the master a conspiratorial glance. "I doubt that you hinder gossip about your powers." She waved a hand at the medicine jars. "Belief in such rumors turns my plants into silver coins."

Not to mention her religious charms, Bertwoin thought.

Na Thea rapped on the table. "This is rowan wood. No witch can sit on this bench or at this table. So I cannot be a witch. And the woman you speak of often sits here with me. Besides, she is keen to further Armendis's welfare and would never harm her."

"So you know her?" Flowia said.

"I do. She's a devout woman who follows the ways of the Apostles. She doesn't deserve trouble from a sniveling, tight-assed scoundrel like Hebert." When the alchemist started to interrupt, she again raised a hand for silence. "She doesn't have the power to lay a curse on anyone. Maybe you should ask Hebert why he wishes to distract you."

Bertwoin turned his head and stared at the snapping fire so no one would see his smile. This relentless woman was queen of her own household, and while in it, dared to command even the learned alchemist.

"Do you have an idea why he would do so?" the master asked.

"It's possible the woman went to see Armendis that day. And Hebert likes to raise trouble for Artal."

"Artal?"

"Yes, Na Guillema's brother-in-law is husband to this woman Hebert accuses."

Bertwoin brayed, "My Aunt Meli?"

No one spoke, and the only sound in the room for a breath or two was Na Thea's pestle rasping in the mortar and the fire's hiss.

The alchemist smoothed his beard. "Why does Hebert wish to punish Artal? Why this hatred between them?"

Na Thea hesitated, glanced at Flowia, and then nodded. "Artal was Ermessen's first suitor, the one she preferred. But her father gave her to Hebert. Poor Ermessen. To muffle her crying every night after her marriage, she must have gnawed her knuckles raw to the bone."

"Ah, the wooden heart," the master murmured.

Na Thea stood up. "There, I've said it. It's good to know the truth of things. I thank you for the wormwood and hope my bit of gossip was payment enough."

"It was," the alchemist said. "I thank you for it. Much that puzzled me is now clearer."

Na Thea stared down at her bowl. "Well, I have to visit a woman who needs my powder. She has failed to bear a child."

"Dried umbilical cord?" Flowia asked, nodding at the mortar. Bertwoin started, making both women smile.

"Yes. If taken with heated red wine, she might have a son, taken with cool water, a girl." Na Thea cackled. "Either way, her husband will have fine sport."

The alchemist said, "We wish you success with her."

Na Thea shook her head, her expression both amused and perplexed. "If she believes strong enough, she may well bear a child. It surprises me how often my cures and charms do what I say they will."

"Does it?" the master asked. "Her belief might open the door so she can receive the blessing. Perhaps you inadvertently call down Heaven's power."

CHAPTER VIII.

The following morning, Bertwoin finished his normal chores, then slipped away. The ground was scattered with fallen branches after the night's brawny gale. This would please his sister Rachel when she came out to gather kindling.

He found the master and Flowia waiting for him, and the three of them immediately set out for Guillema's house in St. Vincent.

Bertwoin rubbed his hands together to warm them as they stepped lively along a forest track. "I want to hear how it went when the *bayle* visited my aunt yesterday."

"Do you imagine the thrust of sharp questions," the alchemist asked, "and Na Guillema parrying them with evasive answers?"

"Well, she's never going to tell him where she sent Armendis, and both of them know that."

"It is to one's advantage," the alchemist said, "to be allied with a woman of her character. She is the spritely agent that spawns reactions or ends them."

"Last night," Bertwoin said, "I remembered something peculiar. Yesterday my aunt's tunic was speckled with blood, but Raimunda's was cleaner than a fish in a brook. Did she not help my aunt move her sister into the house? Wasn't she the one who washed her?"

"She did both," Flowia said. "When she fled to Guillema's *ostal*, she was blood-smeared and distraught and wearing her own tunic. After cleaning the blood off Armendis, she changed into one of her mother's tunics."

"I'm surprised Hebert let her," Bertwoin said.

"Now her mother's tunic is hers to wear
for unlucky Armendis is no longer there,
and grieving Hebert doesn't really care
now that he's in a pit of deep despair."

They lapsed into silence and walked to the unfortified town of St. Vincent, its edge crowding down to a languid stretch of the Aude River. Bertwoin led them to the house in the town's center where his aunt and Jehan lived. Guillema had lost three babies and her husband. Her only living daughter had married and moved a few streets away in Saint Vincent. So, if Armendis married Jehan, Guillema would again have another woman in her house.

Bertwoin knocked on her sturdy door, then opened it without waiting for anyone to respond to his knock.

He paused in the front room to fill his nose with the homey smell of yeast that lingered from the morning's bread baking. Though it was still early, the town's women would already have collected the loaves they gave his aunt to bake for them. No doubt, the women who came were shocked—and excited—to learn more about the murder on Hebert's farm.

His aunt appeared in the doorway of a side room, wiping her wet hands on a hemp rag. She studied the three of them, judged their intent, then relaxed and smiled.

Her hesitation aside, Bertwoin could see that his aunt was more pleased than annoyed by their surprise visit. The alchemist brought an aura of respect to her house. He might also bring further news about the murder.

"You find welcome in my house," she said.

The master dipped his head. "May God give you and all those in this *ostal* health."

"May your blessing come true," Guillema said. She waved them into her baking room.

Flowia seated herself at a table, and the master planted his back in front of the oven to warm his old bones in the heat still radiating from it. Bertwoin leaned against the doorframe, where he could keep an eye on the front door and still see everyone in the oven room. He remembered the time he had stood guard inside the abbey and watched for monks while the alchemist examined the corpse of the woodcutter's daughter. The abbot had denounced them as blasphemers when he learned of their trespass.

"If you've come to see Mendy, I've carted her off to a safer place." Guillema's expression dared the alchemist to find fault with her doing so.

The alchemist laughed. "Sending her on to Artal and Melisende was wise."

Guillema reared back, her eyebrows raised. "You already know where she is?"

"Of course. By the way, Na Thea sent medicine to Artal for the girl."

His aunt said, "Good. It may help her recover her wit. Until then, we must keep her beyond the *bayle's* sharp claws. We need time to judge Mendy's guilt or innocence." Guillema looked displeased. "But she may not be safe at Meli and Artal's house. Not now. Both you and Thea already know where she hides. Others too may find her."

"*We* judge her guilt?" Bertwoin asked in disbelief. Both the master and Flowia ignored him, obviously taking his aunt's side. Did they believe that Guillema and Meli, instead of the law, should judge whether Armendis should hang?

The master nodded. "It's best we keep her hidden for now. What did the *bayle* say when he visited you?"

"He didn't, and that makes me fret. Does he know she's no longer under my roof?"

The alchemist also looked worried. "The *bayle* is a threat to Armendis, but I no longer deem him to be the most pressing danger she faces."

Guillema pushed her tunic sleeves up her muscular forearms as if preparing to fight whoever the master named as a more dire threat. But Bertwoin had misjudged her action. Instead, she turned to the table and tore off chunks of bread, sliced some cheese, and dipped olives out of a wide-mouthed pot for them. She also poured out some of her home-brewed ale, the source of yeast for her bread.

"It's likely," the alchemist said, "that once the drug's madness passes from her, Armendis will return to normal."

"You mean—" Flowia said.

"Yes, the murderer can't let Armendis become clearheaded. Her memory might prove dangerous."

Bertwoin rubbed a fist in the palm of his other hand. "You're saying the killer will now come after her?"

"If the murderer wishes to be truly safe."

"Well," his aunt said, "right now she's a frightened doe and will be an easy victim if she's left alone. She's red-eyed from crying and can't stop asking if she really killed the mother she loved."

Her words "red-eyed" bothered Bertwoin, but he didn't know why. There was something he should remember. He tried to bring it up, but it was hidden too deep in the cave of his mind.

Guillema patted Flowia's shoulder. "I would take it as a kindness if you looked in on her. Guilt has shoved her into a deep, deep darkness. I know of no herb to soothe her. If we could only lighten her mood a bit..."

After looking at the master, who nodded, Flowia said, "I will go immediately."

Guillema put her blunt hand over Flowia's slender hand. "I'll not forget this."

After they heard Flowia close the front door, Guillema muttered, "And I'll not forgive Hebert for accusing my sister of practicing witchery. Let him look to his own safety now. And may all women shun his house."

The master chewed an olive, his expression dreamy as he let its flavor flood his tongue. "Tell us about Ermessen."

Guillema's face hardened and aged at the mention of her bosom friend, then softened into a smile. "As a girl, she was always gadding about, always talking. She made life interesting for those around her, at least when she was young and before she married."

"Any enemies?" the alchemist asked.

"None, other than her husband."

"Whom her father picked?"

"Ermessen's father wasn't a mean man and might have allowed her to marry Artal, but he fell into debt to Hebert. For all his faults, Hebert is a successful farmer. He demanded Ermessen as his wife or the debt paid. Her father sacrificed her for the good of his *ostal*."

The alchemist sighed. "So he thought—"

Someone rapped on the bread room's shutter, and a few moments later, opened the front door. Bertwoin leaned back in the doorway and saw a carpenter's prim wife enter. Her long blue dress looked new, and she held its hem up so as not to catch it on the bundled floor reeds. She paused just inside the doorway and eyed him with surprise. Then she smiled at him. He nodded, glad it was her who had come and not the *bayle*. He stepped inside the baking room so she could enter. Her mouth opened when she saw the master near the oven, and she dipped her head in greeting. He nodded to her.

"Catarina," Guillema said, "I was about to break up one of your loaves and soak it in milk for our pig. What time of the morning is this to come?"

Bertwoin whispered, "Hah," to himself. His aunt was exaggerating. Jehan and she might eat this fine bread if it was not claimed, but never would their pig have a taste of it. It fed on old maslin loaves, scraps, and what it found in the street.

"My man dropped a hammer on his naked foot and now acts like he's crippled for life. He *only* broke two toes. It's a blessing that he's not the one who had to give birth. We'd have no children."

Guillema put her hands on her hips. "Don't tell me, woman, that your old man gets up before daybreak with you. I'll not believe in the miracle of that. The warm bread should've been in your house before he left his bed."

"He did it yesterday evening when I brought you the loaves for baking. Kept me up all night with his moaning."

"That I'll believe." Guillema got two loaves of bread and handed them to Catarina.

Before leaving, the woman turned to Bertwoin, "Congratulations to you, and may your family prosper."

"What?" Had he done something important?

She seemed confused at his not understanding her. "Roul announced your coming marriage to his daughter, Maria." She looked at Bertwoin's face and put her hand over her mouth. "Oh, was it a secret?"

Bertwoin had to sit down on a three-legged stool.

"Not all rumors are true," Guillema told Catarina.

"Oh, devil's bones. Now I have to confess to the sin of telling falsehoods. Well, God grant you all peace." Catarina hurried away, probably to tell others that the latest rumor they had heard wasn't true.

"I'll never do it," Bertwoin announced.

"How can you not do this?" his aunt murmured with pity. She poured all three of them more ale from an earthenware flagon shaped like a crooked man. Hunchbacks brought good luck, even when made of clay.

The alchemist moved over to a bench and seated himself. He leaned his elbows on his knees, his head bowed, and gazed at the flagstone floor.

Bertwoin shook his head. "He can't make me."

"Clanoud will have his way," Guillema said, again with gentle pity. "I know my brother well, and you do too."

"I'll run off and become a shepherd first."

"And shame your father, your house, your family, not to mention Roul. And what of Maria? Would you disgrace her? She—"

"I know Roul," the master muttered, interrupting Guillema. "He's a good man, but I do not comprehend why his daughter should be so favored by Clanoud."

His aunt stomped the hard-packed dirt floor. "Land," she said, as if it were a damnable word. She waved for Bertwoin to explain.

"It's a patch of oaks," he said. "Both my father and Roul claim them. Both are still sniffing around each other with their bristles up, but neither one of them shows any sign of backing away."

"You think your father won't settle this peacefully?" the alchemist asked.

"He says we need those oaks to give us acorns, if not for our pigs, then for us. He says this land will tide us over during the hungry times before harvest and maybe even be the bit that keeps us alive if famine dries up the fields."

"My brother only wants what's best for his family," Guillema said. "I've heard tales of men eating each other and of families killing themselves instead of starving slowly to death."

Bertwoin nodded, remembering a time of hunger when his *maman* had ground acorns into flour to make their barley and rye go farther. "I understand his reasoning, and it makes sense, but I don't want my marriage to be part of the bargain."

"He found a way to share those trees, after all," Guillema said with pride. "Clanoud usually gets whatever he wants. He'll make Roul part of our family."

The alchemist told her. "It is possible that these words have no truth in them."

"Well said, master. Half the rumors I hear have no truth to them. You need to run home, nephew, before you take another breath and see if Maria is sewing her wedding dress."

"Yes," the alchemist said. "Then come to my house. This is something we must discuss with Flowia before she hears of it elsewhere. And let us all pray the rumor isn't true."

His aunt held up a finger. "And if the gossip is wrong, let us pray that neither Clanoud nor Roul hear of it. They may well make it true. It answers their problem well."

CHAPTER IX.

As Bertwoin trudged home, he prayed that his family hadn't betrayed him, but if he had to wager his last silver denier, he would bet the rumor of his coming marriage to Maria was true. His father would think it pig-smart to ally the two farms, and at the same time, rid their family of the threat of his ever marrying Flowia. Even now, his uncle might be frolicking about in that lanky dance he always did when celebrating. His *maman* too might now relax, relieved that the tension in her family had melted away. This marriage to Maria would also settle the nettlesome dispute between the two farms. Instead of fighting over the wooded strip of land, they might now share it like they shared their children.

Both fathers, of course, considered it their parental right to marry off their children howsoever they willed, though he, as the eldest son, should have a voice in the matter, even if it was only a whisper. Maria was expected to obey her father without a murmur. Did she look forward to this marriage or dread it? He barely knew her. She always seemed as shy as a doe.

Please let it not be true.

He detoured into the hamlet of Montredon, seizing the opportunity to visit their church and seek ancestral help. The only way to fight his father now was to recruit a spiritual ally, someone among the dead, to intercede for him. Rather than pray directly to St. Raphael, the patron saint of marriage, he decided to light a sweet-smelling beeswax candle to honor his grandfather. This would bring his plight to the old man's attention. Though dead, his grandfather was still the powerful patron of their *ostal*, the one they, the living, consulted before making major decisions. His father kept a lock of the old man's white hair in a wooden box to bring luck to their house and to keep evil away from their farm.

But no, his gruff grandfather was not the best choice. Instead, he would light a candle in memory of his grandmother—a warm, comforting woman with a gentle voice. She was more saintly than her husband and was more likely to be on good terms with St. Raphael. Besides, his grandfather probably didn't know *any* saints because he was in Hell.

He hadn't known his grandfather well because the old man died while he was still a toddler, but his one abiding memory of him was of teasing the old man, trying to get him to play with him. Irritated, the old bear had knocked him against a wattle-and-daub wall.

Anyway, his ghostly grandfather probably wouldn't help him. He held the same beliefs as Clanoud, his favorite son. He might oppose his grandson's bothersome rebellion. He might agree that love was a secondary consideration in marriage, especially if Clanoud used a wedding to benefit their *ostal*. Increasing their family's honor by adding to the size of their land would widen the death grin on the old man's moldering skull.

Montredon's square, brown-stone church resembled a thick-walled fortress and exuded a soothing air of permanence. A lone cloud passing overhead swept away the sun's glare, covering Bertwoin in its sudden shadow. His dismay leaked away. Might this be a sign that his grandmother would shelter him?

He opened the church's scarred door and crossed the threshold into an aura of spiritual calm. He relaxed in the scent of incense, shedding his worries as if someone had lifted a horse collar off his neck. He knew then he had to hold to his purpose. Bartering away love for land at this altar in this church in this village would profane the sacred wedding ritual.

Their priest, Father Pons, was talking to Widow Bonne under the rear stained glass window. She had assumed the duty of adorning the church with flowers or dried flower decorations every week.

Not having any coins or barter on him, Bertwoin silently promised to pay for the candle on Sunday when he came to mass. His grandmother would smile at his self-serving assumption that the silent Catholic Church had accepted his promise. His grandfather would call it thievery, even if he paid the price on Sunday, and punish him for it. Bertwoin lit the beeswax candle from one already burning and spiked it on a rack near the door.

He sat on a chair in the back and pleaded with his grandmother's spirit to rescue him. Then, going outside, he entered the adjoining graveyard and stopped at the Teisseire family tomb.

"Bertwoin," Father Pons said, flapping toward him in his brown robe. "Well met. I was told just this morning that you are to marry soon. Oh, is that a surprise? Is something wrong? Don't worry, pre-wedding qualms are normal, especially for women, but also for men."

"Then it's true?"

"So I am told." Father Pons was gleeful. "Roul came early this morning. Maria is a fine girl. She'll make you an excellent wife. You must always strive to be worthy of her."

Bertwoin hoped their handsome priest hadn't already been with Maria. He had a reputation for deflowering virgins, something many young women welcomed, since he was much gentler and more attentive than their future husbands would ever be.

Bertwoin kept mum, not wanting to reject Maria publicly and shame her. He would do whatever was needed to stop this wedding, but do it in such a way that Roul would find *him* unworthy of marrying his daughter. Let her father call off the wedding. There must be no stain on Maria. Maybe Aunt Guillema would allow him to join her household after his father banished him.

"Well," he said, trying to keep his tone light, though the distressing news made it hard for him to breathe. "I'm needed at home now. There's still much to talk about."

The priest patted Bertwoin's shoulder. "It's a marriage, my son, an occasion for Godly joy, not for the sorrow of a funeral." He beamed at Bertwoin, full of hearty goodwill. "I must now go inside and prepare for a christening. Maybe before long, I will baptize a child for Eudes and Rachel, and then one for you and Maria. But you must promise me that if you have a boy, you will forgo giving him a *girl's* name."

Bertwoin laughed. Before Laurence was born, his father dreamed that the baby would be a girl and bragged about his foreknowledge. So the baby boy was a disappointment and rather than change his second son's name to Laurent, he reinterpreted his dream to be a sign from God that this son should bear a girl's name. "Don't worry, I wouldn't do that to my boy."

"Good." The cleric slapped him on the shoulder and flapped away.

Bertwoin scowled at his grandfather's grave. "I defy you, old man. I defy your selfish, ungodly ways. You shouldn't have done that to Laurence. And you shouldn't have punched your little grandson and knocked the joy out of him. I'll not sell myself for more land. May your skeleton twist in anger until its bones crack."

Bertwoin ambled over a small rise and looked across the fields, some newly planted and some kept fallow. This was the flat land that he and his brown mules had plowed, the land he and his family had tilled and harvested. The house, barn, and land he cherished as much as a king does his realm. These fertile fields fed them and gave them an honored place in the community.

The *bayle* and one of the lawman's burly cousins were also in sight, marching across the field ahead of him. Why had the lawman hired someone to come with him?

Despite the cold, Bertwoin's family sat outside in the front yard with two visitors—Roul and his daughter, Maria. Everyone around her seemed animated while she sat as stiff as a Madonna statue.

His family saw the lawmen striding toward them and became as still as a fluffle of wary rabbits. Bertwoin set a determined smile on his face. The *bayle* and his cousin were already drinking ale by the time he reached the house. As usual, the lawman stood like a haughty rooster in his horse-leather tunic with a red crusader's cross on his chest. He wore his outer cloak open so everyone would see the cross and mark him as a holy warrior.

His family had relaxed again, as had Roul. A yeast-smelling cloud hung around them. The *bayle* also seemed relaxed, though his eyes were watchful.

He forced a grin. "A celebration? Has the dispute over the borderland been settled?"

"It has," his father said and smacked his lips with satisfaction.

Dread lay heavy as a log in Bertwoin's chest. All the men other than the *bayle* glowed with mirth. The women were more somber, especially Maria. She stared at their front door as if she longed to slip away into their house. The color of her ankle-length, gray cloak probably matched her mood. It certainly did his.

It was now they would tell him their plans for his future. He must take care that Maria didn't see his dismay. As his aunt had said, rejecting her would disgrace her.

Roul stepped forward to shake his hand. "So you've come home. I'm told you've helped the alchemist," he realized his mistake, "er, and the *bayle* solve two murders already."

Everyone looked at the lawman for confirmation. With obvious reluctance, the *bayle* nodded. "He's been useful, though I need little help with upholding the law."

Bertwoin half bowed to show appreciation for this feeble praise. "It was the *bayle* who sent me running to the alchemist on the first murder and started me working for the master."

"Hah," his father barked. He smirked at the lawman, who looked as if he had just tasted a sour blackberry.

His *maman* chastised him with a stern frown. Insulting the lawman would not do their family any favors. Bertwoin glanced at Roul, who seemed not to know how to interpret his future son-in-law's comment. That meant Roul didn't know that the *bayle* had tried to arrest him for the murder of the woodcutter's daughter, forcing him to flee for help.

The *bayle* smirked at Clanoud. "Like I said, I can uphold the law with little help, but ghosts are another thing."

"Ghosts?" his *maman* blurted out.

The *bayle* smiled, pleased at everyone's excited attention. "Hebert claims he saw his wife gliding through the copse of chestnuts. She was wearing the bloody tunic she was killed in. He reckons even burial might not lay her spirit to rest. Wants me to find and punish her killer so her ghost can move on."

Roul rubbed his hands together in satisfaction. "From what I hear, this killing is already solved." He glanced at the *bayle*, who sipped his ale and said nothing. "Yes," Roul continued, "Even Hebert says Armendis did it, and I heard that Raimunda admitted this was so. What daughter would kill her mother?"

Laurence, brisk with suppressed joy, handed Bertwoin a mug of ale. There was a pause as everyone, except Maria and the lawman, watched him with knowing smiles. His-bride-to-be sat in the wicker chair, a seat of honor, with her head bowed, watching him from the corner of her eye. The *bayle* and the man he had brought were wary, probably sensing something important was not being said.

Bertwoin took a sip of ale to calm himself, but the drink tasted sour and almost made him gag. Maybe he could get away. "The alchemist ordered me to come to him. I was on the way there from my aunt's house."

His father made a dismissive sound in his throat. "He can wait." His tone allowed no argument.

"From your aunt's house." The *bayle* repeated Bertwoin's words as if they had a hidden meaning. "Did you see Armendis there?" He watched for Bertwoin's reaction.

"Armendis? Why?"

"Hebert says you and your aunt took Armendis to Guillema's house. That's why I stopped here on the way to talk with your aunt."

"Armendis left us before we reached St. Vincent's."

The *bayle* raised his eyebrows. "Word is that the girl was... unwell. I'm surprised you let her go off alone."

Bertwoin shrugged off the lawman's disbelief. "She didn't need my help to walk. And I have no command over her or any of her family."

"She's not yet family, huh?" The *bayle* glanced around, his smile icy. "Maybe Guillema is lucky to be rid of her. Looks like Armendis has a tendency to murder people in her family."

Bertwoin asked, "Doesn't that still need to be proven?"

"It will be when I find her. And she's guilty until she proves she's not. Only the old alchemist would doubt she did it … and maybe yourself."

"I wouldn't—"

Roul interrupted, "She's sleeping in Artal's cellar." When everyone gaped at him, he added, "My brother knows someone who saw her go there. She may not be in his cellar, but she's at Artal's house."

The *bayle's* cousin hawed. "If we charge into that cellar, heretics will scatter out of it like rats escaping a beaten haystack."

His *papa* and Laurence glanced at each other, then looked at Roul to judge his reaction. Roul carried the reputation of being a devout man. It was plain as daylight to Bertwoin that his father and uncle wondered if their having Good Folks like Guillema and Melisende in the family might prevent the wedding.

Bertwoin doubted it would. When Roul agreed to the marriage, he knew about these heretical aunts. Everybody did.

The *bayle* said, "Well then, I guess we'll make an official visit to Artal's household. I thank you, Roul, for letting me know where the vixen has gone to ground." He turned to Bertwoin. "Gidie came to The Noble Head two days ago. You might want to watch your back." He laughed as if he had played a joke on Bertwoin.

"I'll need to be going," Bertwoin said.

"Before you go, *we've* got a surprise for you," his uncle said with a gloating smile.

It was now when the crisis was upon him that his grandmother sent him a revelation. He fought down the urge to dance a step or two.

His mother watched him with pity, as did Wilfraed and Rachel. Bertwoin smiled to reassure them and said, "I've got a surprise for you, too. It's the main reason I stopped here on my way to see the master."

His uncle dismissed the importance of his coming revelation with a mocking sound, then said, "But ours is a *big* surprise. One that concerns all of us. You'll never guess what it is."

"My surprise is also big, at least for me." He knew he needed to charge in with his lie to forestall them from telling him what they had decided to do. He wanted to argue over his decision, not theirs. "I've decided to become a priest, or at least, a monk."

The stunned silence was so profound they all seemed to be underwater. They gaped at him as if he had just announced he could fly and would now prove it to them. Bertwoin saw Maria's relief before she turned her face away.

"A priest?" Wilfraed said, his voice hoarse with surprise and excitement.

"It's a joke," his father told everyone.

"I am resolved to become one."

"A priest?" his father shouted. "A soft-pawed church cat petted by old ladies." His left hand flicked the idea away. "If you even touched a Church Bible, it would burst into flames. You know little of what's in the Good Book and can't read. The closest you ever got to being religious was when you were in the bishop's dungeon."

"Father Pons can't read either. And I can learn. I could also become a lay brother if I can't be a true priest."

"You're a plowman," his father scoffed, "and always will be. You'll do what I tell you to do. You'll do what's right for your family and marry Maria."

Roul cleared his throat. "We might have seen this coming. He *is* the one who gave his tunic to a leper."

"He's the one," Clanoud shouted, "who killed a young boar when he was a boy. He's more David than Good Samaritan. How can I believe him, knowing as I do how little respect he has for clerics? Anyway, he'll do what he has to do for his family. There's religion in that too."

Roul frowned at Clanoud. "I'll not lure a man away from God's service." He crossed himself. "So, what do we do now?"

The *bayle* stood up to leave. Bertwoin began walking away.

"Where are you going?" his father called.

"Latrine."

After he circled their house, he took off running. He had to reach Artal's *ostal* before the *bayle* did.

CHAPTER XI.

Trotting along at an easy but ground-eating pace, Bertwoin turned onto a footpath most people avoided even in the daylight. He used it now because it was the shortest route to Artal and Meli's *ostal*. He also wanted the fewest people possible to see him running toward St. Vincent. If the *bayle* figured out that he had warned Artal, the lawman might stick him in the pillory for a cold, uncomfortable day or two.

So Bertwoin braved the haunted crossroads at the Devil's Doorstep. It was here that condemned criminals spat out their souls while kicking at the end of a hanging rope. It was here the majestic Gallows Oak held sway and cast its gloom over the surrounding forest. It was here that Armendis might hang.

There was a permanent gallows set up in Bourg's central square, but the *visconte* and bishop preferred to rid their domain and diocese of transgressors on the Gallows Oak. Dying in this evil part of the woods emphasized to all that a soul loosed here wafted straight to Hell.

When Bertwoin came within sight of the accursed place, he was relieved to see no rotting body dangling at the end of a hemp rope. No corpse meant he didn't have to contend with a furious ghost.

Bertwoin made the sign of a cross and whispered, "Keep me under Your wing," before he sprinted under the oak's sturdy branches.

His Uncle Artal and Aunt Meli lived on the edge of St. Vincent. Since Artal was a farrier, he had a barn where he could stable a horse or mule overnight if need be. Not only did he shoe mules and horses, but he also tended to those that came down sick.

Bertwoin knocked on a front shutter and breezed inside without waiting for anyone to open the door for him. The house felt as empty as an upended mug. Were they hiding? He glanced in a side bedroom, then climbed the ladder to the *solier*. As expected, both were vacant. Meli had prepared a straw mattress against the room's far wall. This was unusual because guests normally slept in the cellar, especially those hiding from the law. The cellar had two exits while the *solier* was a trap with only one way in and one way out.

He climbed back down. Even though it wasn't yet evening, his aunt had already damped down the hearth fire. He pulled open the kitchen door to the cellar and cold air blew into his face. He was surprised to see light beaming in it through the other door that led outside.

A man in a black robe with a rope belt sat on a stool in one corner. He wasn't a monk because he didn't have the tonsure, the monastic crown. So, his aunt and uncle were hosting an itinerant True Christian preacher, a *bonhomme*. The Catholic Church would call him a *perfect* because he was a perfect heretic. This one had been using the light coming through the open outside door to mend a leather mitten.

Bertwoin recovered from his surprise and remembered his manners. "God give you peace. I am Bertwoin Teisseire, son of Clanoud Teisseire."

Without getting up, the *bonhomme* raised a hand chest-high in blessing. "And may the Good God bless you. I am Prades Authie. You know Artal and Melisende well?"

"They're my aunt and uncle." Bertwoin glanced around and saw only one bed behind two beer barrels. So, the Good Man was alone, which was odd. "Is Armendis here?"

"No," the *bonhomme* said. "The alchemist's virgin came by, examined her, told Melisende what Armendis must eat, and advised rest in a darkened room. After she left, your aunt began preparing a bed in the *solier*. Artal had a fierce argument outside with Armendis, and he left in high choler. Armendis came inside crying, then she too disappeared. Melisende ran off to search for the young woman."

"And no one knows where she went?"

"Mayhap, she now felt unwelcome in Artal's house."

Yes, his uncle was plain-spoken and might have said something cruel. Thinking the *bonhomme* would want to know that they were about to have unexpected company, Bertwoin said, "I came to warn my aunt and uncle that the *bayle* is on his way here to arrest Armendis."

"Here?" The *bonhomme* rose and began stuffing his few belongings into a hemp bag.

"I'm going to my Aunt Guillema's home," Bertwoin told him. "You can come with me if you wish. If she can't board you herself, she'll know where to send you."

The *bonhomme* studied his face, clearly judging his intentions. "That is kind of you. I know her well."

Before leaving Artal's *ostal*, Bertwoin stopped by his uncle's barn. A roan horse watched with calm curiosity as he quickly made sure Armendis wasn't hiding anywhere in the stable. The *bonhomme* also watched him.

His uncle's mule and small cart were gone. As a farrier, Artal was often away from home during the day, but Bertwoin doubted he had started new work this afternoon. Perhaps he had a small chore to do and had used it as an excuse to be away. Meli was sure to chastise him for arguing with Armendis.

Bertwoin and the *bonhomme* hurried away down a crooked dirt street toward St. Vincent's center.

Bertwoin said, "I thought Good Men always traveled in pairs."

"I have a companion boarding elsewhere."

"Ah, I see."

"Do you? It is less of a burden on an *ostal* if we divide the cost, and it only takes one of us to bless the bread. Most families of our faith consider it an honor to host us."

"So, you are not hiding?"

"Not yet," the *bonhomme* said. "As of now, the Church tolerates us because it hopes to convert us back into the fallacy of its teachings. But already, there are those in the Church who believe they serve God by hounding us. Some of us have been beaten, one or two killed. Bishop Othon encourages these brutal acts against us. So, for protection, we often travel in pairs."

"Does the *bayle* also harass you?"

"The lawman dislikes us, but he causes us little trouble if we keep within the law. Though, if he found me in Artal's cellar, he might banish me. Once a crusader, always a crusader." The *bonhomme* smiled. "As I am sure you know. I have heard of your father."

Would his aunts one day be in danger? Could his fierce father help them? It was true the Catholic Church now only used words as its weapon against these heretics, but rumor said the Pope was growing impatient. Argument did little good. Church officials often lost when they faced off against the Good Folk elders in public debate. The Good Folk claimed they followed the footsteps of the apostles and were converting more and more people to their simple faith every year.

Bertwoin changed the subject. "Do you think someone warned Armendis that the *bayle* was coming for her?"

The Good Man frowned as he considered this. "No. She would tell your aunt that the lawman was coming and tell her where she was going." The *bonhomme* stopped and stretched his arms toward the bright sky, his lips moving in silent prayer, before he walked on. He asked, "Why do you now go to see Guillema?"

"Armendis may have run to her. She still expects Guillema to be her mother-in-law. And I'm looking for my Aunt Meli. She needs to know the *bayle* is coming to search her house."

The *bonhomme* smiled at Bertwoin. "The girl is fortunate. Guillema protects her, Melisende cherishes her like a daughter, and you care for her welfare."

Bertwoin shrugged. "She needs to stay free until the alchemist proves her innocent. She doesn't need to be hung for a crime she didn't do and be buried in an unmarked grave." He shrugged. "I also want to know why she ran away."

They kept to the crooked, narrow, dirt lanes instead of St, Vincent's three cobbled streets. They saw no one except two dogs and a sow that made them walk around her. As they passed windows, Bertwoin smelled cabbage and onions, and of course, ale. His empty stomach gurgled, and his throat felt dry as parchment.

When they entered Guillema's front room after a quick knock on the shutter, his Aunt Meli stepped out of the baking room, her face hopeful. Her disappointment at not seeing Armendis was as plain as a black swan among a bank of white ones.

"Did Armendis come back?" she asked *Bonhomme* Authie, her expression that of a worried mother searching for her lost child.

"No. Let us hope she doesn't do so. The *bayle* is now on his way there to arrest her."

Guillema stepped into the long front room behind her sister. As soon as she saw Master Authie, she dropped to her knees, clasped her hands, and bowed three times, each time saying,

"Bless me, Lord, and pray for me." Then she ended with, "Lead us to our rightful end."

The *bonhomme* raised a hand in blessing and intoned, "God bless you, Guillema. In our prayers, we ask that God make you a Good Christian and that He lead you to your rightful end."

His aunt rose, her expression serene and joyful.

Disconcerted at witnessing a pagan rite and not wanting to see anymore, Bertwoin asked Guillema, "Is it possible she is with Jehan?"

"No, even now he searches every street and looks behind every bush for her." She stared at the kitchen hearth a moment before saying to Bertwoin, "She may be confused. You need to find her."

Meli wrung her hands. "I have to go defend my home from the *bayle*. The men he keeps company with would steal coins from a church box."

"Remember," the *bonhomme* cautioned, "we do not lie."

Meli huffed, "What could that girl be thinking? Running off like that? Did Artal come back?"

Surprised that his aunt had rudely ignored the *bonhomme's* warning, Bertwoin said, "No. Is he out searching for her?"

Meli shook her head. "He left before she did and doesn't know she ran off."

Guillema told Bertwoin, "Go by Hebert's farm."

Meli flapped her hands, dismissing this. "Jehan has already gone there. And Armendis would never go back home."

"Yes," Guillema argued, "but she may have forgotten something. We packed in haste and came away with little. The alchemist has faith in Bertwoin. Says he is the mastiff that can sniff her out."

When Meli looked at Bertwoin as if he was now certain to find Armendis, he raised his hands. "I'll do what I can, but if she's not there, I can't conjure her up."

Disappointed, Meli asked her sister, "If Bertwoin finds she hasn't gone back to the farm, where else should he look?"

"Maybe the pottery. Garnier still insists his son, silent Tumas, should marry Armendis. Maybe Tumas took her. He's strong as a bear."

"True, true," said Meli. "Tumas means to scare Jehan off."

Guillema pushed the sleeves of her long woolen tunic up to her elbows. "Jehan will not be turned aside." She looked at Bertwoin as if surprised to see him. "Standing here won't find her."

He laughed. "You'll earn me a beating. My father will punish me for shirking my chores."

Guillema put her hands on her hips. "Don't you worry about Clanoud. Tell him I sent you on an errand."

"I'll want a crust of bread and a scrap of cheese. I need wood to feed the dying spark of strength still left flickering in my belly."

"Fair enough," Guillema said. "You can eat while on your way to Hebert's place. And I'll feed you again when you return and tell me what you found."

CHAPTER XII.

Bertwoin decided to delay obeying his aunt's order to visit Hebert's farm. Since Jehan hadn't visited the alchemist, it made sense to go there first. Armendis might have fled to him. It was where he had run to when the *bayle* came to arrest him for poor Emeline's murder.

As he hurried along the narrow dirt streets of St. Vincent, eating his bread and cheese as he went, he met only a few people, but he noticed a thickset tramp in a threadbare blanket following him. The man kept a fair distance between them.

Who would follow him? And why? He doubted it was the murderer. Ermessen wouldn't have let this ruffian near her. Bertwoin needed to find Armendis instead of confronting the ruffian, so he turned onto a side lane, ran down it, and dodged into another street. He kept changing streets. When he crossed the Toulouse Road bridge over the Aude River, he was certain no one followed him.

Did the master already know about Armendis's disappearance? He might. One of Flowia's duties was to gather and tell him all the local gossip. The alchemist thought it important to know the background and full story of whatever happened in their area. Nobles and officials often lied or told only part of the truth. Sometimes they, themselves, didn't know what really had happened. And even if the gossip wasn't true, it might still be important if people believed it. Was a fire in a peasant's kitchen an accident or had the chandler he cheated set it? Why did Tumas believe he had the right to marry Armendis? Did he? Had Hebert backed out of a binding agreement? The master wanted to know the truth of these things.

As Bertwoin was about to enter the alchemist's poultry yard, he heard Flowia singing behind their cottage. He found her pouring water on the few medicinal plants left in her garden. Her guard pig, Roland, huffed a greeting and trotted over for a back scratch.

"Ready for a cold winter?" he asked the pig, who was now fatter than usual and wore a shaggy winter coat.

"Good evening, Father Bertwoin," Flowia said, smiling to herself as she continued to wet a row of creeping savory. So, she had already heard of his ruse to prevent his father from marrying him off to Roul's shy daughter. Had his not wanting to marry Maria softened her anger against him?

"Well met, maiden" he said to Flowia as he scraped his fingernails down the boar's bristly spine, causing Roland to quiver with porcine ecstasy. "I have come to hear your confession."

She laughed and stared a moment at the ground before chanting,

"Father, I have so little to confess,
my quiet life is plain and truly dull,
everything you can easily guess,
and finding sin in me would be a miracle."

"Even so, we'll need to find a private place where we may discuss your sins."

She rolled her eyes and said to the smiling pig, "Roland, I think you will need to protect *me* as well as my garden." She then asked, "How is Maud faring?"

"Better. Her diarrhea is gone, and she's livelier."

"Good." Flowia said. "I will not disturb your *ostal*, but if your mother needs me, she only has to ask."

Bertwoin almost asked, "And if I need you?" But instead, he announced in an official tone, "I come with news."

She waited, her face expectant. He wanted to tell his tale only once, so he said, "The master?"

She finished watering a row of winter savory. "Does it concern Armendis?"

When Flowia was in a willful mood, she would not budge from having her way, so he surrendered and told her, "She ran off."

Flowia jerked upright, sloshing water on her felt boot. "What?"

He tried not to look smug. It was rare for him to know something she didn't. And he now also knew that Armendis hadn't fled to the alchemist for help.

"I think," he said, "she left while my Aunt Meli was making up a bed for her in the *solier*."

"And you know this to be true? She's gone? I just spoke to her at your aunt's house."

"I came there just after you left. She's run away."

Flowia set the bucket down and pointed at the master's workshop, its wattle-and-daub walls and shingle roof now in the spidery shadow of a naked oak. Roland watched them, peering from face to face, sensing that something important had happened. He followed them to the hut's sturdy door.

Flowia knocked once and led Bertwoin into the workroom. The room smelled like burning fat. On a rowan bench sat the master with a tallow candle near him, its light washing over his noble features as he read a book. The leather cover of the tome was decorated with entwined golden vines and gilt lettering. Its pages were also made of fine leather. He was studying the illustration of a long-necked pelican. It bit its breast so drops of blood would splatter down and feed its three chicks.

"Ah, Bertwoin," the master said, "the plowman who wishes to stop scratching furrows in the earth and start furrowing the brows of sinners with homilies?" The alchemist laid a costly silk ribbon in the book to keep his place and closed it. "I wait with barely controlled anticipation to hear your first sermon."

"Roul says he will not thwart a man from serving God. So Maria is saved from bondage to me." He nodded at the book. "Do pelicans really wound themselves?"

"Not that I'm aware of. It symbolizes a mother's sacrifice for her children. In this book," the master patted the leather cover, "it is a symbol of the Lord's sacrifice for us."

Bertwoin stared at a glass beaker the alchemist had placed on top of his warm brick oven. It was half filled with a clear liquid that covered a goose egg. Scum lay across the liquid's surface like a slimy skin.

"And your family?" the master asked.

"I'd rather be here or out searching for Armendis than be at home right now."

The alchemist sat up straighter. "Searching for Armendis?"

Flowia said before Bertwoin could explain, "She's gone missing from Artal's house."

"Fled or taken?"

Flowia glanced at Bertwoin, letting him answer.

"No one knows," he said as he remembered the empty straw mattress he had seen in the *solier*. "But the bed made up for her showed no signs of a struggle." Bertwoin told them about Roul telling the *bayle* where Armendis was hidden, of his running to Artal's house, of his meeting the *bonhomme,* and then of their hurrying to his Aunt Guillema's house.

The alchemist listened attentively until Bertwoin fell silent. "So Artal left before Armendis disappeared. Let's hope no one stole her away. Does she follow the faith of the Good Folk?"

"I don't know."

"Hebert is not one of them," Flowia said. "And though he cares little for priests or the Church, he and Ermessen attended mass." She fluttered a hand toward Bertwoin. "Armendis was to marry your cousin. Would she not convert to their faith?"

"Aunt Guillema is one of the Good Folk, but Jehan still attends mass. He obeys his mother in most things but rebels against joining the True Christians. I'm told she prays daily for her Good God to set him on the path to save his soul."

"Might Armendis not be off attending one of their ceremonies," Flowia asked, "or seeking advice from one of their preachers? Or even one of our priests if she's still loyal to the Church? She might even claim sanctuary?"

"If she wanted to speak to one of their Good Folk preachers," Bertwoin reminded her, "there was one in the cellar below her. And Armendis seems too polite to run away without telling Meli."

The alchemist took a deep breath. "Ah well, where do you intend to search now?"

"My aunt ordered me to search Hebert's farm again, though Jehan has already done so. Then I am to visit Garnier because he insists his son, Tumas, has the right to marry Armendis."

"She may also have fled to her best friend, Sibilia," Flowia said.

"Jehan already talked to her. Of course, Sibilia might lie to protect her friend. If so, it'll do me little good to visit her. Sibilia will never tell *me* if she's hiding Armendis."

"True," the master said. "It will be best if you take Flowia with you."

"I'm busy here," she said.

Bertwoin felt like kicking a nearby bench. She still despised his company. Would she never forgive him?

"I know you are, daughter," the master said, as he used a small ladle to skim the scum off the liquid in the beaker. He then scooped out the egg. "Our young plowman here also has duties at home. Yet he sets them aside. We must find this young woman before the killer does, if he hasn't already done so."

"I will meet you here tomorrow morning," Flowia told Bertwoin, her face stern with disapproval. "Now, I need to finish working in my garden." She flung open the door and shut it with a thump.

Using his fingers, the master sloughed the shell off the solid inner egg as if it were a loose pelt.

"So," Bertwoin said, "you're certain Armendis didn't kill her mother?"

The alchemist raised his eyebrows and spread his hands. "Certain? No. She might have been drug-addled or demon-ridden. But I don't think her mother scratched anyone's face. So I wonder who wounded Armendis's cheeks?"

"The murderer? Why?"

"Who knows?" The master cleared his throat. "And while I doubt Armendis has fled home, and Hebert would never tolerate her being there, I agree that you and Flowia should go by his farm. We need to know where Hebert and Raimunda are and what they are doing."

"You suspect them?"

"I am uneasy about their safety. One of them might become the second victim." The master waved a hand to retire their discussion. "By the way, plowman, I assume you do not intend to become a cleric." When Bertwoin nodded, the master rubbed his age-spotted hands together. "It was a clever idea."

"My dead grandmother sent it to me. But I'm not sure my father won't force me into this marriage anyway, especially when he doesn't see me trying on black or brown robes for size."

"Why does Wilfraed not marry Maria?"

"He's not the eldest son."

"I know this, but wouldn't his marrying Maria also tie both families and farms together? He's only a small step behind you in years."

"Well said!" Not able to stand still, Bertwoin walked in a tight circle. "Maria and Wilfraed know each other well. Roul may accept him, and my father will get what he wants."

"Good, now that we have settled the fate of two young people to please you and further the scheme of their fathers, I will leave it to you to make our plan happen." Smiling, the alchemist bounced the egg a few times on top of his brick oven.

Bertwoin watched, wide-eyed. "It's like a muscle. Can you turn it into something else?"

"Is not turning it into a muscle enough?"

"Not if it doesn't do anything."

The alchemist considered the egg. "It amuses me. It is also a symbol, like the mother pelican in my book. Are we not trying to slough the shell off Ermessen's death to reveal what the murderer has hidden from us?"

"So what you do in here with a simple egg may help you solve the murder? Even if it does nothing itself?"

"It also reminds me of the shell of assumptions and beliefs that hide the true nature of this mystery. I need to it slough off in order to reveal the killer."

Bertwoin looked at the closed door. "Well, I'll bid you good night."

The alchemist chuckled. "May you and Flowia have success tomorrow, gleaning clues." He smiled a moment, then laughed out loud. "May you also transform her active anger into passive contentment."

As Bertwoin trekked homeward, he had the feeling that he was being followed, but he saw no one.

CHAPTER XIII

Bertwoin slipped as silently as a weasel into their dark barn with no one in his family seeing him, not even his snoring brother. Wilfraed had taught him a trick, a bit of magic he had learned from their grandmother. Before falling asleep, he would tell himself when to wake up, say at sunrise or when the moon reached a certain point. It always worked if he wasn't sick or too exhausted. So Bertwoin undressed, covered himself with his woolen blanket, and told himself to come awake at false dawn.

In the morning's first gray light, he woke to find Belle snuggled against his side. Bertwoin listened and judged that the idiot wind was also asleep. Good, he wouldn't have to shove through a strong breeze all the way to the alchemist's house. He wouldn't get a sore throat.

He slipped out from under his blanket, dressed without waking Wilfraed, and crept to the barn's door. He had misjudged the wind. It grabbed at him like a wrestler trying to get a grip.

A strip of light from their hearth fire gleamed along the seam between the roof and the wattle-and-daub wall of their house—his *maman* was already up and baking bread. His empty stomach growled at the thought, but he had to leave before his *papa* came to rouse him.

The sun had just risen with slow dignity over a mountain peak on the southeastern horizon when he arrived at the alchemist's house. Roland met him at the front opening in the mulberry hedge, his bristles raised, his eyes alert for danger. Recognizing his friend, he huffed a greeting, which Bertwoin returned.

Bertwoin ran his fingernails down the boar's spine. "So, the idiot wind has made you restless too, heh? Let's calm you down."

He left the pig grunting in a trance of delight and crossed the enclosed poultry yard. The geese, alert but not alarmed, watched him with the superior air of ladies-in-waiting.

He tapped on a closed shutter and waited. Flowia opened the door, her expression and attitude so aloof that it reminded him of her geese. "I'll be right out."

"Could I have a bit of bread with a slice of cheese? I've had nothing to eat."

"I'll bring it out to you, and you can eat it on the way."

He ambled to the opening in the mulberry hedge, escorted by Roland, and told the pig, "I'll bet your sows are sometimes snappish too."

Flowia glided out wearing goat-skin shoes, blue leggings, and a long blue dress under a green cloak that suited her slender figure. Her long hair under the coif hung down her back in a thick braid. She handed him a slice of wheat bread and a square of cheese. The expensive bread melted on his tongue.

"Maud?" Flowia asked.

"Still doing well, thanks to you. *Maman* is beside herself with relief."

"Good." Flowia took in a breath and let it out slowly, as if mustering her willpower for the chore ahead of her. "We should go to Sibilia's house first."

"The master told me he wants to know where Hebert and Raimunda are and what they're doing."

"Will you tell on me?"

"Not if you give me a kiss."

She laughed. "He'll forgive me."

"Maybe he should be an example to us all."

She glided away in a direction opposite to Hebert's farm, chanting over her shoulder,

"Right now, our best chance
of discovering lost Armendis
is to take a snooping glance
at where her best friend is."

So she thought Armendis may have run to Sibilia. It *was* a possibility.

He sighed and caught up with her. Would marriage to Flowia be a never-ending battle of wills? Which house they visited first was a small matter and her argument had merit, so he found it easy to yield to her this time. But what would they do when they had different opinions about life-changing problems?

Roland assumed it was his duty as Flowia's bodyguard to chaperon her, and she had to order him more than twice to return to the poultry yard.

"He's loyal," Bertwoin said.

"And effective. The pilfering from my medicine garden has stopped."

"Loyalty is valuable."

"It is. Roland would never let anyone attack me *in any way*."

That hadn't ended the way he had wanted. He said, "I know Sibilia on sight, but I know little about her. What's she like?"

Flowia's expression changed into one of quiet respect. "She's just as skilled as her elder brother at helping her father build boats. She's also the opposite of Armendis in some ways. Like Hebert, Armendis often keeps to herself and doesn't like to talk with people she doesn't know well. Sibilia has a busy tongue and will converse with crows or crickets if no one else is about.

"Her father built a boat for a wine merchant, and the man refused to pay for it when he saw it. Declared it had defects. Her father and brother argued and yelled, then stomped away, muttering threats. Sibilia stayed and explained why they had built the boat the way they had. She made it clear they weren't cheating him. What the wine merchant believed were defects in the boat's shape were necessary features to make it ride the water like a swan. In the end, the merchant bought it. Not only had she helped build the boat, she had also sold it."

"And one of her arms is shorter than the other because of an accident, right?"

"She climbed a tree and tumbled out of it. Broke or cracked the bone in her left arm. It healed, but the injured arm never grew as long as the other one. Perhaps the healing used the energy her arm needed for growth. Anyway, it hasn't hindered her from plucking chickens or sawing wood or smoothing planks."

"And if she knows where Armendis is, what makes you believe she'll tell us?"

"A lie will toll in my ears like a funeral bell."

"You're sure?"

She stared at the ground as she strolled along. "Remember, I've lived among those whose livelihoods depended on deceiving people. Believe me when I say the sour note of falsehood will clang in my ear with the sound of an iron bar dropped on flagstones. If I hadn't learned this skill, I would be someone's slave right now."

He thought of the innkeeper's wife selling her to a traveling troupe of actors. How many lies had she told to survive on the road? People said a thief recognized a fellow thief. Might that also be true for liars?

"But even if she admits to knowing where Armendis is hiding, will she tell us? A closed mouth is as good as a lie."

"If she lies, we may assume Armendis is well hidden and is as safe as possible. If Sibilia knows where her friend is hiding but won't reveal her location, we'll simply let the master know. He may be satisfied to leave Armendis safely where she is."

"And if he isn't?"

"Then he must tell me how to wring the information he wants out of our reluctant boat-maker. Or he can try to coax the secret out of her himself."

Sibilia lived not far upriver from Hebert's farm on a bend where the Aude became smooth and lazy.

Their workshop sat on dry land just out of reach of the Aude's seasonal flooding. It had the shape of an oversized ship—a shape a boatbuilder would well know how to build. Bertwoin smiled as he imagined them hauling a new boat out of it. It would seem as if a mother ship had just given bloodless birth to a baby boat.

They looked inside the shed first, but it was as empty as a hangman's heart.

As they began walking toward the house, they saw Sibilia kneeling on the bank of the Aude with a long pole in one hand. She kept her other hand tucked into the armpit of her green cloak for warmth. Seeing them, she stood up without lifting her hemp fishing line out of the swirling water.

She and Flowia greeted each other with relaxed courtesy. Sibilia was thin, her figure still more girlish than womanly. The hand holding her rod was red from the wind and maybe from the river's cold water. A humped-backed perch lay on the bank with a stake through its tail to keep it from flopping back into the river.

"Worm?" he asked her.

Sibilia shook her head and lifted her thin line out of the water, showing him a minnow on a bone hook. "These work faster. It's cold out here."

Bertwoin saw no hesitancy in her manner, no wariness, and began to think she didn't know where her friend was hiding.

Flowia asked how the boat business was going and if everyone was well. Sibilia was talkative and kept glancing at Bertwoin's face. She seemed amused by his presence.

Then Flowia asked without warning, "Do you know where Armendis is?"

Grief aged Sibilia's face. "Wasn't I just going to ask you that self-same question? And now your question gives me my answer."

"So, when did you learn of her disappearance?"

"Jehan tells me this, but does he tell me any details? No. Then two biddies come later to borrow a sieve and tell of it. My Mendy gone." A tear crept from the corner of one eye. "The women said she may of ridden off with a devil, the same one that caused her to murder her long-suffering *maman*. That's a wicked thing to say, and I tell them so. Mendy worshipped her *maman*. And as to her being possessed of a demon, she knows charms to keep them off her. And didn't she have a soft heart in her chest? Hebert once beat her to her knees, because she shirked away from killing a chicken."

Flowia reared back. "So Ermessen had to do it?"

"Or Raimunda."

"Was Armendis afraid of anyone?"

"Hebert, but he'd not kill Ermessen or want to lose Mendy. He knew who pulled his cart for him. The heartless women say he accuses Mendy of this murder?" She slapped her thigh. "The shock must've turned his brains to porridge."

"He believes it," Flowia said. "I heard him say it myself. Was Armendis afraid of anyone else?"

Sibilia squatted beside the water as if to begin fishing again but instead stared at the cold water. "Maybe Tumas, though that wasn't so much because he would hurt her as it was that he might become her husband. He keeps his eye out for her."

"She does love Jehan, then?"

"Their souls are sewn tight together. Makes you smile to see how moony-eyed they are around each other." The momentary delight fell off Sibilia's face. "Did Ermessen die, as the biddies say she did? Was Mendy really found wallowing in the warm blood of the mother who birthed her?"

Flowia nodded and said in a gentle tone, "We mean her no harm, Sibilia, and would never turn her over to the *bayle*. We only want to make certain that her leaving was her choice, not someone else's."

Sibilia put a hand to her mouth. "You think someone might of taken her?"

"It's possible."

"I just hope we find her so we can help her," Bertwoin mumbled.

"What do you mean?" Flowia asked.

He blew into his clasped hands to warm them. "What happened shocked Armendis to the core. She's not sure she didn't hurt her mother. She'll never forget it until she finally rests in the churchyard." He gave them a helpless look. "It reminds me of a fledgling wren I found. It had fallen out of its nest, so I took it home to raise it. Kept it warm and tried to feed it worms, but it couldn't eat and starved to death. I hope we can feed Armendis's body and soul once we find her."

The two young women glanced at each other, and he saw they knew something he didn't. "What?"

Flowia looked at him with soft pity. "The parents teach fledglings to fly only after they've jumped out of the nest and are on the ground."

"You mean. . . . You mean they would have kept it alive?"

"You didn't know," Flowia said. "Your intentions were good."

Sibilia scanned the forest crowding down to the water as if an enemy might charge out of it. "It's all come the Devil's way now, hasn't it? That morning I saw her, everything was so set and so right, so normal. How could their *ostal* change like that?" She snapped her fingers.

Flowia huffed. "You were there that very morning?"

"Mendy needed to borrow my celebration ribbons from me, so I brought them to her. I come in to find Rai and Mendy in the kitchen, laughing over something."

"Did they get along?" Flowia asked.

"They argued as sisters do. Rai can be sour sometimes—well, most times. Mendy stayed cautious around her. Their *maman* didn't favor Rai at all."

Flowia watched her face. "Where was Ermessen?"

"She was out somewhere, maybe getting a few sticks of firewood."

"Maybe?" Bertwoin asked.

She threw her hands wide to show she wasn't sure, then admitted, "She might've gone out to meet Artal."

"Artal?" Flowia said in disbelief. "You saw them?"

"No, it was just something Rai said that made me think he was there."

Bertwoin chuckled. "Wouldn't Hebert have run him off?"

"I guess so if he had been there. Anyway, Rai was in a good mood and made special mutton pies just for Mendy and me."

"Would Armendis not run to you for help now?" Bertwoin asked.

Sibilia's bottom lip trembled. "Yes. Ten times yes. She knows I would hide her—even from my own family."

Bertwoin said, "Why would she ever leave the protection of my aunt and uncle?"

Still squatting and huddled in her cloak, Sibilia's body began bouncing with sobs. "Sh-she wouldn't. She and Artal might argue, but he would never harm her. He would protect her even from the *bayle*."

"Argue?" Flowia asked. "About what?"

"Artal opposes her marrying Jehan. He has another husband picked out for her."

"Tumas." Bertwoin said.

"Yeah. Mendy told me he wanted her to wed silent Tumas. Said Jehan thought himself a little prince and was no more worthy to marry her than a lapdog."

Bertwoin understood now why Tumas thought Armendis belonged to him.

Flowia laid a sisterly hand on Sibilia's thin shoulder. "If she does come to you, please tell us. The master wants to know she is safe. He may also need to talk with her if he is to solve her mother's murder."

"I will, I will. God give you help in your search. Mendy is the sister I never had at home."

Bertwoin asked, "Did you see anyone else at the farm? Anyone who might be called a witch?"

"Hebert laid that slander on your Aunt Melisende. He keeps black hate stored in his heart for her. Thinks she killed his prime ram. Oh, you don't think, . . ." she put a hand over her mouth. "Your aunt did visit the farm and talk with Ermessen early that morning."

"His ram?" Bertwoin asked. "What about it?"

"Someone slit its throat."

"So now I know why he accused her of being a witch."

"I think," Flowia said, "it's time Hebert told us what befell his ram. And we must ask Raimunda whose doll was found on Ermessen."

CHAPTER XIV

They walked along the Aude's bank where the clean, crisp smell of early winter surrounded them. Gusts of biting wind rippled the water's surface, turned their cheeks red, and tried to shove them sideways into the forest. A wind that made people feel restless. A wind that birthed arguments. A wind that laughed at their cloaks and slipped cold winter in their bones. A wind that people said could blow the ears off a rabbit.

"Hebert is closer than Garnier," Flowia said, again justifying a decision she had already made. "So we'll visit the farmer before the potter."

"I'll not argue against plowing the nearest field before going to one farther away." Bertwoin held up a finger. "But I think questioning Hebert again is a waste of words. Hebert is rock-hard ground for us. Our questions will grow no crop there. And Armendis would never run home. She'll only be there if she was taken by force, and if that's true, she'll be *in* the ground somewhere on the farm. Hebert will make certain we never find her."

Flowia shrugged. "Your aunts and the master demand it, so we obey."

Bertwoin grunted. He didn't mention that she hadn't precisely obeyed the master when she wanted to go to Sibilia first. "You never obey me?"

Bertwoin sucked air in through his teeth. His words had sounded pouty instead of manly, but once spoken they couldn't be taken back. He needed to be more like Roland, who never embarrassed himself.

"Not true," she argued. "You just see it that way. If you tell me to do three things, and I only do two of them, you remember only the one I didn't do. And you have no right to order me about."

"Neither do my aunts."

"They command my respect."

"And I don't."

"I had more respect for you before you let your uncle abuse me without saying *one word* in my defense."

"I would never have let him hit you."

She dipped her head to one side and admitted, "I saw you stand where you could stop him from hitting me. But words are weapons too."

She would not let herself be appeased, and his limping excuses would not change her opinion, not at this moment, anyway. When would they settle this and return to being a couple again? "Even God forgives sins," he reminded her, again sounding whiny.

"Not always in the Old Testament." She smiled when he made the sign of the cross. "But even if a dog forgives you," she added, "that doesn't mean you didn't kick it. And the dog may not completely trust you again." She frowned. "Why do you seek my forgiveness, anyway? You've already forgiven yourself?"

When he said nothing, she studied him. "Having my respect means something to you?"

"It means everything to me."

Her expression softened. "I always heed your words and give them their due, but obeying you is not my habit."

"You're a dunghill rat," he quipped, meaning to praise her self-reliance.

"I was raised in alleys," she said in a serious tone, taking the banter out of him. "And I still hurt because you didn't gainsay your uncle."

"What does it take to earn your forgiveness?"

"It'll come unbidden. I can't think away this feeling."

He threw himself on his knees at her feet, stretching his hands pleadingly toward her face. "Oh, sternest of goddesses, I beg you to forgive my sin. Let me be your devoted servant."

Surprised, she laughed before she caught herself. "You'll not joke your way out of this, plowman. And besides, goddesses keep strict rules. You didn't follow the ritual properly."

"What ritual? I'm on my knees."

"You didn't clean yourself properly before you prostrated yourself in front of me and adored me. There's a crumb of cheese in your beard. A large one."

"What? You let me talk to Sibilia without telling me this?" No wonder his presence had amused the boatbuilder's daughter.

"I'm more of an avenging goddess."

He patted his beard, and yes, dislodged an embarrassing morsel.

Flowia smiled down at him, kneeling before her. "I'm certain Sibilia found it endearing. But I doubt she would obey you, either."

A man's voice behind Flowia said, "I heard tell that the plowman was generous to beggars, but I didn't know he was a beggar himself. Have I come upon a plea for a virgin's favors?"

Bertwoin jumped to his feet, stumbling a bit, his face warming with blood. Hebert grinned at him. How long had been he listening to them?

"Have you found my wife's killer yet?" the farmer demanded, all levity gone.

Without answering, Flowia turned and walked down the path toward Hebert's house. Bertwoin caught up with her, and the farmer fell into step behind them.

"You're wasting *my* time," Hebert said. "Pestering me about Mendy is useless. Pray tell me, do you believe in your heart the bitch would come hieing home, knowing that I will beat her senseless if she does? Knowing I'll turn her over to the *bayle*? If you think that, then you've not got the sense God gave a goose."

Bertwoin called over his shoulder, "What enemy hated your wife so much? Or was it you the murderer meant to punish?"

Hebert gathered phlegm in his throat, spat at their heels, and stayed as silent as a Benedictine monk.

Flowia stopped and turned. "What about your ram?"

Hebert glowered at her. "So you've heard of that, have you? Who's talking against me? Rai?"

"So," Bertwoin said, "the killings were alike?"

"Leave me be."

Flowia glanced at Bertwoin to get his attention, then nodded toward Hebert. He crowded close to Hebert. "You can answer us now, or after I beat you into a lump of bloody meat."

"You think you can beat me into talking, scamp?"

"You'll be more polite after I break a finger or two."

Hebert grinned. "And what of the *bayle*, ox fart?"

"I'll say *you* started the fight. You're known to be surly."

The farmer grabbed for the knife hanging on his belt. Before he could pull it, Bertwoin clamped a hand over Hebert's hand to keep it in its sheath.

Nose to nose, Hebert sneered up into Bertwoin's face. "She's no virgin, ox fart. And I doubt there are any virgins in your house, either. That includes your sister, the one that's about to marry."

Bertwoin grabbed the front of Hebert's tunic and jerked him forward, then put him into a choke hold. Hebert struggled, but his face turned red as he gasped for breath.

"The ram," Bertwoin prompted.

Hebert waved a hand in surrender. After catching his breath, he wheezed, "I found it skinned with its throat slit."

Flowia asked. "And why would anyone do such a thing to your ram?"

Hebert glared at Bertwoin. "You've no right to choke me, pus-boil."

"I didn't bust your nose."

Flowia asked, "Do I need to repeat my question?"

"Ask Mendy. She's the one doing the killing."

"Armendis? Why would your daughter wish to punish you in this way?" Flowia looked ready to slap him. "And what does killing your ram and your wife in such a manner mean to you? Think!"

Hebert massaged his sore throat as he considered her words. "Ah, you're right. Mendy probably didn't kill my best ram. Some other bastard did it during the last full moon. But maybe she got the idea of murdering her mother from the ram's killing."

"Full moon." Flowia prompted.

Hebert continued to knead his neck.

"I didn't hurt it that much," Bertwoin scoffed.

"The full moon shows it had to do with that black-hearted witch," Hebert told Flowia "Charmed my ram before performing a blasphemous rite on it. Probably killed it while it fed from her hand. Bled it and flayed it. Maybe she wanted to do the same devilish rite on my wife, but instead of doing it herself, she laid a spell on Mendy."

"If my Aunt Meli were a true witch," Bertwoin muttered, "she'd of crippled and blinded you long ago, or else turned you into a white-skinned leper."

Looking as displeased as a duchess, Flowia frowned at Hebert. "So if Armendis didn't kill her mother, who did? Who means to destroy you? The killer seems to be giving you clues, so you'll know who he is."

"If that's true," Hebert muttered, smiling at her, "he's too cowardly to declare himself to me."

"Still, you must know who has a grievance against you."

"Ah, don't badger me, maiden. And you won't need to come inside my house. I have no ale for the likes of you."

"The master wanted us to talk to Raimunda," Flowia said.

"You've no need to bother her. She's got chores to do." He muttered under his breath, "She's the only woman left to me now, when I can find her."

"Find her?"

"She's always gone when I need her."

"Still," Bertwoin said, "we mean to talk with her."

"You've no right," Hebert said.

Bertwoin raised a fist in front of Hebert's face. "Speaking of rights, nothing gives a puffed-up toad like you the right to call my aunt a witch? If I hear you repeat that lie, I'll break your teeth."

Hebert glared at him, his face twisted with hatred. After a breath or two, he walked around them and strode down the forest's narrow path toward his house.

When the farmer was beyond hearing them, Bertwoin asked, "Do you think he killed his wife?"

"During last threshing season, he beat Ermessen senseless. For days, she was too dizzy to stand or walk and couldn't lift her arms. The hedge-born dumbass crippled his wife during harvest time when he needed her labor the most. If someone had beaten Ermessen to death, I would point the finger at him. But cutting her up like that, no, that's not Hebert."

"Why did he beat her?"

"They argued over the wooden heart she always wore. Na Thea probably knows the why of it. It was she who nursed Ermessen back to health."

"Hebert should thank her for curing his wife, not despise her."

"He remembers only the hurts done to him, never the kindnesses." Flowia grinned. "Of course, Na Thea is not one to keep her opinions to herself. She told everyone at Sunday mass that Hebert was as stupid as a rooster that destroys its hen's eggs. When Hebert threatened her with his fist, Artal rose to Na Thea's defense. A priest had to shove between them to prevent a fight inside the church."

Bertwoin looked down the path toward the farmer's *ostal*. "Hebert's greatest enemy is Hebert."

"That's one antagonist, he will never outrun."

Raimunda opened the door and waved them into the cottage. She didn't look either of them in the eye.

Bertwoin rubbed his hands together to warm them. The house was chilly, but at least they were now inside and away from the stinging wind. Ermessen's corpse was no longer in the front room. Was she stored away in a bedroom? Why was she not lying in the front room where people could pray over her and pay their respects?

"So you're the ones that put *papa* sour," Raimunda whispered. She scowled at Bertwoin. "Especially you. He never wants to see you. I'm not sure I do."

"He went for his knife," Bertwoin said. "Didn't like our questions. We wrestled a bit."

"You've done more than that to us."

"That wasn't me. My *papa* said no because of what your father did."

"Well, he's angry at everyone now, even God." She led them through the front room into the kitchen, where barley porridge simmered in a black pot on a low hearth fire.

Flowia made a point of looking around the empty rooms. "A death usually brings a crowd. Where are the women? Have you no help?"

Bertwoin wondered where Hebert was—in a bedroom or out with his flock? He eyed Raimunda. His father had once thought it a clever idea for Bertwoin to marry her, but he changed his mind.

She was the opposite of Flowia in many ways. She was what his uncle called a breeder—stout hips, breasty, with comfortable thighs. Children would feel safe in her lap. As the eldest daughter, it was an insult for her younger sister to marry before her. Many farmers would find her suitable. So why was she not married? Had Hebert prevented it?

"Have you found my sister?" Raimunda asked.

"Not yet," Flowia told her.

"Ale?" Raimunda mumbled.

Flowia shook her head. "Your father said he would give us none. We'd best not raise his anger against you."

Raimunda snorted, got the jug down from the shelf, and poured two mugs half-full for them.

"Is your father not getting you some help?" Flowia asked.

"We have a cousin coming after Sunday mass, but. . . ." She rolled her eyes. "She's older than dirt and more of a burden than a help to me. When she comes visiting, she warms her bones by the fire all day and orders me and Mendy about." Raimunda wrung her hands. "Are you really no closer to finding her? She was in no state to be out on her own when she left here."

Flowia glanced at the simmering porridge, picked a potato off the kitchen table, and began dicing it into the pot. "We came by to see if Armendis sent you a message, or if you have even a glimmer of an idea where she might be."

Raimunda shook her head. "People came by earlier and said she'd run off from Artal's."

"So you knew," Bertwoin said, "that your sister had moved from Guillema's *ostal* to Meli's?"

Raimunda nodded as if it took effort to move her head.

"What about Ermessen's parents?" Flowia asked. "Might she have run to them?"

Raimunda grimaced. "Doubt she's ever said more than a passing greeting to them. I know I haven't. Our farms are near, but we dodge down another path if we see them coming. And they do likewise. *Maman's* brother especially despises us. Did you try Sibilia?"

"We did." Flowia stirred the diced potato into the porridge. "Sibilia said she visited you on the morning your mother died."

Raimunda frowned a moment, then sighed. "She brought Mendy some ribbons." She stared at the floor, her expression woeful.

Flowia caught Bertwoin's attention and nodded at a bucket. He said to Raimunda. "Water?"

"We use the river."

Was she grateful for his offer to bring water or for him to leave? Bertwoin pushed his way through the wind to the Aude. He took his time, knowing Flowia would get more information out of Raimunda if he wasn't there. Poor Raimunda, how could she even stand up, let alone take care of guests? She'd lost both her mother and sister. Not only that, but she had also lost any chance of becoming a bride. Hebert would never let her leave his *ostal* now unless he found a husband who would move in with him. That would give Raimunda two men to care for.

Bertwoin sat on the bank within sight of the farm and listened to water splash over the rocks. He scanned the mountains to the south and wondered what Michel, an outlaw shepherd he knew, was doing. He probably wasn't in the high pastures now. Nearly all of the shepherds had already moved their flocks to the warmer lowlands. It was time to set the rams among the ewes.

Michel had once courted Armendis. Odd that Michel had also liked Emeline, who was killed. What were the betting odds of two young women wooed by one shepherd becoming victims of gruesome murders?

And what was he going to do about his own wooing? His lie about becoming a cleric wouldn't hinder his father more than another day or two. He had to go home and face his family. His father was sure to box his ear for slipping away while Roul was there, and then he'd get a kick or two for neglecting his farm chores. No doubt, Wilfraed and Laurence were cursing him at this very moment for having to do his chores along with their own.

When he re-entered the cottage, Raimunda had her tunic raised and was showing Flowia something on her leg. He saw a flash of white thigh before the hem dropped. They waited with their arms crossed under their breasts while he set the bucket down by the front door and went outside again. Had Raimunda wounded her leg?

He strolled to the copse of chestnuts where they had found Ermessen. Its silence was oppressive. Birds and animals seemed to shun it. Even the rankling wind seemed to tiptoe through it. The copse was not a spot he would ever visit after dark. Not now. Murdered women often haunted the places where they had died.

Flowia and Raimunda were in the poultry yard when he returned. Poor Raimunda, was someone with a grudge against Hebert murdering his family? Was she next?

Flowia came to the gate and told him, "I will remain here to help Raimunda."

"Is her leg okay?"

"Just a small boil. She's already smeared it with bee salve."

"Don't forget to ask her who the poppet belonged to."

"I already did. It was her mother's."

"So, what does that tell us?"

"It's a riddle only the master can solve. Anyway, come fetch me tomorrow morning. We'll visit the pottery."

Throaty screeches and the snorting of distressed mules woke Bertwoin. The restive mules had crowded against the rear wall where he and Wilfraed slept and were almost trampling them.

Outside, he heard his *maman* yell, "Fire!"

"What's going on?" Wilfraed grumbled, still dream-addled.

Bertwoin lifted a shingle at the edge of the roof to let moonlight into their barn. He scanned the shadowy interior but saw nothing dangerous.

He heard his father yell, "Move your asses! Fetch me a shovel or hayfork."

Bertwoin hurried through the dark barn to the large pine-wood door and flung it open. Sticks of flaming wood scattered across the ground. Disbelief paralyzed him for a moment. Someone had lit a blaze against the door. He saw Rachel hand a shovel to his father, who scraped the burning sticks and small logs apart and began beating the flames out of them. Wilfraed came and stood next to Bertwoin inside the barn.

Laurence ran across the yard with a bucket and began pouring water on the scattered fires. He soon said with satisfaction, "We've got the burn out of it now."

His father stepped back to judge the damage and almost tripped over Maud, who was holding Poppet up to see the excitement. "Get out from underfoot, girl."

Maman used a scrap of old blanket to brush ashes and heat off the scorched barn door.

His father put his hands on either side of his waist and said, "Yeah, the fire looks to be out. Thank God we caught it before it took hold." He smiled at Bertwoin. "We might've lost our mules."

Laughing, Rachel said, "Wilfraed would've slept until the fire bit his toes."

"I'd of gotten out through the back hole," Wilfraed muttered.

Bertwoin went back into the barn to stroke and calm their restive mules. He heard his father say, "Well, let's get out of this cold. Wilfraed, you stay out here awhile and make sure that the fire doesn't rise up again."

"But Bertwoin's still out here," Wilfraed whined.

"Do as I say." His father then yelled into the barn. "Come out, Bertwoin. We need to study on who set this fire, and you're the dog with the nose to find the scurrilous pustule. You can prove to us that the alchemist taught you something."

The mules were still a bit nervous but not fretting, so Bertwoin left them. As he passed Wilfraed, who squatted just inside the barn with a ragged blanket over his shoulders, Bertwoin said, "I'll bring out some ale."

In the kitchen, his father and Laurence sat at the table, blowing warm breaths into their cupped hands. *Maman* was blowing on embers in the hearth while Rachel poured cold ale into mugs for all of them, including little Maud.

"Who'd do this?" Laurence asked.

His father sat frowning at the oak table top, saying nothing. Bertwoin sat down beside his uncle, but his *maman* shooed Laurence and him away from the end of the table and began setting out bowls, a wooden spoon, and the ingredients she would need to make bread dough. She told Rachel, "Bring me up some barley and peas." She pointed her chin at the bucket. "Then go fetch us some water."

Their father looked at her. "How'd you learn there was a fire?"

Maud yelled with glee, "The cat told us."

"I didn't ask you, Bug."

Maman explained, "Maud came and woke me. Said Jolie was slinking around with her ears back. Kept looking at the wall facing the barn and slinking away from it. Maud thought maybe the leprosy imp was prowling around outside, trying to get in."

Clanoud slapped his thigh. "The cat? By God, she saved our barn. The daubed walls might not have burned well, but the frame and wattling inside them is as dry as tinder."

Laurence said, "We need to find the cowardly fart-licker that did this. If he comes again, Jolie might not announce him a second time." A sly smile slid on Laurence's face. "Well, Clanoud, like you say, we've got the man right here who knows the ways of hunting down criminals."

"I'll do anything I can," Bertwoin said. What would the master do if he were here now? Would he not start asking questions? "How many enemies do we have who'd do a thing like this?"

"I've got twenty-three enemies I know of," his father said with pride, "but only five or six would be bold enough to try something like this against us."

His uncle pointed an accusatory finger at Bertwoin. "Maybe the whoreson wasn't trying to hurt our household so much as he was trying to get back at you."

"Me?"

"You're the one who sleeps in the barn, right? And I heard someone say they saw one of the squires you unhorsed walking about. What was his name? Oh, Gidie."

Bertwoin hummed. "He'd hurt me if he could, but he'd make sure I knew who did it. The other possibility is Hebert."

Laurence pointed at him. "That's an idea that might pull some weight. He doesn't have the balls to attack us straight out, but he might sneak in at night to get at us."

Bertwoin told them about putting Hebert in a chokehold.

Maman added, "He also still hates us because Bertwoin didn't marry Raimunda. We shamed him."

Clanoud spat at the hearth fire and missed. "I'll not link up with a cad who spurns his own kin. But why would he wait until now to get back at me? That was two harvests ago."

"Maybe," said Laurence, "having Bertwoin in his face because of Ermessen's death reminded him of how much he hated us."

"Maybe. But it's more likely he meant to punish Bertwoin for besting him in a fight. That's fresh in his mind. So, bloodhound, what are you going to do?"

"Ah, I'll look around after sunrise, but I doubt there's much profit in doing so. The ground is harder than pottery, so there'll be no footprints. Then I'll have to go see the alchemist. He's the expert."

"You can do that a little later on when he's up," his father said. "Right now, we'll get out of the women's way and use this opportunity to get an early start on the day's chores."

CHAPTER XVI

After sunrise, Bertwoin walked through a wind-ruffled forest to the alchemist's house. He watched his back trail and didn't see anyone following him.

Flowia glided out as soon as he got there, and they set off, butting through the spirited breeze, their cloaks clutched closed at their necks. She seemed under a cloud of dark thoughts, so he stayed quiet.

Finally, she shook her head and said, "We must take care with Garnier. While you were outside at Hebert's, Raimunda told me that her father had agreed to a marriage between Armendis and Tumas, but he later decided not to honor his word. She said Garnier blames Ermessen for changing Hebert's mind. There is bitter bile now between the two men."

Bertwoin remembered walking with his aunt after Jehan had taken Armendis away on his cart. "Garnier? He accuses the wrong woman. It was not Ermessen, but Guillema, who changed Hebert's mind. She bought his accepting of Jehan as his son-in-law."

As Flowia skimmed along, Bertwoin moved closer to her so their shoulders almost touched.

"I can understand," he said, "why Hebert thought Tumas would make a good husband. As the eldest son, he'll take ownership of the pottery someday and be able to provide a living for his family. And more than that, Tumas's twin is a farmer. If the two families joined together, Hebert might persuade the twin to move in with him. That would give him a farm worker and an heir at the same time."

Flowia turned off the path onto the road leading to Bourg. "A farmer? Why was his twin not picked to marry Armendis instead of Tumas?"

"I hear the twin spreads his tail feathers for another woman. And I doubt he dares to get in his brother's way."

"Is that why Tumas doesn't marry Raimunda?"

"Probably. Tumas wants Armendis instead."

He smiled at Flowia, wishing she would go into the woods with him, but he knew better than to become amorous now. He saw forgiveness coming like the first light preceding the dawn, but the sun hadn't yet peaked over the mountaintop.

"Raimunda thinks her sister killed their *maman*," Flowia said. "But she told me that if that's not true, Tumas might have done it. He is wild with rage over Hebert's betrayal."

"He's reputed to have a temper, but I've yet to hear of him doing anything criminal. He's also said to be honorable, which could be the problem. Honorable men are sometimes doubly savage when cheated. And though he has no voice, I hear he doesn't lack wit. But wouldn't he be more likely to attack Jehan than Ermessen? That would remove the other suitor, and at the same time, show everyone he intends to let nobody hinder him."

Flowia laughed. "Raimunda called Tumas a demon hiding in a young man's body. Her face had a dreamy look when she said this."

"What?"

"I think she would find it to her liking to step into the place her sister spurned and be the wife of the potter's son. Maybe Raimunda can change Tumas's mind."

"Hebert would then get the benefit of Tumas's twin joining his household and also get my aunt's money."

Flowia made a dismissive sound. "Maybe so, but Hebert has a genius for chopping off his own foot with his own axe. When he and Garnier argued over the matter, he beat the potter to the ground and threw him into the Aude. Hebert was lucky they were alone. It might have been the other way around had silent Tumas been there to protect his father."

"And it was just after this fight that Hebert's favorite ram was mutilated?"

"So it seems." Flowia huffed, her face tight with anger. "The animal had to die. How the innocent suffer."

"I know the feeling," he lamented.

She raised her eyes toward the sky and chanted,

"And so the cunning fox
makes his false defense
by dressing the guilty ox
in a fleece of innocence."

"By the by," she said, "Raimunda told me that not only did your Aunt Melisende come by that morning, but so did Artal. And they did not come as a pair. He came to see Ermessen while Hebert was away. And she argued with him."

"So Meli came to see Armendis, and Artal to see Ermessen? Sibilia also visited them. I still don't see a murderer among them."

"No, but I felt Sibilia was not telling us everything she knew."

"So she might well know where Armendis is hiding? Did Raimunda see her mother after Artal left?"

Flowia hesitated. "I don't know. I didn't think to ask her. But Raimunda acted as if Artal's seeing her mother was suspicious." She shook her head. "But he has no reason to kill her that we know of, and especially not in such a violent manner."

They marched into Bourg, one of the three towns crowded around the bottom of the citadel's hill. The pottery was located just off the central plaza where the gallows stood. They found Garnier sitting in a large room, its walls covered with shelves crowded with raw pots and mugs and bowls and jugs that were drying so they wouldn't crack, break, or explode when he fired them in his brick kiln. For a moment, they watched his nimble fingers mold a clay pitcher on the potter's kick wheel between his knees, a wheel specially made so he could rotate it with his bare foot.

"God bless you, maiden," he said.

"And you, Garnier. May you and your family have health." She scanned the packed shelves. "And may you sell all your wares. I've come to pick up the heart molds for the master if they are ready."

He nodded. "They are, as promised." He pointed to one of the shelves. "I pulled them out of the oven just yesterday. I think the glaze came out well. Tomorrow morning, I'll begin making that special form he ordered."

While he talked, Garnier continued to turn and shape the pitcher, stroking the pliant clay with practiced hands.

"Does all go well with the master alchemist?" he asked.

"His health is more than satisfactory, but this murder vexes him."

"Ah yes, Ermessen. I heard of this killing. Who has not?"

"Did you know her?"

"Only to know she was Hebert's wife and to see her once or twice when I did business with him. She had little talk in her."

Bertwoin asked, "Did you blame her for persuading Hebert to pick Jehan over Tumas?"

Garnier shook his head. "I knew she wanted Jehan, but I doubt she could change Hebert's decisions. Tumas thinks Hebert was against him because he's silent. Hebert might think that being speechless is the same as being stupid."

"I've not heard anyone accuse him of that," Flowia said.

"Then you keep good company, maiden." Garnier glanced at Bertwoin as if trying to decide whether he was good company.

"Many people believe a silent tongue means a silent brain. It is his cross to bear. They make jokes about him. Behind his back."

Yes, Bertwoin thought, Tumas was said to have a choleric temper. Could Flowia cure an excess of yellow bile?

Flowia shook her head. "The master says that silence is to wisdom what rain is to a seed."

Garnier looked at her with gratitude. "I must remember that."

Tumas slipped into the room through an open back door, his leather apron streaked with dried clay. He stood just inside the doorway with his thick forearms crossed over his chest, as if on guard duty.

Flowia glided to the shelf Garnier had indicated and picked up a stack of three heart-shaped dishes. "These molds are well wrought. The master will be pleased."

Garnier acknowledged her compliment with a grin. "It pleases me to aid his art, whether it be magical or not. Usually, I fashion the same pieces I've made a thousand times before. I spend my days making one basic object in many forms, usually a clay belly with an open mouth. Not so with the master alchemist. He brings me problems that kindle my interest and use my skill."

Flowia moved back to the room's center, her steps leaving footprints in the clay dust on the floor. She paid him with a silver coin from the leather purse hung on her belt. "Have you heard how Ermessen died?"

Bertwoin glanced at Tumas, who still blocked the doorway. Did something secret lie on the other side of the back wall, something he didn't want them to see?

"Yes," Garnier said, "and if the rumors be true, she suffered as no Christian woman should. One wonders who would do such a thing to her. I would not wish such a death even on Hebert, but I could understand it better if it had been him. He boasts more enemies than a stray dog does fleas." He lifted his cloth cap from his head and scratched his scalp, which was as bald as the bottom of the smooth pitcher he was shaping. "Ermessen was said to have only friends. That's the shock of all this."

Tumas shook his head and clicked his thumb against his middle finger.

"I think your son disagrees with you," Flowia said.

"His heart is weighted with disappointment. Hebert and I had agreed Armendis was to marry Tumas. We were disappointed to learn Hebert's pledge was only breath with no true intention behind it. He's not a man of honor."

"I heard you fought with Hebert," Flowia probed.

Garnier's laugh had no joy in it. "It was more of a skirmish than a battle."

Tumas thumped the butt of a fist against the plastered wall behind him.

"I think," Flowia said, "the fight would have ended differently if Tumas had been there."

Sudden pride showed on Garnier's lined face. "Yes, maiden, it would've ended otherwise. Fighting Tumas is like fighting a wild boar. His strength brings him honor, and he wins far more wrestling matches than he loses."

Garnier made a chucking sound with his tongue. "Hebert, though, is as stubborn as a stump with deep roots. It's likely that even if Tumas had beaten and bloodied him, he wouldn't have honored his vow to us." The potter studied Flowia's face. "Think not, maiden, that I trouble my thoughts for long over that rascal. I do not stew in anger or sneak around looking for revenge. I have been knocked down before. And know too, maiden, that I held no grudge against Ermessen, though she opposed us. Tell the master this. No Christian would kill her or anyone else in such a savage way."

"You heard about his ram?"

"Oh yes, many have heard that tale. Hebert is not one to keep a grievance to himself. He thinks he makes them grow more terrible by telling everyone about them. To my way of thinking, a man who bleats for pity is no man at all."

"Would you have any idea where Armendis might be?" Flowia asked.

Garnier shook his head. "Tumas neglects his chores and searches for her every day. Has she run away? Why? Did someone take her? If so, it wasn't us. We are not the kind who'd take her by force." He smiled. "And if we were, my wife would be certain to help her escape."

They all chuckled, and even grim Tumas smiled at the thought of his *maman* thwarting them.

"We will not disturb you any longer," Flowia said.

"Your visit is a pleasure, maiden, not a disturbance. It seems you do not believe Armendis killed her mother?"

"The master is not yet convinced."

"Ah well, then Armendis may well be innocent. The alchemist is a man of reason and not easily fooled. Have you asked Artal if he has seen her?"

"My uncle," Bertwoin said, "doesn't know where she is. How did you know she had been at his house?"

"I didn't, but she might well have run to him."

"Why so? I know my Aunt Meli is fond of her and often visited her, but I don't remember hearing that my Uncle Artal had much to do with her. We heard he visited Ermessen."

Garnier looked at him a moment with his mouth open in disbelief, then realized Bertwoin was sincere. "Hebert is a cuckold. Artal is Armendis's real father, and he took our side in the argument. He wanted Armendis to marry Tumas, not your cousin, Jehan. As her real father, he should have some say in how she marries."

CHAPTER XVII.

Flowia and Bertwoin walked for some time in silence before she fluttered her hands like restive sparrows and said, "We can now guess what Artal and Armendis argued about. So, did he take her away? And if so, was it to hide her somewhere safe, or was it to keep her away from Jehan? Or did she run away from him?"

"Either way, my Aunt Guillema will swoop down on Artal with all her talons out. She might tell my father to talk to Artal."

"Your father will help?"

"It's a family problem. He will think it's duty to see that Guillema and Armendis get what they want. Artal is family, and if Armendis is his daughter, then she too is family. And Guillema was going to tie Armendis even tighter into our family."

Bertwoin felt uneasy, but wasn't sure why. They were on a little-used, rutted road the width of two mule butts—just wide enough for a cart. The wind disturbed the forest. Was it the wind that chafed his mood? He glanced behind them and might have seen a flash of blue disappear behind a hackberry trunk. He stared at the tree but saw nothing beyond the ordinary.

Flowia stopped with him. "What's wrong?"

"Thought I saw something. Probably a bird." He shrugged and began walking again. "Though I don't know what kind it could be."

Flowia stalked along like a grim egret hunting frogs. "The master will glue the clues we bring him together like Garnier glues pieces of a broken pot together. He will name the killer and save Armendis for your family."

"Then so be it," Bertwoin said. "It's Armendis we need. . . ." He stopped and scanned the crowded shrubbery around them.

With a hand on his knife's hilt, he stood rock still, his senses as alert as those of a rabbit that smells a musty fox. Something was amiss. Then he understood. It was as if the forest was trying to hide. The wind slipped through the trees without sound. There were no bird sounds and nothing moved. The back of his neck prickled as if death's clammy fingers tickled across it. Was someone? . . .

Two unkempt men strolled out onto the path and faced them, clearly intent on blocking their way. One was Gidie, the squire he had unhorsed with a hoe. He was barefoot now and wore a gray tunic and a woolen cloth draped around him in place of a cloak. His tangled reddish-brown beard was a squirrel's nest. The other outlaw was young and as thin as a chicken's leg. His wispy beard had no brawn to it. His brown cloak only came to his knees but looked well made, something a merchant might wear. Bertwoin assumed the knave had stolen it only days ago, because it was still in good condition.

He glanced at Flowia, who was half-turned and staring behind them. Another man had stepped out onto the path, a short man in a green tunic with two brown blankets, one over each shoulder, held in place by a rope belt at his waist. His left arm ended in a stub. Likely, the rascal had lost the hand for thieving. He would find it almost impossible to hire himself out and so had no choice but to become a beggar or brigand. Robbing travelers paid better.

Bertwoin balled his fists in angry disgust at himself. Even if outlaws rarely worked so near towns or citadels, he knew better than to let himself be so distracted in the forest as to be blind and deaf. But this wasn't the usual brigand attack, was it? His uncle had mentioned that Gidie might be stalking him. He had seen someone following him.

Why had . . . stop! Now was not the time to distract his thoughts. He cleared his mind and focused on staying alive.

He put his back to the forest. "Behind me," he growled.

Flowia slipped into the woods without a word, her dagger already drawn. Fleeing through the forest would bring her no advantage. One of the outlaws would chase her down while the other two brought him down. The youngest villain eyed her, his face feral with lust.

Gidie and the two outlaws strolled closer, all three of them grinning, their eyes shining with the excitement of hunters closing in on trapped prey. The one-handed beggar crept in on the left, the other two on his right. Gidie swung wide on the path so he could attack Bertwoin from the front. He and the young villain carried clubs in their right hands with knives in their left hands. The one-handed man had only a cudgel.

Bertwoin let his eyesight expand until he could watch all three of the outlaws at once. Details receded and white light blurred the edges of his sight. The least twitch would now catch his attention. His body could react without thought. He pulled his knife.

"You can't fight three of us," Gidie said, his voice gentle, coaxing. "We only want your purses, not your lives." He paused and smiled. "And, of course, your knives. And if the bitch is wearing a necklace, we'll want the chain and whatever it holds between her tits."

Of course, if he and Flowia surrendered their knives, they would be as helpless as midges tangled in a spider's web. And the sly way the young knave leered at Flowia made it as clear as air that he wouldn't be satisfied with just trinkets and coins. Gidie too would want more revenge than just robbing them.

Bertwoin relaxed, readying himself. He must get in the first blow and end the fight quickly. The longer they fought, the more the odds of winning turned in the outlaws' favor.

Gidie scratched his beard and watched him with mock pity. "You don't want to fight us. It'll only get you hurt." He chuckled. "You don't have a hoe this time."

Bertwoin stayed silent. Spewing threats or insults would make him seem desperate and weak. He smiled, which wiped the amused arrogance off their faces. They tensed, ready to attack.

Bertwoin jerked his head up and stared past Gidie's shoulder as if surprised. Gidie half turned to see what was in the forest behind him. The other two scoundrels also glanced rearward.

Bertwoin charged forward. Gidie turned back toward him, bewildered, and Bertwoin head-butted his nose and face. The ex-squire recoiled and yelped in pain. He dropped his club and knife, clasped his nose and mouth with both hands, and began backing away. Blood dripped off his chin. Bertwoin stepped closer and struck his jaw, knocking him to the ground.

While the other two outlaws were still stunned motionless, Bertwoin jumped to his left and attacked the one-handed beggar. The man tried to swing his cudgel, but Bertwoin was already close enough to block his arm. Bertwoin stabbed at the man's eye but missed. His knife's point slid along the side of the beggar's head and sliced the top of his ear. The man screamed and twisted sideways. Bertwoin smacked him on the nose hard enough to knock him to the ground.

A kick to the back of his left leg brought Bertwoin to one knee. He twisted and saw the fierce young outlaw standing over him, his club raised high to strike. Bertwoin threw up his arms to protect his head.

The knave shrieked and arched backward, dropping both his club and knife. Amazed, Bertwoin stared upward. The rogue clawed at the small of his back, jittering, taking stiff jerky steps sideways, mewing in agony. As the outlaw moved aside, Flowia came into view behind him, her dagger bloody.

Movement on his left caught his eye. He rose just in time to meet the bleeding, red-bearded Gidie's charge. They grappled, grunting like wrestlers, each trying to force or throw the other to the ground. Gidie was solid as a boulder and also agile, but Bertwoin was taller and plowing fields had made him a match for most men. Still, Gidie had a knight's training. He twisted and threw Bertwoin off his feet.

Bertwoin saw Gidie step over and grab Bertwoin's dagger lying on the ground. Gidie's club lay near him. He grabbed it. Flowia came in from the side with her dagger and threatened Gidie, who turned and slashed at her with his knife. She dodged his blade.

Bertwoin scrambled up and swung the club with all his might as the outlaw turned back toward him. It thunked against Gidie's temple with a sickening sound. Bertwoin knew it was a killing blow. He watched the ruffian fall with disbelief.

"I killed him," he told Flowia. His voice sounded as if it came from far away.

She patted his forearm and whispered, "You had to. You had to save us from them."

Bertwoin remembered the other two outlaws. The young one lay twitching on the ground. Flowia had wasted no time before cutting his throat to hasten his death. The beggar wearing brown blankets had vanished into the forest.

"Doubt we'll find him now," Bertwoin said. "God's truth, Flowia, in a fight, I'll always want you behind my enemies. You've got the stomach for it."

"These men meant to kill us both after they had their sport with me," she said in a guttural voice that sounded more animal than human. "A rat has more right to live than they do."

She knelt beside Gidie's still-warm body and cut a small leather bag with embroidery on it off his belt. Her face hideous with hatred, she held the lady's purse up for Bertwoin to see. "How many women do you think they raped and killed before now?" She blew out her breath. "Well, these two will do no more harm in this world. May their souls go straight to Hell."

While Flowia collected their knives and pulled a ring off the young outlaw's finger, Bertwoin grabbed Gidie's wrists and dragged his corpse into the bushes. He then did the same with the other body. They didn't deserve burial. Let the animals have their fill of them. Let whoever was unlucky enough to smell them take care of their rotting corpses. He doubted anyone would ever point a finger at Flowia or him for these killings, and if it should happen, if the one-handed villain should talk, they had the right to self-defense. No one would take an outlaw's word against theirs.

Bertwoin's legs trembled as he escorted Flowia homeward, but he felt distant from his emotions. Flowia skimmed along, her manner as silent and grim as an angry saint. When they came to a crossing path, she stepped up to him, put her hand on his chest, and kissed his cheek. She turned and glided down a side path, clearly wanting to be alone and expecting him to keep going straight.

Bertwoin trudged homeward, trying to think of what he would say to his father and family when he got there. No, he had somewhere else to go first. He dodged off the path and waded through the woods toward Roul's farm. If he could talk to Maria alone, he had something important to say to her.

CHAPTER XVIII.

As Bertwoin ambled down a forest path toward Roul's farm, he relived the fight. He had done as well as any man could be expected to do against three gnarly ruffians who were practiced at preying on people. No, *they* had done well—one man *and* one formidable woman.

Sensible, lethal Flowia had saved their lives. He knew not how to praise her enough. Yet something about her manner and the emptiness he had seen in her made him draw his cloak tighter around him. He cupped his red hands around his mouth and blew warm breath into them. As she cut the lady's purse off Gidie's belt, he had gazed at her grim face and stared into the eyes of a wolf. These were the same eyes that had shone with excited love for him. What other devils haunted this woman he cherished more than his own life? What —

Something thrashed through the tangled underbrush. He leaped sideways and drew his knife. Whatever it was, it fled from him. He sighed, took a deep breath, and released it slowly, relaxing the tightness out of his chest. Most likely, he had startled a pig foraging for mast.

Why should Flowia's fierce manner make him uneasy? It was worthy of praise. It was a relief to know Flowia would always protect his back. And he had noticed that after the fight, she too had trembled. She had done what was necessary, then her true nature had returned. He skipped three or four steps like a gamboling child, then walked onwards.

Almost before he knew it, he reached the edge of the forest and found himself looking across a fallow field on the outer edge of Roul's prosperous farm. Maria sat alone on a small bench in the early winter sun near a bare chestnut tree, sewing a small white cloth. She looked up and noticed him, then glanced at her house. Had she felt his gaze? He hadn't meant to scare her.

He didn't see Roul or Maria's mother. He raised his eyes toward a sky blown cloudless and smiled his thanks. Again, luck had folded its soft wings around him.

As he strolled toward her, she continued to sew but kept glancing at him like a hare that is unsure about an approaching animal. He saw she was stitching chin straps onto a coif—linen, not cheaper wool. She laid her sewing on her lap when he came close and waited for him to speak. He didn't quite know what to do with his hands.

"May God bless you and all in this house," he intoned.

After greeting him, she said, "My father has gone to Montredon. He should return soon."

"It was you I came to see, not him."

This startled her. She tilted her head to one side and watched his face, trying to judge his mood. "Me?"

How to start? "I thought we might come to an understanding." That sounded too formal, almost as if he were about to propose marriage. He didn't want to scare her. He blurted out, "I mean, uh, I didn't come to propose marriage or anything." That was as blunt as a cudgel. Why had he ever put himself in this position?

She laughed, relaxing a bit. "So my womanly charms have not lured you away from a life dedicated to serving God?"

"You didn't believe I was going to become a cleric, did you?" He sounded more like a croaking toad than a cooing dove.

Amused now, she shook her head. "No, and neither did anyone else except my *papa*. Everybody above the age of three in the *visconte's* domain knows you worship the alchemist's virgin."

His face grew warm, which broadened her smile. "Worship?" he said, rolling the word around in his mouth as if trying to taste it. "That might be too hefty a word for it. Anyway, it only concerns me and my family."

She raised her eyebrows. "Maybe Flowia won't agree with you on that. It concerns her. If she joined your family, would your father ever heed her?"

"I doubt it, but I think he'll have no choice but to hear her opinions. She's as outspoken as a saint filled with the Spirit."

"She has the freedom to do so." Maria looked him in the eye. "That you adore her is as plain as a one-legged man. Some men think you are silly and weak because of it, but most women don't. We think Flowia is fortunate. None of us would spurn being adored by the right man."

Her bold honesty embarrassed him, yet also warmed him. It would be nice to add her to their family, even if not as his wife.

"By the way," she said, "my *papa* will never trust you again after he understands you lied to him. How is it with your father?"

"I don't know, but I'm going to find out sooner than I want to. I expect he'll beat me. He can tolerate lying except when it's done to him."

After a moment of thoughtful silence, she said, "You proposed that we come to an understanding." She said the word "understanding" slowly, as if savoring its meaning.

"I do. Wilfraed."

Her eyes flared, and she turned her face away from him, but not before he had seen the face of a barren woman who had just realized she was with child.

Encouraged, he rushed onward. "Our fathers want what they think is best for both of our houses. I believe you and Wilfraed can do what's best for both *ostals*. My brother is fond of you. That's as obvious as the one-legged man you mentioned."

"And I am fond of him. We played together often as children. But will your father agree to this? It isn't normal for Wilfraed to marry before you."

"But do you agree to be his wife?"

She looked down at her hands. "I do."

He nodded, keeping calm, though he wanted to throw his arms in the air and shout with pagan joy. "My father might agree, especially when he realizes it's either my brother or nothing. I'm not saying you aren't desirable, but as you say, I am bound to another."

"She is lucky."

Bertwoin wasn't certain Flowia thought herself so fortunate after his failure to curb his uncle. But she had kissed his cheek after their battle with the outlaws. There was hope in that. "I want you to be lucky too, as long as my brother is what you want."

She clasped her hands together. "More than anything. This silly dispute over some trees hinders our seeing each other."

So Wilfraed had sneaked away to visit her when he could. Bertwoin squinted toward the border between their farms, where a pile of rocks marked ownership of the disputed land. He smiled. "Coming here, I noticed my father, or maybe my uncle, had moved the pile of rocks so we again own that strip of land."

She giggled. "My father will move the stones back tonight."

Bertwoin chucked his tongue. "Strong-willed fathers are sometimes a blessing, sometimes a curse. Do you think your *papa* will agree to Wilfraed taking my place at the altar? As you said, he isn't the eldest son."

"*Papa* loves me in his own way. He just thinks that I will love any man he picks as my husband. My *maman* did. I think, though, *maman* will take my side and help me change his mind." She looked coyly at him. "Besides, why would my parents ever want a son-in-law who lies to them?"

Maria sat with her back to her house, so she didn't see her *maman* open the front door and step outside. Her *maman* jerked as if slapped when she saw him, then she strode toward them, her gait that of a mother hurrying to defend her daughter.

"I think," he said, staring over her head, "you are about to find out if she will argue for or against you."

Maria looked behind her, picked up her sewing, and stood up. Her *maman* joined them and put her hands on her hips, not bothering to ask for an explanation but clearly expecting one.

"God bless you, Na Petra."

"And you Bertwoin Teisseire."

Before he could stutter his way through an explanation for his presence, Maria said, "Bertwoin came to talk with me about the disagreement between our families. He thinks he knows how to end it." She paused to let her *maman* say something, but Na Petra remained silent. "He proposes that I marry Wilfraed instead of him."

"Why then does he talk to you and not your father?"

"I would not propose this marriage if Maria spurned it," he said.

Na Petra looked him up and down, then accepted his excuse with a nod. "I'm sure it would please my daughter to marry Wilfraed. I will talk to my husband. I doubt he cares which Teisseire she marries. But I think it would be best if you weren't here when he comes home today." She jerked her head at Maria. "We need to talk to him first. Godspeed, plowman. And thank the Lord for putting a brain in your head."

Na Petra marched back to the house, and Maria sat back down on the oak bench.

Bertwoin thought of the bruising task ahead of him. "At least now you have your mother on your side. My *maman* would rather I married you instead of Flowia."

Maria stroked the coif on her lap. "You may not get permission for Wilfraed to marry me. Your leaving embarrassed your father in front of my *papa*. After you left, your uncle blamed your running away on Flowia. Said she had bewitched you. Laurence hates her like our bishop hates a heretic, and he let us know it. Your father seemed to share his opinion, though he stayed silent. Your marrying me would solve the problem of Flowia for them."

"My father also values the *bayle's* opinion. Another ex-crusader."

"Ah," she said and giggled, "but the lawman surprised us, didn't he? Your uncle called Flowia a canker in our midst. Said she should be run out of the domain. He turned to the *bayle*, expecting as we all did, that the gruff old warrior would agree with him. Instead, the lawman defended her. Said he had been glad of her services when his wife got the flux. Flowia had brought them medicine from her garden and helped nurse his wife back to health." Maria slapped her knee, chortling. "Your *papa* stared at the *bayle* with his mouth open, and your uncle almost staggered in surprise. My father laughed all the way home."

"Maybe my uncle's tirade against Flowia helped our cause."

After a moment's pause, Maria said, "Wilfraed said you were helping the alchemist solve the murder. Does the master still doubt that Armendis is guilty?"

"He believes there's a reason to dig deeper into this foul killing. What does your *papa* think?"

She shrugged. "He accepts what Hebert says. Even if Armendis was out of her mind, she still did it. That's why he told the lawman where Armendis was hiding. He believes that anyone with eyes can see that Ermessen's blood on Armendis was a sign of her guilt. He thinks Artal and Melisende were wrong to hide her and should also be punished."

"What do you believe?"

His question startled her. "No one cares what I think."

"I do."

She frowned at the ground, choosing her words with care. "My father is usually right, but the alchemist is wise. Maybe he'll find that *papa* is right. But," she smoothed the coif in her lap, "why would Armendis ever kill her gentle mother?" Then she smiled. "I hope you become my brother."

"I want you to be my sister." He smiled. "Rather than I become a brother at the abbey."

She grinned. "Flowia would think you a churl if you did."

Flowia already considered him a churl. "Well then, I will follow your *maman's* advice and trot off before your father comes home and finds me here."

"Thank you for coming to ask my permission instead of just talking to my *papa*," she said. "Flowia is lucky."

"Let's hope we too get lucky and convince our fathers."

She folded her hands in her lap again and looked up with the hopeful expression some statues of the Virgin Mary had. He felt the same.

On the way home, he debated whether to visit his grandmother's grave again before facing his father's anger. He could use another miracle. He decided instead to stoke up his courage and return home. Besides, going to Montredon would double his debt to the Church for the candles he used.

CHAPTER XIX.

All the way home, Bertwoin rehearsed arguments he might use to convince his father that Wilfraed was the better choice for Maria's husband. He decided it was better to leave home than to take another beating. He would outrun his father instead of accepting blows from him. Maybe Guillema would take him in if he ran to her.

He stopped as the trees thinned and looked at the furrowed land he had plowed and helped plant with barley and oats. Here was the wattle-and-daub house with its hearth, and the fire-damaged barn where he and Wilfraed slept with the mules at night. Here were the people he loved.

He smiled at the ancient almond tree with the hole in its trunk where he hid his small hoard of silver coins. It stood as proud and lonely as a soldier on guard duty. As a boy, he had fallen out of it one summer. At first, his *maman* thought he had broken his forearm, but if so, it healed as young bones do. And unlike Sibilia, his arms were the same length. Thinking of the hidden coins reminded him that he needed to pay the Church for his grandmother's candle. He would light another one to honor her memory if she would give him another miracle now.

He squared his shoulders and marched across the side field, his hands cold in the wind that was again gathering force. When he came within sight of the house's front, he saw that despite the wind, his family had again gathered in the front yard to enjoy the winter sunshine. He saw their grim stares, as if he were bringing them the plague. Even his *maman* sat unsmiling as he strode toward them. Wilfraed looked concerned, almost frightened.

His arguments, which had seemed so promising while he marched through the forest, now turned to ash. They were nothing more than desperate excuses no one would heed.

They watched in silence as he walked past them, went inside the house, and came back out with a clay bowl half-full of ale.

"You were seen with the alchemist's virgin," Laurence accused.

"We had to talk with Garnier."

"Shouldn't have taken that long to talk to the potter," his father said.

"Where've you really been?" his uncle asked. "And when are you going to come home and do your work here?"

"Fought three outlaws," he muttered.

Wilfraed and his father sniggered, and the others looked at him with disapproval, then with confusion when they realized he wasn't joking.

His *maman* took half a step toward him. "Are you hurt?"

"No." It amazed him even now to realize that he wasn't. Three men had attacked him, and he hadn't even suffered a telling blow.

"Outlaws," his father muttered with mistrust. "Where was this?"

"They came out of the forest on the way back from Garnier's pottery. Close to Roul's *ostal*." He decided not to mention Flowia. "I killed two of them and the third one ran off into the bushes with part of his ear cut off. Gidie was their leader."

His father said, "Well, you did a day's work if you sent him flying to Hell." He added with suspicion, "Roul's place? Speaking of Roul, we're hearing rumors that you aren't serious about preaching to us sinners. We're hearing that people are laughing at us."

"The alchemist made a suggestion about Roul," he told his father.

"The alchemist," his uncle sneered. "That interfering old man has already caused us enough trouble. He's the reason we all have our claws out and are hissing at each other. He makes you think that being only a plowman and supporting your family is beneath you."

Bertwoin didn't need to defend the master or himself. That would be yielding to Laurence. With deliberate calm, he said, "He suggested Wilfraed marry Maria and bind the two families together."

His father stared at him as if he had turned into Hilario the halfwit. He hacked and spat on Bertwoin's cloak.

Wilfraed, who had been leaning against their house's front wall, slid down it into a squatting position. He set his mug on the ground with a trembling hand so as not to spill his ale. "Can that be?"

"Why not?" Bertwoin looked around at their disbelieving faces. Only Maud gazed up at him with a friendly expression. "The *visconte* has set no law against it. And Father Pons will have no objection to marrying them."

"But I do," his father shouted. "You'll do as you're told. No son of mine will contradict my word. I can't go to Roul and say he gets the second boy, the second best. Wilfraed hasn't yet established himself. Far from it."

"Neither have I." Of course, this argument was now about more than just joining the two farms together. This concerned his father's standing both at home and in the community. He had promised his eldest son as Maria's husband. Not only did Roul know this, but so did everyone else by now. If it became known that Bertwoin had disobeyed him, it would diminish his father's reputation as the powerful master of his ostal. "You didn't know Wilfraed and Maria were fond of each other when you and Roul decided on me as the husband. That would be reason enough to change your mind."

Clanoud swiped away this justification with a flick of his hand. "Fond? Fond of each other? What has that to do with anything?"

When his uncle laughed, Bertwoin felt hot hatred bubble from his stomach into his chest. The bowl shook in his hand. He willed himself to concentrate on his father. "It means he is more established with Maria than I am."

"Established?" His father pointed at the fields between their farm and Roul's. "Are you addled, boy? We're talking about land, something you can walk on, not some maiden's emotions. We're talking about making a living after I'm in the ground. We're talking about having standing in the community and keeping the family fed."

"I'm talking about marriage," Bertwoin said.

"You're talking about love, not marriage. Love." His father spat out the word as if it tasted bitter. "Can you grow barley on love? Can you eat love? Will love increase your flock? Will it give you wool to keep the winter winds from freezing your family to death?"

Bertwoin said quietly, "Marriage and survival are two different things, *Papa*. Besides, Roul will not want me to marry his daughter now. I lied to him about something he thinks is important."

"You lied to us all. Something I won't forget. Believe me on that."

"I've heard you lie when it was to your advantage."

"Not to family."

"That's because you never need to. Right or wrong, you always get your way."

"Wrong?" His father glared up at him, incredulous that anyone would dare to say he was ever wrong. "That's the last ale you'll drink in this house until you come into your right mind again."

Bertwoin's stomach lurched. He took a heaving breath, then let it out slowly to relax the lump in his chest. He stayed silent, and they waited. Without his family, he would be a social leper. Without a family, many farmers would refuse to let him plow their fields, especially if his father told them he was against their doing so.

"Go on." His father flicked his hand at the barn. "You can sleep with the dog and study on what you need to do to help your family."

"*Papa*, our dog died before All Saint's Day."

Bertwoin stared a moment at his father. The shocking thought that Clanoud, the king of their household, was not all-powerful, overwhelmed him. His father wasn't completely in control of this situation. His father could punish him, and the price he would pay was heavier than iron, but his father couldn't force him, the eldest son, to stand at the altar with Maria. The power was his if he was willing to do the unthinkable, to lose his family and throw away the life he was building as a farmer and plowman. But on the other side, he didn't want to imagine life without Flowia.

He took a long sip of his ale, its taste bitter on his tongue, to clear his throat so his voice wouldn't quaver. "*Maman* brews excellent ale, but I can do without it."

They all stared at him. Rachel began crying, and his *maman* looked like she was about to do the same. He expected his father to charge him, his fists flying, but instead he sat looking flummoxed on his stool.

Hurting them made him feel like a stray cat that had scratched a hand holding food out to it. But he had done what he could. He had brought them a solution that would resolve their disagreement, even if no one was entirely happy with what he proposed.

It was time to stop arguing. "It's simple. If Roul accepts Wilfraed, will you agree?"

"That's not the way it's going to be. You'll marry the girl, and that's the end of it."

"I can't do that, *Papa*. And it's not because I don't respect you."

His father set aside his special mug in the shape of a boar's head and stood up. "You think you can take me, boy?"

"I think it'll take you all winter to heal after you fight me. And you'll still be sore come spring. Thrashing me is as useless as talking to a dead man. You'll never change my mind about this. That's something I learned from you."

"Don't need to. Just need to make you do it."

"And," Bertwoin added, "if you pound me into raw meat and break a bone or two, come spring, you won't have me to plow our fields or those of any other farmer's. Laurence or Wilfraed will have to cut the furrows for the *visconte*. And come harvest time, you'll need Eudes to sneak old bread out of the *chateau's* kitchen for you."

"Where will you go?" his uncle sneered. "The alchemist's?"

Bertwoin thought again of his Aunt Guillema and wondered if Rachel and Eudes would have a place for him after they married. "Maybe. But there might be better choices than that. And being alone is better than living with my enemy."

"Then get off my land," Clanoud muttered. "Now."

"If he goes, so do I," his *maman* said with quiet certitude.

Stunned, all eyes turned toward her. Rachel put her hand to her mouth and whispered, *"Maman."*

His father said, "That'll never happen."

When Laurence laughed at her, his *maman* snarled at him, her face twisted with disgust. "You scorn love and worship hate. You've brought no woman into this house. No children call you *Papa*. You live in your brother's shadow."

He looked ready to hit her but had better sense than to do so. "At least, I'll have a place to live. Where can you go, woman?"

"Rachel will marry soon. I can move in with Eudes and her. They'll be glad for my help." She glanced at her youngest daughter. "I'll be taking little Maud with me, of course."

"You've been stung with stupidity, woman," Laurence told her. "We can make do here without you."

"I'll piss on your grave, Laurence, after you've killed yourself and Clanoud with your cooking." She laughed, sounding pleased at the thought. "Who's going to gather the herbs Clanoud likes so much for his soups? You? You'll pick deadly nightshade for your salad, thinking it's spinach. And forget early bread. You're too fond of your sleep to get up in the dark of night to prepare it before dawn."

"You're not going anywhere," Clanoud told her.

"I'll be leaving too," Wilfraed said.

"I guess you'll go to Rachel's new family too?" Laurence scoffed.

"Why not?" Wilfraed nodded at his sister. "Rachel's new house will accept me. They can always use my labor."

"Or," Bertwoin said to his father, "you could just let him marry Maria. It would level the path if he had your permission. More dignity for you that way and for the whole family."

Laurence stared at his brother, waiting for him to take charge of the situation. Clanoud just stared at the ground, breathing hard through his nostrils like an irate boar.

"Who's that?" Rachel said. She held a hand over her eyebrows and squinted at something out in one of their front fields.

They all turned and saw a boy trotting toward them. Bertwoin sighed with relief, as did his *maman*. Thank God the alchemist had sent a boy this time and not Flowia to fetch him. Maybe his grandmother was still watching over him.

Bertwoin answered Rachel's question. "An angel without wings."

CHAPTER XX.

Clanoud stood with his legs spread, hands on his waist, leaning toward the intruder. He watched the boy as if vermin crept toward him.

Bertwoin could almost feel a thick aura of menace radiating off his hostile father. His family waited in hushed silence. The boy had slowed to a hesitant shuffle, his frightened eyes never leaving Clanoud's face.

If the alchemist had sent this messenger to fetch him, it meant something important had happened. Had they found Armendis? Or had the killer now murdered her too?

Bertwoin stepped forward to meet the boy.

Behind him, his father told him, "We're not done here."

But they were done. Neither of them would change the other's opinion.

The boy said loud enough for everyone to hear, "My uncle sent me to find you. He wants you to come to him now."

Expecting a message from the alchemist, it took Bertwoin a couple of breaths to adjust his thoughts. "Who's your uncle?"

His question surprised the boy, who must have assumed he would be recognized. "Hugon," he chirped.

Bertwoin placed the boy then. Why would Sibilia's father need him? Did this have to do with Ermessen's murder? Why then did the boatbuilder want to talk to him rather than to the alchemist?

"What's your name?"

"Hugon."

"I thought you said he was your uncle."

"Got the same name. I'm little Hugon."

"I see. Was the alchemist there when you left?"

The boy shook his head. "Didn't see him."

Then the boy stared at Clanoud and stayed quiet, so Bertwoin asked, "Why does your uncle want to see me?"

"Something happened to Sibilia."

A bit confused, Bertwoin stared at the boy. He and Flowia had just talked to her. "You, uh, you don't know what happened to her, do you?"

Little Hugon shook his head, then waited, saying nothing. He had finished his task and clearly wanted to leave.

Behind Bertwoin, his father said, "I'll come too. Ellyn, fetch my cloak and winter boots."

The boy's eyes flared. "My uncle's at his house." He turned and ran away.

Why would his father want to come? Was it to show him who was head of the family? Did he want to keep talking about his marrying Maria? Or was he just butting in because he knew his son didn't want him to come? "This is about Armendis's disappearing, *Papa*."

"I need to see for myself what it is you do when you're away. I need to see if we should continue doing all the work around here by ourselves. Besides, it doesn't hurt for me to get out once in a while and get the stink off me."

His stubborn father stayed silent as they walked to Hugon's place on the Aude River. Hugon met them on the path leading to his house. He was short and wiry. It was said that women found him handsome, though Bertwoin judged his looks to be no better or no worse than normal. What set him above the ordinary, besides his ability to build boats that floated like bubbles on water, was his singing. Gossip had it that grateful fairies had given baby Hugon a honeyed voice as payment for something his father had done for them.

Hugon's cheeks and beard were wet, probably from tears. He didn't bother to greet them. He glared at Clanoud, as if he might tell him to leave, then turned without a word and led them to his boathouse. His outside workshop—a roof without walls—stood on its deck and two large steering oars reached from a platform at the stern to the ground. Instead of climbing up onto the deck and entering the workshop as Bertwoin expected, he faced them and said, "I've sent for the alchemist and the *bayle*." He gulped and said in a voice hoarse with pain. "Some whoreson killed my girl." He waved toward his cottage. "Women are tending to her body."

Bertwoin felt a jolt in the hollow of his stomach. Who would kill Sibilia, so skilled and girlish? The women had been quick to come wash her. Were they wiping away clues?

"The alchemist will want to see her in the clothes she was wearing."

Hugon snarled. "The alchemist be damned. They had to sew up gashes all over her body. She deserves a decent burying." He shook himself, gasping for breath, his nose running. "The master has a way of finding these killers. Let him come and do it. He doesn't need to see the shame done to her. Nobody does, except the women who clean her up. I'll tell him what he needs to know. I found her naked and dead." He put his face in his hands. "Her clothes are gone."

"Did the killer leave a doll on her?"

His father scowled at him. Hugon stared at him to see if he was being mocked.

"The killer left a poppet on Ermessen," Bertwoin explained.

"No poppet," Hugon growled.

"What do you want from me?"

"When you know the killer's name, I want you to tell me before the *bayle* arrests him."

"You're asking me to betray the master."

His father said, "Revenge is every father's right."

Hugon nodded in gratitude. No doubt, he thought that if the father agreed, then the son also had to agree.

Bertwoin felt tired. If he deceived the alchemist, the master would never trust him again. But how could he refuse this grieving father?

"If the master makes me swear to keep the man's name secret, I'll not betray him. But he's unlikely to do so. I'll tell you the name. Whether the seneschal hangs him or you kill him, it matters not to me."

Hugon spat into his hand and held it out. Bertwoin spat into his palm, clasped the bony hand, and sealed his promise. His father nodded at the rightness of the agreement.

"That's neighborly of you," Hugon said. "What did Sibi tell you when you visited her?"

"We asked her if she knew where Armendis was. She said no. She told us to ask Hebert about his ram."

Pain clenched Hugon's face, and he closed his eyes. Tears continued to seep from them. He moaned. "She was throat-cut like that ram." His whole body shuddered. "And the whoreson did something more. He . . . he cut off her nose," he said in a shrill voice. "They've got to sew it back on. Why? Why do this to my lamb?"

What was the sick killer telling them by cutting off Sibilia's nose?

His father tapped Bertwoin's shoulder. "The alchemist should be here soon. When he's done with you, get your ass home. You still have a problem we need to discuss."

"You don't think," Hugon said to Bertwoin, "that the killer followed you to my house and saw you talking to my Sibi, do you?"

Was he accusing Flowia and him of leading the murderer to his door? Did he blame them for his daughter's death? He reminded himself that the boatbuilder was half-crazy with grief.

"No," he said, "we would've noticed anybody tracking us. And the murderer wouldn't waste his time following Flowia and me. We're not that important. He would spy on the alchemist or the *bayle*, not us."

Hugon gazed at him with boarish suspicion while he considered this answer. Then he nodded. "Let it be so." But he didn't sound convinced.

"Sibilia and Armendis were best friends," Bertwoin said. "The murderer may have believed your daughter was a danger to him. She may have known something she didn't think was important, but the killer thought it was."

"We'll leave you to your sorrow," his father told Hugon. "Bertwoin will wait on the path for the alchemist and keep out of your way."

Hugon gazed at the ground as if he hadn't heard him. His father jerked his head for Bertwoin to follow him.

As soon as they were out of earshot, his father said, "I've seen this before. He failed to protect his girl and needs to lay the blame across someone else's neck. No good will come of this. Stay out of his sight until the alchemist comes. Even after he comes, keep away from Hugon as much as you can. His mind is awry, and there's no telling what might provoke him into attacking you."

CHAPTER XXI.

Bertwoin sat on a limestone block, probably a boundary marker for Hugon's land? He watched a smattering of clouds skim overhead as if he were underwater and watching the bottoms of boats pass overhead.

Had Armendis again become demon-stricken and killed her friend? Sibilia would have welcomed her friend with open arms. Where was Armendis hiding?

Bertwoin heard men talking and strolled around the bend in the path. The alchemist stood at the boat shed, talking to Hugon. How had he gotten here? Was Flowia already in the house with the women? He hurried over and greeted the master.

"God give you peace, plowman." The alchemist's voice was hushed, probably in respect for Sibilia's death. He raised his bristling eyebrows in surprise when Hugon's expression turned hostile on seeing Bertwoin.

"Ah well, my assistant is here now." The alchemist patted Bertwoin's shoulder.

The boatbuilder snorted. "He's been hanging around. I already talked with him and Clanoud."

The alchemist eyed Bertwoin. "Oh, so your father came with you. Have you been waiting long?"

"He has," Hugon grumbled before Bertwoin could answer. Something near his house caught his attention.

Bertwoin turned and saw a priest wearing only a cassock and cincture, no cloak, marching up to the front door. Maybe his faith kept him warm.

"I need to tend to him," Hugon said and hurried away.

"Is Flowia in the house?" Bertwoin asked.

"She is, and I am not. Hugon would rather I not—disturb is the word he used—his daughter. I will comply with his wish." He sighed. "No matter, Flowia will fare better without me in there. The women will be more at their ease. By now, they may even have anointed the girl's body. Flowia brought oil. The girl's clothes seem to be missing, as were Ermessen's."

"Souvenir?"

"That would be my guess, though there is another possibility. Hebert did see his wife's ghost. Perhaps what Hebert saw was the killer dressed like Ermessen."

"Sibilia's nose was also cut off," Bertwoin said.

"Hugon mentioned that." The master stroked his beard. "I believe that might be a telling clue."

"Another souvenir?" Bertwoin suggested.

"Perhaps. Or was it the killer's way of telling us why Sibilia had to die? Had she been too nosy? Let's not forget the children's story of the cat whose curiosity caused it to have its nose chopped off." He pointed a bony finger at the workshop on the boathouse. "Hugon found her in there. He could barely talk about it, and who can blame him for that? The killer used one of the carving knives stored in the shed rather than his own dagger. Did it amuse him to kill Sibilia with one of her father's tools? I suspect that our murderer has a malicious sense of humor. Walking around as a victim's ghost might also please him."

"It's like a devil is loose among us."

"Yes, evil often likes to make itself known. It can't just be washed away." He clapped his hands and rubbed them together. "Anyway, I've already examined the work shed. There was little to find there except the dried blood and feces one expects after a violent murder. Hugon's boat knife . . . ah, we have visitors."

Bertwoin turned. His Uncle Artal and Aunt Meli had rounded the bend in the path. On seeing them, Meli darted forward, leaving Artal slouching along behind her.

"Sibilia dead," she cried. "How can this be? Have you heard anything more about Armendis?"

"No," The master studied her as if she were a page in one of his rare books. Then he turned his gaze on Artal, who stopped beside his wife and nodded to them.

Meli wrung her thin hands. "We must find her soon. She may be starving or hurt. Or. . . ." She looked at the house, no doubt thinking of Sibilia's mutilated corpse. Word of the murder and its gruesome details—some probably exaggerated beyond truth—was public gossip in all three towns and the citadel by now.

"I doubt Armendis is dead," the alchemist assured her.

She relaxed with a grateful sigh and leaned against her husband, who put his arm around her waist to support her. "You know this?"

"The killer makes certain we find the bodies of his victims immediately."

Bertwoin felt a prickle shiver up his spine and glanced up at the boathouse. Was Sibilia's ghost already haunting the work shed?

Artal smiled down into his wife's face and said, "That's true," to reassure her. Then he asked the alchemist, "Do you think Sibilia knew something about the killing?"

"Perhaps, but she mentioned nothing of significance to Bertwoin and Flowia when they questioned her. Though she did tell them about Hebert's slaughtered ram. So, did the killer practice for Ermessen's brutal death? Or was he just sending Hebert a savage message?"

Meli pressed her lips together and looked as if she would like to find this killer and practice her butchering skills on him.

"Hebert says you visited his farm shortly before Ermessen was killed," the alchemist said to Meli.

His aunt started. "Yes, I was there early and had left long before Ermessen was killed, no matter what Hebert might say. I asked Armendis what she wanted for her coming marriage to Jehan. She is like a daughter to me."

His uncle sighed and gazed out over the lazy river. They were childless, a quiet yet public sorrow they bore with fortitude.

"You saw nothing amiss with Armendis?" the alchemist asked.

"No," Meli said. "She was happy and so-o excited." Her face relaxed as she remembered their meeting. "We talked of nothing but her marriage. She almost swooned with joy at the mere mention of Jehan's name."

"And you didn't see her," the alchemist said to Artal.

"Not then, no." He smiled. "She is also like a daughter to me, so we sometimes talk."

"At your house?"

"She came by when she could, and I saw her often at Guillema's, though she usually spent her time there mooning around Jehan."

The alchemist perked up. "And you looked forward to this marriage?"

Artal glanced at his wife. "Meli and I differ when it comes to Jehan. I thought Armendis might do better. I think he's a lot of fun, and the women dote on him, but he has not yet proven his mettle. His mother shields him from a man's toil and woes."

Meli's face tightened with disagreement. "You judge him too harshly, husband."

"He has always drunk from a golden cup. When he was a young pup playing at the game of being a carter, he earned almost as much coin as some men did, but never had to do the work of a grown man."

"Tumas then?" the master asked.

Artal's eyes flared, and he looked like a child caught with his fingers in the honey crock. "How did you know that?"

Bertwoin said, "Garnier mentioned that you thought his boy should replace Jehan as the future husband."

Artal stared the alchemist in the eye. "Tumas has an affliction, but still, everybody knows not to trifle with him. And if the need to protect Armendis ever arose, he's the man to do it. He also will inherit his father's pottery."

Meli crossed her arms over her chest. "It's no more useful than a mill with a broken wheel," she told the alchemist, "to discuss husbands for Armendis if she's never found."

"Could she have taken sanctuary with any of the Good Folk?"

"And me not hear of it? No True Christian would act in such a way, knowing I spend my days and nights fretting about her. They know I have searched in every hole and around every corner for her?" She wiped a woolen sleeve across her eyes. "I came here hoping she might come out of hiding and visit Sibilia's body. They were very close."

"What if she fled to someone she trusted and made them promise not to tell anyone, not even you?" the alchemist persisted.

"She would never hurt us like that, and True Christians do not make vows. Besides," she sobbed, "I've already looked everywhere among us."

"I'm well aware of the girl's plight, Na Melisende," he said gently. "The law is now just as dangerous to her as her mother's murderer. We need to hide her from the *bayle*. Some in the *château* have already pronounced her guilty."

"She's not."

"I agree. Bertwoin and I will continue our search. We will bring her to you immediately if we find her and will leave it to you to find a hiding place for her."

"Thank you." Meli touched the master's sleeve, then turned to Bertwoin. "We stopped at your house on our way here. It was as tense as a chicken coop with a fox prowling around of it. What happened?"

Bertwoin glanced at the alchemist, who looked away. "It's best if *maman* tells you the tale."

"I'm asking you, not her."

"My father wants to force me to marry Maria to settle his boundary dispute with Roul. I refuse to do so." He glanced at the master as he told this to his aunt, "I've proposed that Wilfraed marry Maria. They are fond of each other."

She gave him a sour look. "Why do all of you young folks have so much trouble with marriage?"

"It's our parents who cause the problems."

She laughed. "My brothers always were selfish louts."

She nodded to the alchemist and told Bertwoin, "Stay strong." Then she put her nose up and strode away. Artal nodded to them and hurried to catch up with her.

The alchemist watched them march halfway to the house in silence before saying, "Your job now, plowman, is to follow Artal wherever he goes."

Bertwoin hummed agreement. "I did mark that he doesn't seem overly concerned about his daughter's disappearance while my aunt is almost hysterical. How does she not notice his cool manner?"

"She is focused only on finding Armendis."

"I think not all women would be so distracted. Some would feel that something was wrong."

The alchemist raised his eyebrows. "Flowia perhaps?"

"Well. She seems to sense things others miss."

"I've noticed," the master said. "But your aunt *is* preoccupied, and Artal may have more practice at keeping secrets than you do. When talking about Armendis, he said she *is* like a daughter to him, not *was*. Is he just keeping his hopes up, or does he know for certain that she isn't dead?"

CHAPTER XXII

Bertwoin sat hidden in the forest on the lichen-crusted trunk of a fallen oak, hoping Flowia would come out of Hebert's house before Artal did. He needed to talk to her. The chore of following his uncle reminded him of clearing rocks from a field—monotonous, mindless toil. What was keeping Flowia? His eyes felt raw, and he had to fight to keep them open.

A noise startled him. He raised his chin off his chest, realized where he was and that he had catnapped. He remembered why he was there and kept still, listening. Had anyone gone past him while he slept? On the path, he saw Artal and Meli's clothes flash between the bushes and tree trunks as they passed his hiding spot.

His aunt shrilled like an angry wren. "You need to stop biting Jehan in the back. My sister will hear of it."

"And if she does?"

"It will cut her to the heart. She was so-o happy about Jehan and Armendis's marriage and still wants it to happen. She thinks we are on her side in this."

Staying in the shrubbery close to the path, Bertwoin slid like a fox around bushes and brambles and followed them.

"I've got the right to have a say in who Armendis marries," Artal said. "That bastard, Hebert, sold her for money."

"Jehan is spoiled," his aunt admitted, "but he's a good lad and will treat her with more kindness than Tumas ever will. And marrying our nephew keeps Armendis close to us. We'll see her almost every day."

He grunted. "Having more in-laws than Guillema and Jehan wouldn't harm us any. Garnier's brother raises horses, and his need for a farrier would be a boon to me."

"You mean to do as Hebert did," his aunt shrilled. "You want to sell her like a loaf of bread at the market."

Artal made a hacking sound in his throat. "Don't insult me, woman. You're the one people are calling a witch. You're the reason some people now shun me. We're losing business because of you. I need to find more work."

"All I know is that Guillema would never shame a child of ours."

"Maybe that's because we'd raise it right. I'd see to that."

"It's always easy for people to say how good they'll be. But it often proves otherwise when they find themselves in the situation."

"Well, I can't prove my point, can I? We *don't* have a child." It was clear as the wind who he blamed for that.

Bertwoin slipped onto the edge of the path and peeked around a bush. His aunt stalked along stiff as a walking statue.

Bertwoin kept them in sight. They marched the entire way to their home on the outskirts of St. Vincent without moving closer together. After they went inside, Bertwoin posted himself on a dirt lane with a view of their front door.

Bertwoin didn't have to wait long before his uncle slipped outside and looked up and down the street as if he didn't want to be seen.. Bertwoin shoved his back against a plastered wall and peeked around the corner.

His uncle looked excited, his manner brisk. He was a loner, not an easy man to know, but Bertwoin still wondered if his uncle might be going out to lift a tankard with a friend or two. Or was he going to visit Armendis?

Artal hurried along narrow streets, stepping around debris and foraging pigs, until he stopped to knock at the door of a butcher shop only a street away from the river. He was let in and soon came back out carrying a hemp bag. Then he hiked out of town, taking a road not far from the Aude. Was he bringing Armendis food?

Bertwoin lost sight of his uncle on a curve and hurried around it, expecting to see him striding along ahead of him. But Artal had vanished.

Bertwoin dodged into the underbrush. How could he have lost him? Was his uncle now going through the forest? Had he noticed that someone was following him?

Bertwoin waded deeper into the woods, then turned and hurried as best as he could in the same direction Artal had been going. He heard water that sounded too small to be the Aude close to him. Maybe it was a stream feeding the river.

He sneaked forward, wary as a mouse. Something solid showed off to his right, probably the wall of a hut or shed. He crept toward it.

The alchemist and Flowia would be pleased beyond words if he found Armendis. But why would Artal hide his daughter and not let Meli know she was safe? Was she safe? What if Artal had killed Ermessen? But that wasn't right. They had been and maybe were still lovers, and he didn't seem the type who'd drug his daughter and blame her for her mother's murder.

He heard the crackle of twigs behind him and was turning, all his senses alert, when his head was knocked forward. Piercing pain paralyzed him, and stars exploded inside his eyes.

He came awake, stretched out on the ground, a weed fluttering beside his left eye. His eyesight was bleary. Clumps of hazy tree leaves shivered above him. He moved an arm and a blaze of pain flashed through his head. He remembered something striking his skull. Had his uncle knocked him senseless? If so, the whoreson would learn to regret it.

When Bertwoin sat up, the forest began whirling, so he eased back down onto his side. Behind his closed eyes, pulsating light sickened his stomach. He turned his head and retched down one cheek, smearing his beard with vomit.

He scooted an arm's length on his side away from the vomit and lay still until his eyesight returned to normal. Then, with slow care, he climbed to his knees and pulled himself up a young pine tree branch by branch to a standing position. He leaned into the prickly limpness of its limbs, gasping, and waited until the spinning forest stilled.

He discovered his knife was missing. He searched the ground for it, but it was nowhere to be found. His attacker was also a thief.

Now for the stomach-wrenching trudge homeward. He was a Teisseire. He could gut it out. No, instead he would go to Guillema's house. Then he would search for the three people he must find—the bastard who had attacked him, Artal, and Armendis. And if Artal proved to be the one who had smacked his head, then he only needed to find two people.

CHAPTER XXIII.

When something snuffled his cheek, Bertwoin jerked open his crusty eyelids. He found himself within kissing distance of a sow, her alert eyes staring at him with interest. He pushed her snout away and hawed to let her know he was irritated. The pig stuck its nose into his armpit. He felt too weak to fight her, and so let her investigate. She would soon sate her piggy curiosity and move on.

He stared up at the underside of a roof, the rafters slightly blurred. A beam with an iron hook in it crossed the middle of the room. A ham dangled from this hook. Bertwoin chuckled. Pork on the ground and pork in the air.

He was lying on a straw-filled pallet. He remembered being struck down and wading through the forest but nothing after that.

A flock-filled mattress in a wooden frame lay on the floor near him. An oak trunk with an iron lock was shoved against a plastered wall. The shutters over the room's single window were open. It was day, but the light was subdued. Outside, two men walked past the window, talking. Someone greeted them. He decided he was in a town. He also felt he had been in this room before.

Guillema bustled into the room. The pig moved toward her, watching her hands. "I've got nothing for you," she told it. She showed it her empty hands and shooed it out of the room.

"So, Chubby, returned to the world of the living, have you?"

"Think so. How'd I get here?"

"That's my question as well. A neighbor saw you wandering the streets, raving like a wounded fiend. And shame to me, she recognized you as my nephew. So she led you by the hand to my door. This is your second day here." She watched him for a moment. "What happened?"

"Someone sneaked up and clubbed me from behind."

"Why?"

"Don't know," he half-lied.

She became alert, and he knew she had sensed that he was keeping information from her. "Was it a thief?"

"My knife is missing."

"You're lucky it's not stuck between your ribs. Where were you?"

"I was in the forest close to the Aude."

"Where exactly?"

"Heading toward Pennautier."

"Pennautier? Why ever were you there?"

"The alchemist sent me there."

"*In* the forest," she said, suspicious as a stray cat approaching food held out by a stranger. "Do you mean on the road?"

"The master didn't want people to see me. He's the one to tell you why I was there and why I was hidden, not me. He expects me to keep his secrets."

She put her hands on her hips, but all she said was, "Well, somebody saw you. I certainly hope this had something to do with finding Armendis?"

"I can't be telling about it, but do you think my father would let me shirk my chores for anything other than helping to solve Ermessen's murder or finding Armendis?"

His aunt nodded, satisfied with his answer. "Flowia came by with a poultice for your head. She and your mother sat up with you for part of the night. Ellyn wants you under her roof, where she can nurse you back to rowdiness so you can go out and get bashed again." She shook her head and pretended to despair over his foolishness. "Jehan will carry you home in his cart."

"I don't want to be any trouble."

"Then stop getting knocked on the head."

When he explained to his father that while searching for Armendis, someone had bashed him on the back of his head and taken his knife, Clanoud slapped him. Bertwoin, still as weak as water, staggered sideways and almost fell.

Clanoud thrust his face close to his. "You *lost* your knife?" he yelled. "No *man* lets *anyone* take *his* knife from him."

His *maman* slid between them, and as she guided Bertwoin to a stool, said, "Clanoud, he's hurt. Leave him be."

"Hurt? He doesn't know what true hurt is."

"You'll damage him even more. Let me tend to his head." She gently peeled the bandage away. She then pulled clumps of his hair off the wound with brusque fingers, causing him to hiss at the sting of it. "Good, it's not leaking blood anymore," she said. "Skin was split open, but we needed to let it bleed a bit before sewing it up. The bone has no crack in it."

Clanoud hawed. "Of course not, he's got a Teisseire's head."

"Rachel," his *maman* said, "get me a needle and thread. I'll close it now. Maud, there's just enough water in the bucket. Bring it and a rag. Wilfraed, we'll need the black salve."

His father moved a stool beside them. "Now that you're *finally* here again, we can talk about your marriage to Maria."

"I'm not feeling up to talking, *Papa*. Or thinking."

Clanoud slapped his knee. "No need for you to talk or think. Just sit still and listen." He rubbed his hands together, eager to settle this matter with an easy victory.

Maud set a bowl of water on the floor beside their *maman*, and Wilfraed did the same with a small pot of black salve. They watched her with solemn curiosity as she washed the back of his sore head.

Rachel brought the needle and thread from a bedroom and laid them in his *maman's* lap. Bertwoin sighed. She would sew his scalp together. But what needle and thread could they use to sew shut the split in their family? His father still insisted he marry Roul's daughter.

"You could change your mind," his *maman* said to his father.

He rolled his eyes. "Once a man gives way, where does he stop?"

"Maybe with a better decision. One that pleases everyone."

"There's no way to please everybody, so it's best just to please yourself." He smiled, clearly enjoying an argument he was confident of winning. "Besides, that's no goal for a man to have, pleasing everyone. A man makes his own decisions and abides by them."

"Even a king has counselors and takes advice."

"Woman, you need to stop countering everything I say."

Bertwoin swallowed a hiss when the needle pricked his scalp. "What if Roul agrees to let Wilfraed marry Maria instead of me?"

"Never happen. Roul and I agreed that it'd be you. He's not about to go back on his word. It's a matter of honor."

"It's not going back on your word," his *maman* said, "if you both agree to change the pact."

"Like I said, he's not going to say that."

"But he will," Wilfraed said.

Everyone stared at him. He swallowed and said, "Maria convinced her father to accept me instead of him. It's just down to us agreeing to it now."

His father jumped to his feet, knocking his stool over backward. "Us?"

"You," Wilfraed quavered.

"How do you know this?"

"Maria said so."

"You talked to her?"

Wilfraed reared to full height. "Why wouldn't I? She's no enemy. Far from it. I love her."

"Love?" his father said with scorn.

His *maman* stopped sewing to study her youngest son. She nodded and prepared to begin stabbing her other son's scalp again. Bertwoin put on his warrior's face.

"Smart men know when to change their mind," she said to the back of Bertwoin's head. "That's one of the things that makes them wise."

"And wise women know when to keep—"

Laurence threw open the front door and strode inside like an emperor entering his throne room. He had been drinking at The Noble Head and it showed. "Ah, you're here," he bellowed to Bertwoin as he swaggered into the kitchen. "Made it home, I see."

"Why wouldn't I?"

"I met your good buddy, Tolarto. He said he saw you staggering about in St. Vincent, drunk as a duke. Asked me to ask you where you bought such strong ale. He wants to go to the same place you did."

"That blackguard," Bertwoin said.

"There's no argument there," Laurence agreed. "He's a man I've always found it easy to hate."

Bertwoin thought of Flowia, the woman his uncle also found easy to hate, while his *maman* smeared his head wound with a black salve that smelled as if it had fermented in a dunghill, which wasn't beyond possibility. She swore that only the blessed Savior was better at healing wounds than her black salve.

"I'm being told," their father said to his brother, "that Roul is ready to accept Wilfraed as his son-in-law."

Laurence opened his mouth, then closed it, probably more surprised by his brother asking for his advice than by Roul's change of plan. His face twisted with disgust. "Meaning we get the Saracen bitch for a daughter-in-law?"

"No," their father said in the tone of one explaining something to a four-year-old boy. "Meaning only that Wilfraed does the marrying instead of his elder brother, which is not the normal way of doing things. Bertwoin wants to believe he's free to do whatever he wants, but he's not free, at least not while he sits at my table."

Laurence frowned down at the bundled reeds on the floor, his sight turned inward. "Meaning," he said with deliberation, "that either way Maria comes into the family, and the spat over that strip of land between our farms is over. Meaning you get credit for coming up with the idea that settled this entire issue."

"But I said Bertwoin would be the groom."

Laurence waggled his shoulders. "Doesn't matter who does the marrying. Your idea has weight and works even with a different son standing in front of the altar. It's flexible. That makes it smart."

For a moment, Bertwoin forgot his aching head. Was his uncle really siding with him?

Laurence looked at him. "As long as the alchemist's little witch doesn't enter this family, I'm all for Wilfraed doing the honors for us."

Wilfraed stared at his uncle as if he were adoring Saint Valentine.

His *maman* wrapped the bandage Flowia had put on the wound around his head again, tied it as Flowia had, then pinned it in place with the needle.

Clanoud crowed. "My idea *was* flexible, wasn't it?" He shook a stern forefinger at Bertwoin. "I'll let you get by this time, boy. But *only* this time."

Wilfraed whooped.

Pleased with himself, their father continued, saying to Bertwoin, "What you deserve is a beating for betraying me. But you've been injured enough for one day. Remember," his finger helped make his point, "I'll not let you turn against your family again. Not if you want to stay in it."

His head throbbing, Bertwoin staggered to standing. "I'll be in the barn." He smiled at Wilfraed. "You'll be a better husband to her than I ever would be."

"We'll call you," his father said to him, "if we've got a footrace to run or need a stump dug out."

Bertwoin groaned at the thought of such exertion, which made his father guffaw.

Laurence said, "You're lucky it's wintertime, and your chores are light."

"I've still got to find Armendis, and now I've also got to find a thief. No cowardly pustule is going to hit me on the head and walk away unmarked."

"Damn right," his father said. "You've still got a family name to protect. Rachel, fetch me and your uncle some ale."

CHAPTER XXIV.

Bertwoin lay suffering in their dimly lit barn for three days. He was slow to answer simple questions, and his words tumbled into each other. Light hurt his eyes.

On the fourth day, his father stomped into the barn and roused him, ordering him to quit lazing about and get back to doing his chores. But even he had to admit that his son's balance was off-kilter. So he left, muttering about a younger generation too weak to even march to a crusade, let alone fight in one.

His *maman* allowed him only spring water, no ale. She fed him sage soup and meat to heal his head, saying these would put iron in his muscles. Belle, of course, assumed Bertwoin was in the barn full-time for her convenience. When not hunting or playing or exploring, she snuggled against the warmth of him.

The alchemist honored him with a surprise visit. He told Bertwoin that Ermessen had been buried, and the cemetery had been as crowded as the town square on market day. The master told Bertwoin's family the best cure for him was rest and assured them he would recover to full strength before two or three Sunday masses had passed. Clanoud told the old man he was pleased because he wanted Bertwoin to finish hauling stones out of their new field. The master understood the hint and said he expected Bertwoin, Flowia, and he would solve the murders not long after Bertwoin was well enough again to help find the killer.

Two days after St. Martin's Day, Bertwoin felt he had the strength to visit the alchemist and Flowia. He settled himself at the table with a tankard of ale and answered their questions about his health. He then moved the conversation to business. "It shouldn't have taken me so long to come to full strength, but I would've been more of a hindrance here than a help."

The master said, "I've seen men laid low for far longer after sustaining a head wound. You need to offer no justification for the time required for your recuperation. The blame for delaying our investigation lies with your attacker." He looked at Flowia and said, "Ah well, maybe some gain will come from this, heh?"

Flowia picked up an apron with a ragged hem that needed mending and sat down beside Bertwoin on the bench. "It depends on when Artal realized someone was following him." She threaded her needle.

"I don't know that Artal ever saw me. But if he noticed me, it was probably not until we were a fair way beyond St. Vincent. We were the only two on the path by then."

"If that is true," the master said, "then he may have unknowingly led you a good way toward his intended destination. We searched the area in the woods you mentioned when I visited you and found a fisherman's hut. But it gave us no clue as to whom he met there, if that was even where his rendezvous took place."

Flowia patted Bertwoin's shoulder. "If we know the food's destination, then we know where Armendis is hiding."

"But we don't," Bertwoin grumbled.

"Correct." The alchemist tapped the table twice with a bony index finger. "But the person he came to meet probably lives in that direction. Even if Artal was walking only part of the way to where Armendis is hidden, it is not a stretch of logic to assume both parties would trek the shortest distance possible to their rendezvous. They might each come halfway."

"I don't know if it means anything," Bertwoin said, "but while I was resting, I remembered Artal once mentioned that he has cousins near Pennautier. They own a vineyard."

"Excellent. We make progress."

Again Flowia patted Bertwoin's shoulder and warmth spread into his chest.

The master asked, "Do you think your Aunt Melisende knows where the girl is?"

Bertwoin watched Flowia stab the linen apron with her needle and felt a prickle on his scalp. "She doesn't act like it."

"My thought too," the alchemist said. "When we talked to her at Hugon's boat shed, she seemed genuinely upset and worried about the girl. Too bad Flowia wasn't with us." He glanced at her, his eyes warm with affection. "Of the three of us, she is the best judge of people."

"But I *was* there," she said. "Melisende came to Hugon's house to help prepare the corpse. She was frantic with fear that Armendis too would suffer poor Sibilia's fate. Her dread was genuine."

"Well, then." The alchemist cracked his knobby knuckles. "There we have it. Artal moved the girl from their cellar, and in doing so, he may have saved her. The *bayle* did learn where Armendis was hiding, and he did search Artal's house for her. But what reason keeps Artal from telling his wife where he has hidden his daughter?"

"Perhaps he has set her aside so Tumas can have her," Flowia said.

"Then we will thwart him," Bertwoin said. "If my uncle still carries food to Armendis, then I'll follow him a second time."

"He will be doubly wary now," Flowia warned.

"Then instead of following him, I will hide near the cousins' house and just watch it."

"Yes," the alchemist said. "That might be the better strategy."

"But now that he knows he is being watched," Bertwoin said, "will he not already have moved her?"

"That might be the wise thing to do, but your uncle may not have many choices of hiding places for her."

Flowia laid her sewing in her lap and gave Bertwoin her full attention. "How far is it from the cousins' house to where someone attacked you?"

"A fair distance."

"Then your uncle may think we have little idea of where he is hiding her. He may even think his attacking you was warning enough to prevent you from following him again." She smiled. "He married a Tessiere and knows well how obstinate they can be, but he may believe our generation is less brave than his generation. Anyway, if we see him go there, what then? Are they going to allow us to search their house?"

"She may not be in the house," Bertwoin said. "A vineyard will have many places where people can hide." He rubbed a finger around the top rim of his tankard. "Do you think Armendis let Artal hide her?"

"No," Flowia said.

"I agree. I doubt she'd do this to Jehan or my aunts."

The master surprised Bertwoin by pulling dice from a hemp pouch lying on the kitchen table and throwing them. He studied the results of his throw and didn't look pleased. "She may be so well hidden that even if the *bayle* searched the vineyard, he would fail to find her. Artal may also think Armendis is safe there, because if we did discover his daughter's location, we would never reveal it to the *bayle*. She is safe because no one other than the lawman has the authority to trespass onto his cousin's property."

Bertwoin studied his reflection floating on the ale in his tankard. "How will I ever watch the property day and night? I've never even been there."

The alchemist turned a die to change the result of his throw, as if that would change the answer he had gotten. "You might not need to. Where does this path Artal uses lead to?"

"Ah, I see," Bertwoin said, his excitement almost making him stand up. "I only need to watch the path."

"Yes, first we need to prove that Armendis is in the vineyard. Hide somewhere in the woods and watch the path or road leading to it. Be especially alert at the same time of day when you were attacked. Your uncle might continue to bring her food at the same hour. Watch for his visit to his cousins' property, or if he only walks halfway, as I believe he does, watch for someone who uses the path and goes to the vineyard, someone carrying a bag that might contain food for Armendis." He shook his head. "Food? Maybe not. Surely, your uncle's cousins would feed Armendis. So, what does Artal give to whomever he meets? And is it even for Armendis?"

Flowia sat frowning down at the table for some time before she said, "She might be hiding somewhere near the vineyard but not on it,"

"Or," Bertwoin suggested, "it is food, but his cousins don't feed her because they don't know Artal has hidden her on their property."

The master clapped his hands. "Well said. Onward then."

Bertwoin slid off the bench. "I'll tell my *maman* you've given me an errand and slip away tomorrow while my father is busy. But today I must show him a son's obedience."

Bertwoin was surprised to see no one outside in their yard or near the barn. He hesitated at their front door and listened to lively voices inside. Either they were arguing about something, or they had company. He opened the door slowly.

His aunts, Guillema and Meli, were in the kitchen with all of his family.

"What news?" Meli called to him before he had even closed the front door.

All of them waited like alert geese. "They haven't found her yet," he called from the front room, as if keeping a few strides between them made the news less disappointing.

Meli turned her face aside, and Guillema put a sisterly arm around her.

Bertwoin's instinct was to reassure her, to tell her the alchemist had given him a task that might lead them to Armendis, but he stayed quiet. He couldn't even tell her Armendis was probably alive. The food Artal carried proved this. What would she do when she found out her husband had hidden Armendis away from everyone, including her?

Laurence said, "We all have our crosses to bear." Rather than sounding sympathetic, his sanctimonious tone seemed to slap his youngest sister for her lack of fortitude. "God does as He sees fit. We deserve what we get."

Meli raised her bowed head. Her expression turned from mournful sadness to feral hatred. "You also are childless, yet no one calls you less of a man. No one lays blame on you, saying you are being punished for your sins. What cross do you bear, Laurence?"

He shrugged. "You need to bear up, Meli. It's a sin to question the ways of God."

"Then maybe it was right for God to keep Aalis away from you. You wouldn't be any improvement over the bastard she ended up with. You're only the shape of a true man." She smiled when he clenched his fists and took half a step toward her.

"Aalis?" Bertwoin croaked. No one even looked at him.

"You withered-up witch," Laurence yelled.

"What is a witch? A knowing woman, a woman crazy with sorrow, an old unmarried woman, a bogeywoman? What sin is in them?"

Laurence stared at her, his mouth slack.

"Count your blessings that she isn't," Guillema told him. "And who are you to preach to anybody, you self-righteous prick?"

"We've had enough of this kind of talk," Clanoud said. "It stops here and now."

Meli rushed to the front door, flung it open, and ran out.

Laurence said to Guillema, "Contrary to what you say, Meli's a witch deep down in her crone's heart."

"If she were, don't you think she would've given herself a child?" She shook her head. "Lord, I sometimes wish I were a witch myself. Then I might punish all the smug bastards who know what God thinks and what God wants. All of those who tell me how to behave."

Bertwoin remembered Na Thea making a fertility potion for a barren woman. Was that woman Meli? "Has she consulted Na Thea?"

Guillema gave him her adult look. "Of course she has. But God didn't see fit to answer her prayers."

"And I heard right when Aunt Meli said Laurence loved Aalis, Tolarto's Aalis?"

She gave him a triumphant look. "The very one. Laurence can tell you all about her."

So the woman who might have been his aunt, the one his uncle had loved and lost, was Tolarto's abused wife. No wonder Laurence hated Tolarto.

CHAPTER XXV

Bertwoin brought a borrowed knife, a chunk of leftover bread, and an overripe apple to bed with him that night in the barn. He woke before dawn, breakfasted on the apple and bread, then slipped away without waking Wilfraed. As usual, his mother and Rachel already had the hearth fire ablaze in the house and probably had porridge simmering while they kneaded bread on the kitchen table.

He didn't know exactly where Artal's cousins lived, but luck folded its grandmotherly wings around him again. He met a wandering friar who told him the path they stood on led to a road that passed the vineyard's front gate.

It was cold, of course, but the wind only whispered through the trees now, and as long as he kept his neck warm with a scarf, he didn't need to use his hood. The quiet morning seemed to welcome him, and few people walked the path.

The obvious wealth of the winery's house, stables, storage buildings, and its other outbuildings—all built castle-like out of rough brown stones—set him back on his heels. The impassive outer walls formed a protective square around an inner courtyard, and the few windows set in the outer walls were small with iron bars across them. If Armendis was cloistered inside this vineyard's silent fortress, maybe the alchemist should let her stay there. Artal had chosen her refuge well.

He settled behind bushes in the nearby woods, expecting to watch carters, workers, and family members come and go through the winery's front gate.

Bertwoin watched the gate until the late afternoon sun beamed directly through it. He accepted disappointment and left, giving himself plenty of time to get home before dark. His trembling leg muscles made it clear he wasn't up to full strength yet.

The following day, he was again at his post early, and like the previous day, it proved to be another boring slog until he noticed a boy of about twelve coming along the path—a boy in sabots and stockings carrying a hemp sack. He had seen him the previous day but had dismissed him because he was with a woman, probably his mother. Why had he assumed Artal must give the food bag to an adult?

But the boy didn't go through the gate. Instead, he turned off the path at the front edge of the vineyard's imposing building and disappeared down its side.

No one was in sight, so Bertwoin sprinted to the building's front wall and peered around the corner. A rutted cart path ran along the wall, but the boy wasn't on it. How could he have vanished? There was one small door set in the winery's wall, but Bertwoin found it locked.

He continued down the cart path which led him into the rows of grapevines standing at attention like an army of soldiers. He wandered about, searching, and after some time discovered a small hut built like the main house out of brown stones. The boy wasn't there, but the hemp bag he had carried hung from an iron nail driven in the hut's oak door.

Just as he was about to creep closer and investigate, he heard voices. He crouched in a ditch. Two jaunty young men strode to the hut, took the bag and a key off the nail, unlocked the door, and eased it open.

"No need to hide, Armendis," one of the men called out and laughed. "It's only us again."

Bertwoin hurried away. He had found her, and he now knew Armendis hadn't chosen to hide by choice. She was a prisoner.

Something nagged at him. He felt he had left something undone. He put the feeling behind him and continued on his way before anyone saw him.

Bertwoin found the master and Flowia in the workshop. She was washing glassware in a bucket. The master leaned over a wrought-iron table, burnishing two small silver objects with a stone. The molds Flowia had brought from Garnier's pottery also lay on the table.

The alchemist seemed pleased to see him. "Well met, plowman, it is meet that you came at this moment." He glanced down at the objects on his table. "I am working on something that may be of interest to you in the future."

When Bertwoin took a step toward him, the alchemist held up a thin hand. "In the future. Now is too early. So tell us of your adventures."

They listened with frowning concentration. When he finished, instead of seeming happy at his success, they both looked as if a cherished friend had died. He had expected praise and maybe a cup of the master's expensive wine in celebration.

The alchemist took a deep breath. "The door was kept locked, you say?"

"Yes, master."

"And the key hung outside of it?"

A spasm of dread twitched Bertwoin's stomach. "Yes. But why would my uncle ever imprison her? He's fond of her."

"It is still uncertain that your uncle took her. Someone else may have done so, someone who is now blackmailing him into supplying her with food." The master scratched his chin and stared across the room. "That might also explain why he hasn't told his wife where Armendis is hidden. He may not know her exact location."

"It's odd then that she finds herself held captive in a winery owned by his relatives?"

"True, but that might not be a coincidence. Perhaps one of his cousins visited Artal's house, saw Armendis there, and later came back to take her."

Flowia held a bulbous glass ball with a long spout up to the window's light to see if it was clean. "Would Artal not tell Melisende he knows his daughter is alive, even if she was taken by force? His wife is in anguish."

"Artal might not know for certain that she is alive. Maybe he hasn't seen her."

"Still," Flowia insisted.

The alchemist leaned back. "Artal's sins are of little importance right now. Tomorrow we must rescue Armendis. How do we do that?"

"She may be shy as a doe and not willing to go with just anyone," Flowia warned.

"Wouldn't any rescuer be better than staying shut up in that hut as a prisoner?" Bertwoin asked. Flowia seemed more worried about the girl's feelings than her freedom.

Flowia bit her bottom lip a moment, then asked in a quavering voice, "Who were these two churls who took food into the hut?"

Bertwoin watched her, not understanding why she was so upset. "Men sent to feed her,"

She pitied him with a look. "It takes two men to give her food?"

It hit Bertwoin like a punch. He stepped sideways and dropped onto a three-legged stool. "You're saying. . . ."

Her face hardened with hatred. "That two shitheads are deriving pleasure from her imprisonment." She rushed to the door, flung it open, and banged it shut behind her.

Bertwoin smacked the butt of his fist against the brick oven. "May the Devil take them if it's true." He knew that Armendis's situation probably called up grim memories for Flowia. He told the master, "I saw them both and can recognize them."

The alchemist took a deep breath. "First, we must rescue her. We will get retribution after she is somewhere safe. If Flowia is right and you come to rescue Armendis, she may be loath to go with you. She may fear being alone with you in the forest."

"I know someone she will welcome. My cousin, Jehan."

"Of course. He may be the only man she trusts now. Is he up to the task?"

"I'll see that he is."

"Good, but remember to get her away first. If you fight her two attackers, others may hear you and join them. Make certain that her fiancé also shows restraint." The master nodded at the rightness of his decision. "Now, where does Jehan hide her? We don't want to rescue her, then have her fall into the *bayle's* iron grasp."

"My aunt and the Good Folk are used to hiding people."

"It'll have to do. Guillema needs to be told of our suspicions concerning Artal."

"I'll go see my aunt now."

"Godspeed, plowman."

Bertwoin's leg muscles felt soft as smelted lead, but he pushed beyond his fatigue and trotted to his aunt's house in St. Vincent.

He opened the door and went in after rapping on an open shutter. His aunt and cousin sat at the kitchen table, eating.

"Ah, just in time for supper," Guillema joked. She stared at Bertwoin's face as he came closer and frowned, her levity gone. "What happened?"

Jehan jumped up. "Armendis?"

"I know where she's hidden," he told them. He watched relief, then joy, flood his cousin's face. "And yes, she's alive."

"So you don't have her yet?" his aunt asked.

Bertwoin stared at the kitchen's back wall. Like her son, Guillema was elated, but she immediately recovered, took control, and got back to business. What did it take to get her to thank him? He had done what no one else could do, but she still wanted more.

Jehan said, "Thank you, Ox."

Bertwoin nodded to him, then told his aunt, "No, I don't have her, and I'll need Jehan's help to rescue her."

Jehan rose and came toward him. "I'm ready."

"Good." Bertwoin realized there was no need to wait until tomorrow. "We'll need your cart. Darkness will shield us." He hesitated. "I think things may go easier if your mother came along with us."

His tone turned their joy into concern. His aunt studied his face, hunting for a hint of why he wanted her to come with them. Jehan began weeping. Guillema rose, silently picked her knife off the table, wiped it clean, and shoved it into the sheath hanging from the braided belt around her waist.

CHAPTER XXVI.

While Jehan was in the barn hitching his brown mule to his cart, Bertwoin told his aunt what Flowia feared had happened to Armendis. He expected his practical aunt to show some doubt about the rape, since it was only a guess. Instead, she told him it was best not to mention this to Jehan. Armendis would decide who should know what . . . and when they should be told.

Bertwoin knew Jehan sometimes spent days wandering the *visconte's* domain while being lost on purpose. His goal in life, other than marrying Armendis, was to be the carter who knew their area best. He explored every unknown road and rough track wide enough for his cart until he knew all of them within a two-day journey of St. Vincent. For him, every rutted byway had its special personality. Some would bully him if he let them, while others were friendly. He took special pride in knowing those that were shy and seldom used.

He said the path Bertwoin had used to find Armendis, the one linked to the road running past the vineyard, wanted to be grander than it was. It was too narrow for his four-wheeled cart. So instead of using it, he set out to rescue his fiancée on the generous road that most people used when traveling to Pennautier.

Guillema sat hunched on the long, boxy front seat beside her son while Bertwoin lounged on the bed behind them. Though he needed sleep, he found getting any impossible with his head and body bouncing on the cart's rough slats.

He studied his aunt's righteous posture, which he imagined was like that of an avenging angel, though this one had no wings. Her stiff back had no compromise in it. If what Flowia feared was true, there would be "eye for eye, tooth for tooth" revenge.

No one spoke during the ride. They rattled through the dark and saw only one horseman, a mysterious rider, who passed them without greeting. In quiet Pennautier, Jehan turned onto the road that would bring them past the winery's front gate. The crescent moon above them was not overly bright, which suited their purpose.

Jehan whispered, "We're about to reach the winery."

Bertwoin sat up and scooted close behind them. "Drive beyond the front gate. The forest is thick on the other side of the vineyard."

They stared through the closed iron gate as they rumbled past the winery, watching the main building for danger. Candlelight shone between the slats of a few shutters looking out onto the inner courtyard, but no one was in sight. Bertwoin let out his breath.

"Keep going until nobody can see our cart from the windows," Bertwoin said, "then pull into the woods. Will your mule be skittish?"

"He's used to waiting. Usually just dozes, though I doubt he'll do so tonight. He won't trust the forest after dark."

Neither will I, Bertwoin thought.

Jehan didn't need to drive far before he found a suitable gap in the woods. With Bertwoin's help, they backed his cart into the bushes so they could flee quickly if need be. Jehan tied his mule to a thin nettle tree and helped his mother climb down.

She adjusted her leggings and stomped her boots as if her feet needed to feel solid ground.

Bertwoin led them down the road to the fortress, turned right onto the smaller rutted cart path, and hurried along the winery's side wall. They slipped into the quiet vineyard without seeing anyone.

They stopped when they came within sight of the small stone hut. In the ghostly moonlight, the building reminded Bertwoin of a forsaken tomb. No one seemed about, so he crept to the front door and slipped the key off the iron nail. His aunt stepped forward and took it from him. She then stepped back and nodded to her son.

He took a breath and knocked gently on the door. "Mendy, it's me, Jehan."

They listened but heard nothing. Bertwoin swallowed. Had her captors moved her? Maybe the two young men ate the food themselves and had called out her name as a joke. Maybe they laughed at foolish Artal for bringing them food.

"This is me, Mendy. We've come to take you home."

A wail rose inside the hut, causing the hairs on Bertwoin's forearms to prickle erect.

His aunt unlocked the door. She looked at Bertwoin, her face stark and determined in the bleak moonlight, and twitched her head toward the winery. He nodded and crept to a spot where he could watch both the brooding fortress and the hut. The gnarly grape vines standing in rows around him, their fruit already harvested, now seemed like souls writhing in hellish agony. He made the sign of the cross.

Bertwoin heard crying and murmurs, then thankfully complete silence. Now, at least, no one would hear them. He waited with rising concern, fidgeting, trying to stay still. What if someone came to check on Armendis, or the two young men visited her again? Bertwoin tightened his hands into fists. He almost wished they would.

Finally, Jehan slunk outside alone. Bertwoin hurried to him and realized his cousin was sobbing. Inside the hut, the women's voices hummed.

"We need to get away," Bertwoin whispered.

Jehan looked at him as if nothing mattered now and shrugged. Bertwoin mentally slapped himself. What did he expect his cousin to do? It was as plain as a hen's beak that something bad had happened. His aunt needed time with Armendis.

"Does she want to come with us?"

Jehan shook his head, not in answer to the question, but to show he was too bewildered to know.

His aunt slid outside as alert as a ferret, scanned the vineyard, then darted back inside. Almost immediately, she lurched through the doorway again, half carrying Armendis. The girl's face, like his aunt's, was haggard and aged. Moonlight glowed on her cheeks, making the furrows in them darker than normal. Bertwoin had forgotten that her cheeks were scratched. Startled at seeing him, Armendis whined and shrank into Guillema's embrace.

"It's Bertwoin," his aunt cooed in the voice of a mother soothing her hurt child. "He's the reason we've come. He's the one who found you and now wants to take you home."

Bertwoin smiled at her, trying to look like a friend she could trust.

One corner of her lips twitched upwards into a brief smile. "Thank you, Bertwoin."

Not sure what to say, he nodded. "Let's get you away from here."

Jehan stepped forward to take over supporting Armendis. She cringed at his sudden movement, recovered in an instant, and put her hand on his shoulder, allowing him to slide his arm around her waist. His aunt pulled the hut's door closed, making as little noise as possible. She locked it, but instead of hanging the key back on its nail, she carried it with her.

They hobbled along the shadowy pathways through the silent rows of grapevines and slipped into the quiet forest. His aunt threw the key into the shrubbery. They then crept along the road's edge, alert and ready to dodge into the bushes if anyone appeared.

Guillema climbed into the bed of the cart beside Armendis and motioned for him to join her son on the box seat. Armendis wouldn't want to be trapped in the back with him, and she might not have the strength to sit up front beside Jehan.

Though Bertwoin had thought of walking home after they rescued Armendis, he now climbed onto the seat beside his cousin. He felt too limp to hike all the way home. Should he ask his aunt to let him sleep at her house? No, she had enough to worry about tonight without him getting in her way. Besides, a man other than Jehan in the house might make Armendis uneasy.

As Jehan pulled onto the main road and turned toward the winery, Bertwoin said, "You can let me off when we reach the edge of St. Vincent. I can walk from there."

"No." His aunt reached up and patted the small of his back. "He'll take you the full way to your farm. You've done well today."

"But you need to get home and get some rest."

She laughed as if he had made a jest, one that was backhanded instead of funny. "There'll be no warmth of a bed and blanket for me tonight."

Without warning, Armendis lurched from a sitting position beside Guillema up onto her knees, her face clenched with grief. Crying, she began pounding the cart's boards with the back of her fist.

Guillema flicked a hand at her son and Bertwoin, letting them know they should turn their noses around and see to getting them away. Then she too rose onto her knees and pulled Armendis to her, cradling the girl's head against her breast. "They'll suffer for it," she said. "I promise."

They passed the winery's front gate in angry silence. His aunt muttered, "May your vines rot and all your sons be drunkards and your daughters be barren."

The mule plodded through Pennautier and along the road and sped up only as they neared St Vincent. Bertwoin's mood also lightened.

When they stopped beside his aunt's house, Jehan jumped down to help Armendis climb out of the back, and Bertwoin helped his aunt. He told her he could walk home from there, and she shook her head. "Jehan will have his mule carry you at least as far as Montredon."

She patted his shoulder. "You did well, nephew. We'll not forget this. If my brother gives you any grief for being gone, let me know."

"I just did what I should do."

"When someone praises you, nephew, accept it. Don't dismiss a compliment, especially not one from me. I give out few of them as it is. Not everyone would have done what you did and done it so quickly."

"I guess I am a hero," he said with a mischievous grin.

"Let's not claim too much glory for ourselves," she said, laughing for the first time that night.

"Um," he said. "Before you hide Armendis away, remember the alchemist needs to talk to her. She's the only one who can tell us what happened to her mother."

Armendis whimpered and stared at the ground.

His aunt nodded. "In a day or so, after you've rested, come see me. I need to hear again how you found her at the winery. And I need to talk to you about Artal."

"I will," he promised.

She raised a finger. "And Meli doesn't need to hear anything about this."

"I'll be as quiet as an oyster."

She waved him toward her and kissed his cheek.

CHAPTER XXVII.

Bertwoin shuffled out of the barn the following morning. He smiled up at the blue sky where a few fleecy clouds grazed and breathed deeply to rid his lungs of the barn's musty air. They had rescued Armendis. There was warm satisfaction in that.

Now the alchemist needed to talk to her about her mother's death. Would Armendis be any help? Did she know who had drugged her? What if—God forbid—she believed, as Hebert did, that Meli *was* a witch and had caused her to butcher her *maman*?

Near the outside corner of the barn, he watched half-grown Belle pounce on a leaf scooting across the ground. Grabbing it in her front paws, she fell onto her side and shredded the leaf with scrabbling hind claws.

"I think you killed that mouse," he told her. "But I don't think you'll eat it."

He went inside the house into the smell of milk and pottage. Most people didn't eat their first meal until midday or later, but his *papa* believed people worked better if they had full bellies. Everyone was at the table, except Wilfraed, who still lay sleeping in the barn.

"Well," his uncle called out, "we are blessed this day to have a guest, Ellyn. I hope he finds your food to his liking."

"I always do," Bertwoin said as he squeezed onto the end of a bench beside little Maud. "Well," he said to her, "I guess I can't call you Wormy anymore."

"And you never should have," his *maman* said.

He tasted the pottage, which was creamier and sweeter than usual, meaning his *maman* had blended in a goose egg and added a dollop of honey. He hummed appreciation, which put a smile on her lips.

"You left early and came home well after dark," his father accused.

To make peace with his *papa*, Bertwoin said, "I think my part in helping solve these murders is coming to an end."

Little Maud stared up at his face with round eyes. "Murders?"

Rachel shook her head to warn him to be more careful about what he said.

Bertwoin told his father, "I worked for the alchemist part of yesterday, then for Aunt Guillema part of last night."

His father held out a cupped hand. "Then where are the coins you earned?"

"Ah, *Papa*, no one can refuse the master alchemist. And Aunt Guillema is family."

"Family?" His father chucked his tongue. "Lately, favors seem to go only one way with her."

"I'm sure if we needed Jehan to cart something for us, she'd see it got done."

"And I'd pay them for the effort."

His *maman*, standing near the hearth, asked Bertwoin, "So you found her?"

He should have known he couldn't hide anything from her. "I never said that."

"You didn't need to."

When he just shrugged without answering, his father muttered, "Either you did or you didn't. Which is it?"

He glanced at his little sister. She would mean no harm, but if anyone misspoke at the wrong time to the wrong person and put Armendis in danger, it would most likely be her. "Both Guillema and Jehan are happier than a bishop at a feast," he said.

"A lot of good it'll do them," Laurence said. "Won't take but a few days before the *bayle* knows the girl's still alive."

Rachel and Bertwoin looked at each other and sighed.

Thanks, uncle, Bertwoin thought. That made the fact that they had found Armendis plain to Maud. "We haven't found the murderer yet," he cautioned. "Nobody needs to tell anybody outside our family about this."

Laurence puffed up like a roused rooster. "Are you saying I'm a blabbermouth?"

Hadn't he just proved this to be true? After a few drinks at the tavern, might his tongue slip while bragging to his cronies?

It was best not to argue with his uncle. That would keep him here half the day. So he said to his father, "Aunt Guillema told me to visit her first thing this morning."

Like a martyr wanting pity, Clanoud glanced at the ceiling. "This goes on and on. You'll need to stop sleeping so you can work nights for others and days for your family."

"I'm not the one betraying this family," Laurence said, not willing to end their argument.

"I've got three goose eggs you can take to Guillema," his *maman* said. "She'll welcome the giving of them."

By the time he reached his aunt's house in St. Vincent, his leg muscles trembled as if he had carried a sack of flour on his shoulders the whole way. When would he be at full strength again?

He knocked and entered. His aunt and cousin relaxed when they saw it was only him and called out greetings. Armendis wasn't at the table with them. Was she hidden in a bedroom or already somewhere else?

"Join us, join us," Guillema called to him. She waved a hand over the table, offering cheese and bread. "Eat with us."

"I ate just before I came." He laid the three goose eggs on the table beside his aunt.

She picked one up, sliced the top of its shell off with her knife, sucked down its contents, and smacked her lips. "Ellyn's eggs are always appreciated. Tell her that for me."

"I will."

Jehan raised his eyebrows. "Ale?"

"I'll not say no to that."

Jehan slapped him on the back. "You're Mendy's hero now."

"I just. . . ." He glanced at his aunt, remembering her scolding him for not knowing how to accept a compliment. "That's nice to hear."

Jehan clumped a tankard down in front of him. They said nothing as they waited for him to speak, so he jumped into the deep water without first dipping in a toe. "So, Armendis is doing well?"

They glanced at each other. "As well as can be expected," Guillema said.

"I need to report to the alchemist," Bertwoin explained, "and he'll want to know everything about her condition. He'll ask me if she's safe. He'll expect me to know details."

Jehan looked at him with sympathy. "She's well tucked away."

"The alchemist and Flowia need to know everything you know," he said. "And you need to know everything they know."

Jehan patted the table. "I agree. We need to make it easier for the master to find the murderer so I can marry Mendy."

Aunt Guillema stared into a corner of the kitchen, her thoughts turned inward. After a moment, she faced him. "So, are you admitting that you're keeping something from me?"

"I am."

She smiled. "So you mean to be the thread that stitches all of us together, heh?" She clapped, then rubbed her hands together. "So be it. What is it I don't know?"

So he was to go first. He told them that Artal was probably the bastard who had knocked him woozy. Artal may also have been the one who had hidden Armendis in his cousins' vineyard. He certainly had sent food there for her. They sat in perplexed silence until Jehan whispered, "Why?"

"He didn't want you to marry Armendis."

"Tumas," Guillema said in disgust. "Why ever would he betray his family for that ruffian?"

Bertwoin said, "Garnier's brother raises horses."

Jehan frowned a moment before he understood. "Those horses might bring a farrier a lot of work."

"He chose money over family," his aunt muttered, her face tight with disgust.

Bertwoin agreed that this was shameful, but the subject of betrayal was complicated. With a hoard of pagan gold behind her, it was easy for Guillema to condemn Artal. But if she wasn't able to feed herself and her family, she might understand his decision.

Bertwoin sipped his ale. His aunt and cousin didn't need to know that Artal thought Jehan wasn't man enough for his daughter. In a backhanded way, Artal's betrayal might even be seen as his way of protecting his daughter from what he thought was marriage to a weakling. Everybody had their personal view on what profited their family.

"My father would banish Artal outright," Bertwoin said. His aunt agreed with an approving nod. "But I heard Artal tell Meli that he was losing business because people thought she was a witch."

Guillema sucked in her breath. "Does my sister know Artal did this?"

"We're fairly certain she doesn't."

Jehan frowned. "We?"

"The alchemist and Flowia also think Meli didn't know that Artal was hiding Armendis."

Jehan sagged like an empty wine pouch. "I don't think Artal knew what those scum-suckers were doing."

His aunt looked predatory and ready to shred something with her hind claws.

Anger also tightened Bertwoin's chest. "I think we need to visit the vineyard again. Maybe to buy some wine. If I see those two bastards, I'll recognize them."

Jehan raised a fist over the table and shook it at him in gratitude.

"I agree," his aunt murmured. "Armendis needs to know we'll protect her. And everyone needs to know that they will suffer if they attack anyone in our family."

Bertwoin smiled. "You sound like my *papa*."

"I taught him everything he knows." They all laughed.

Bertwoin finished his ale. "Well, I need to report to the alchemist. He'll be relieved to hear we rescued Armendis."

"Tell him," Guillema said, "that I'll bring her by tomorrow morning. There are fewer prying eyes at his cottage than here."

CHAPTER XXVIII.

The following morning, Bertwoin hiked to the alchemist's cottage not long after sunrise. He had reported to the master the previous day and told him the tale of their rescuing Armendis on his way home.

Roland welcomed him with pleasure grunts and got his mandatory back scratch. Flowia then welcomed him with smiles, wheat bread, and brown ale. He settled into the easy camaraderie of being a comfortable guest.

Once fed, however, Flowia set him to work digging up two large shrubs with deep roots so she could expand her medicine garden. Roland, pleased with his company, sat and watched him with what looked like piggy approval.

Guillema surprised him by marching out of the woods behind the cottage with Armendis and Jehan behind her. He had expected her to use the main path leading to the front of the house, but that was goose-brained thinking on his part. It was safer to use the more private back path.

Roland bowed his head and leaned toward them on stiff front legs. Bertwoin patted the boar's shaggy shoulder. "They're friends, Roland, friends. Let them come."

Ignoring the wary pig, his aunt stopped beside the garden and half-smiled. "I'm glad to see you already at work, nephew. Helping Flowia with her garden helps the community."

"I'm only doing it because I thought it might please you," he teased.

Jehan laughed. "*Maman* will be better pleased if you do a few chores at our house too."

"I wouldn't want to get in your way, Jehan."

Bertwoin picked up the axe and shovel and fell in behind his aunt as she marched around to the front of the house.

At the opening in the mulberry hedge, Bertwoin hesitated and scanned the surrounding forest. No one was in sight, yet the back of his neck tingled as if someone were watching him. The path leading to the cottage was empty, and nothing stirred in the quiet woods. Besides that, Roland was calm. And besides that, Gidie was dead.

Flowia pulled open the door before his aunt knocked.

"You are welcome here," she said and waved them inside.

Bertwoin followed Jehan into the front room, which was thick with the earthy scents of moldering floor reeds and bread, and the heavenly scent of cathedral-like incense. He inhaled, savoring the comforting smells.

His aunt approached an oak chest set against a wall, eyeing it, and stopped to examine a tapestry hung over it. The scene, its colors bright and pleasing, showed a seated lady with a unicorn beside her. Bertwoin couldn't tell if she approved of it.

Flowia waved them to the two benches at the kitchen table. Bertwoin sat beside Armendis and studied her from the corner of his eye. She looked normal at first glance. Her scratched cheeks were almost healed, but her shoulders drooped, and her eyes had the guarded look of someone whose safety might be assaulted in the next heartbeat.

The alchemist sat on a three-legged stool near them, drinking from a leather tankard. He rose and waited until Guillema had settled before saying in the tone of a priest celebrating mass, "May God lay His hand upon you, Na Guillema."

"And you," she said. "We're here to talk about Ermessen's murder." A spasm of grief passed over her features. "If it so pleases you."

The master's craggy face tightened with pity. "It is something we must do. Your baking goes well, I hope."

After being assured that her work was thriving, the master greeted Armendis and asked about her health. She grimaced and said nothing. He then talked a moment with Jehan about his work before he bent and tapped the kitchen table. "Please. Our bread will, of course, be inferior to yours, but I find it edible."

Bertwoin smiled at this polite lie. His aunt and cousin didn't eat the same wheat bread that nobles and wealthy merchants ate.

Flowia glided to a side table and asked Guillema, "Wine or ale?"

"Oh, wine would be much appreciated."

Flowia poured some into a glass vessel for her, which surprised his aunt. Guillema picked up the precious glass as if she were afraid the weight of the wine might break it. Flowia served everyone else tankards of ale.

She brought them wheat bread from a cupboard, olive oil to pour over it, and some salted ham. His aunt looked honored.

Still standing, the alchemist murmured, "It is our shared duty to solve this murder, so we may bury it as a sad memory. We don't want to keep you here for long," he said gently to Armendis. "But we require more information in order to solve your mother's murder."

Armendis's face stiffened. "I'll do my best."

"I know you will. Was it indeed Artal who abducted you and took you to the winery in Pennautier?"

She winced. "It was." The question had surprised her. "Does this have anything to do with my mother's death?"

"Perhaps. Do you know why he took you there?"

She glanced at Jehan. "He insisted I marry Garnier's son, Tumas, but I refused."

"Did Artal ever visit you while you were at the winery?"

"No."

"Did Hebert know he wasn't Mendy's real father?" Flowia asked Armendis. "Is that why he beat your mother so brutally that she was bedridden?"

"It was. *Maman* had a wooden heart Artal carved for her. She always wore it. My father . . . Hebert . . . tried to take it away from her." Armendis put her face in her hands. "*Maman's* anger made her lose control. She told him who had given it to her, and that it was dear to her." She smote her thigh with her fist. "It was foolish of her to do so, but you don't understand the constant torture it was to live with him, especially for her. She often turned aside his rage from Rai and me by taking it on herself. So she just blurted it out. She told me later she wished he had killed her."

There was a pause as they all pitied Ermessen's plight.

Then the master murmured, "Tell us what happened to the ram?"

She gaped at him. "Is that . . . is that what *happened* to my mother?"

Bertwoin glanced at his aunt. She had kept the details of Ermessen's death from Armendis.

Their silence gave Armendis the answer she didn't want to hear. Her face crumpled again with grief. "She was killed like an animal?"

Jehan patted his fiancée's back. Flowia rose from her seat, quiet as a ghost. She fetched a hemp cloth from a shelf and went to wet it. She scowled into the bucket and brought it to Bertwoin. "We need water."

Why was there never water in these buckets? He hurried outside with it and filled it half full from a gurgling spring spurting from between two rocks close to the alchemist's door. He hurried back inside.

Armendis sat hunched forward with her tankard beside her elbow, her face in her hands. Cooing to her, Guillema patted and rubbed her back. Armendis looked up, red-eyed and tight-lipped, when Flowia handed her the damp rag. She wiped her face, and the cool wetness seemed to restore her a bit.

The alchemist leaned toward her, his face etched with grandfatherly concern. "Do you remember anything from while you were in a daze?"

Her bottom lip trembled. "No."

"I am told you and Sibilia were friends. Do you remember her coming to see you on that morning?"

"Sibi? Yes, why?"

The master looked at Guillema, who shook her head slightly without Armendis seeing her.

Armendis asked, "What does Sibi have to do with my mother's murder?"

"Sibilia may have seen something, and so, knew something we don't."

"Sibi came early that morning, and to please her, Rai made meat pies for each of us." She smiled at the memory, then became somber again. "Wait. You said 'we *were* friends,' not 'we *are* friends.' And you said 'knew.' Has something happened to Sibi?"

Guillema put a hand on her back and whispered, "She died, dear."

Armendis wailed and beat her forehead with her fists. Guillema grabbed her wrists and hugged her as she curled up and cried like an injured child.

"I think we're done here," Guillema told the alchemist.

"Yes, but I have a question for you. When you sent Raimunda to fetch Hebert, had you already found Ermessen?"

"Yes."

"So Raimunda knew her mother was dead when you sent her to fetch her father."

"I just told her to tell you to come to the farm and then bring her father home immediately. I felt it best that she didn't know that her mother was dead. She would find out soon enough."

The alchemist rubbed his forehead. "But she may have inferred it when you sent for me instead of Flowia. You didn't send for a healer."

Guillema agreed by raising her eyebrows and twitching her head to one side. "Yes, Raimunda is a bright girl." She leveled her gray eyes at the alchemist. "Do you know who the killer is?"

"I believe I do. I have already discussed my conclusions with the seneschal, but he disagrees with me. He remains entrenched in his opposition. He thinks that changing his mind will be viewed as a weakness on his part. People might come to doubt that he is always right, and thus, he might lose stature. I cannot oppose him because I have no tangible proof and no witness."

Guillema pursed her lips. "You've solved murders before now. Why would the seneschal not believe you?"

"He has already made his decision, and his *bayle* also doesn't accept my arguments, and my evidence has no more weight than a ghost."

His aunt shoved her empty glass away from her. "Well, I must be getting back. Some women still haven't come for their bread."

"We appreciate your coming," the alchemist said.

Bertwoin went outside and stood in front of the doorway beside the alchemist and Flowia as they watched his aunt lead the two lovers away. Before they had taken three steps on their way through the poultry yard, the *bayle* appeared and blocked the opening in the hedge. The geese backed into a corner beside the house and watched him without making a sound. Having established his presence, he ambled inside, his face haughty with authority. Two burly men followed him.

Guillema cried out, "No."

Armendis glanced around for a way to escape, but the hedge enclosed them. She fell to her knees, crying.

Bertwoin then remembered his feeling that someone had watched them enter the cottage.

CHAPTER XXIX.

The *bayle* swaggered forward and stopped in the middle of the poultry yard and stood solid and immovable. The crusader's cross on the chest of his leather tunic glowed in the morning sunlight.

He had not brought his sword, so he hadn't expected to fight anyone while arresting Armendis. Still, the *bayle* had brought two brawlers to help him escort the prisoner to the citadel. He had probably picked them up at The Noble Head and offered each of them a couple of tankards of ale for a morning's work. So he may have expected some resistance.

The alchemist, moving with slow dignity, stepped in front of Guillema, Jehan, and Armendis as if he could protect them. Flowia patted the kneeling Armendis on the back. Both women were crying.

The *bayle* glared at the alchemist. "So it's true, old man. You're hiding her from us. The *visconte* will hear of your treason. You show no respect for him or his laws."

The master looked the *bayle* directly in the eye. "That is not true, lawman. The *visconte* knows I hold his word in high regard and only have contempt for those who pretend to carry out his will while making a mockery of justice in his domain.

He knows too that I have been called wrong before and been proven right. This young woman is innocent."

The *bayle* sighed. "I know your argument, old man. There was no skin or blood under the dead woman's fingernails. Pshaw. Your clue found no favor at the citadel, not even with the *visconte*."

"Then guard your soul, lawman, look to your soul."

The *bayle* seemed less sure of himself. "My soul?"

"If you hang this innocent woman, who is a victim like her mother, it would've been better had you been stillborn."

"I think you go beyond your calling when you try to preach, goldsmith." He jerked his head toward Armendis and told his men, "Bring her."

They lumbered toward where she knelt, going wide around the alchemist. Following orders absolved them of responsibility, but shoving the alchemist aside while doing so meant angering the master, and who knew what ill luck that might bring?

Jehan stepped in front of his fiancée to protect her. One of the burly men lashed out and struck his jaw. Jehan staggered backward and fell. Armendis screamed as each man grabbed one of her arms. She fought them, jerking from side to side as they dragged her to the opening in the hedge. Bertwoin started forward, but Flowia grabbed his arm.

"Stay back," the *bayle* shouted.

Guillema helped her dazed son to his feet, and they watched the two men half-carry Armendis away, as she hung slack between them. Both Flowia and Jehan cried. Then Flowia staggered into the cottage, and they followed her inside. She slammed the door as if trying to shut out the world.

Standing in the quiet front room, Guillema rounded on the alchemist. "She expected us to keep her safe, and we failed. So how do we save her now, goldsmith?"

"We find the killer."

"Come into the kitchen," Flowia told Jehan. "I will put something on your jaw to ease the pain and reduce the swelling."

"I'm fine as I am."

"Do as she says," his mother ordered. She then asked the alchemist. "Do you know who killed Ermie?"

"I believe I do, but I could be wrong. And I know not how to prove it. The *bayle* knows whom I suspect but refuses to believe me. The seneschal also opposes me. They see no evidence that points a finger at anyone other than Armendis. I have nothing to argue with—no confession, no witness."

Guillema clenched both of her hands into fists. "Tell me who you accuse."

"A young woman without mercy. Raimunda."

She stared at the alchemist, her mouth hanging open. "Impossible."

"Is it?"

"Without mercy!" Bertwoin shouted. "I knew there was something I missed. She wasn't red-eyed. Raimunda didn't cry when her mother was murdered."

"Why would she do such an evil thing to her own mother?" his aunt asked.

"My guess is that it had to do with favoritism and a lack of love. Armendis is the youngest daughter, and Raimunda feels it is against nature for her younger sister to marry before she does. Many older sisters would agree with her. This marriage insults her as a person. Also, Ermessen showed a marked preference for Armendis."

He waved a dismissive hand. "And Hebert is incapable of showing her any love. Everybody wanted Armendis—her mother, Jehan, Tumas, you, Melisende, and even Artal. No one gave Raimunda a second glance. It didn't help, of course, to see how happy her sister was with your son. And the constant abuse at home must have added to her perversion."

"But to kill her mother?" Bertwoin protested. "Would she not kill Hebert instead?"

"Maybe not. I have seen this before. She blamed her mother for spurning her but not Hebert. She may even have a grudging respect for her powerful father. That is why she placed a doll between her mother's breasts. She was condemning her motherhood."

"Oh," Guillema stumbled to a bench in the front room and dropped onto it. "Jacme! Is it possible? Was Raimunda crazy with hatred? It's too...too vicious." Guillema wrapped her cloak tighter around her. "You're right, goldsmith, Ermie preferred Mendy. Why? Because she was conceived from Artal, the man she truly loved, not the old ram she was forced to live with. And then there was Jacme."

"Bertwoin told me a little about her son. Tell me more."

"Ermessen believed Raimunda pushed Jacme into the river. I didn't believe it. I just thought she was trying to relieve her own guilt. And he may have fallen into the water by accident, but now I wonder if she shoved him into the river on purpose. He could be annoying. And how could she not resent him? He was a boy and stole away all of her parents' love. Then, after the Aude swept him away forever, Artal did what Hebert didn't do. He comforted Ermie, which may have led to Mendy being born not long after that."

"And Sibilia," Flowia whispered. "Why kill her?"

"Ah well," the alchemist said. "I believe Armendis just told us why her friend had to die. She had eaten with the two sisters on Ermessen's death day. So, even though Sibilia didn't realize the significance of what she knew, she had to die. She had watched Raimunda prepare separate meat pies for them. She might remember that Raimunda had the opportunity to poison Armendis without poisoning either herself or Sibilia."

"Why cut off her nose?" Flowia asked.

"Only Raimunda can tell us that. Perhaps she was warning people to keep their noses out of this business."

"And the dress?" Bertwoin asked. "Souvenir?"

"Possibly, but I think she had another reason. She used the bloody dress to turn herself into her mother's ghost. She intended to haunt her father with it."

"And if we found this tunic?" Bertwoin asked.

"That would be fortunate, and if it were in her possession, it might prove her guilt. But it is undoubtedly well hidden. And I believe Raimunda is too smart to keep it where the finding of it would point blame at her."

Guillema put her hands on her hips and demanded, "So, what do we do now?"

"I am at a loss as to how to rescue Armendis. The authorities have her, and in their eyes, the evidence against her is damning. They will never. . . ." He sat down on the bench beside Guillema and stared at the reeds covering the floor. After a moment, he nodded. "There may be a way, after all, to prove Raimunda is the killer. My plan could drop Armendis into deeper danger if it goes awry, but we have little choice."

He smiled at Flowia and Bertwoin. "We must set a trap. The *visconte* genuinely cares for his people. He will not want to torture an innocent young woman. So now all of us must do our part."

"Anything," Jehan shouted.

CHAPTER XXX.

"You're getting off easy today." His father stretched as if watching his son turn the ground in their new vegetable garden put a kink in *his* back. He glanced at Bertwoin's outer cloak on the ground and grinned. "But I see it's enough to keep you warm."

"It does that," Bertwoin agreed with just enough sarcasm to suggest he wouldn't need more warmth if he were inside the house or the barn.

Daylight just naturally gave rise to work like a hen just naturally laid eggs, or so his father believed. False dawn was a soundless alarm to rise, at least for the men. His women—Ellyn and Rachel—were expected to greet each false dawn with bread already kneaded and a hearth fire already stoked into flame. Maud, still young and needing sleep to grow on, was allowed to stay abed until false dawn like the men. In two or three years, she too would have the womanly honor of getting up in the cold dark.

Watching him work always put his father in a good mood. He knelt and grabbed a handful of dirt, smelling it. "Don't spare the pig shit after you loosen the ground up good. But don't add too much. Growing vegetables need to strain a bit to put strength in them."

"Flowia is like dung for people," Bertwoin said.

His father looked wary. "How's that?"

"She makes people better. Heals them. Didn't she just take care of Maud's maw worms and put me back on my feet after I got my head bashed?"

"She's helped us out. I'll give her that. It softened your mother's attitude toward her after Flowia bandaged your head and sat up with you half the night."

"But you're still against her?"

"I'm still not sure she's the best choice for you. What good does it do for a plowman to have a wife who can read? But I've come around to seeing the good in her. And I can't argue against the fact that a healer is valuable."

"She's about to help us even more. She's a main part of the master's plan to free Armendis."

"We'll owe her if she helps save the girl. Well, I've got to go talk to Roul." He tossed a dirt clod at Bertwoin, hitting him in the back. "You missed a good wife when you rejected Maria. She'll not need more than a slap or two now and then. Not sure that's true for Flowia."

Did that mean he might consider letting him marry her? "I'm happy for my brother."

"Well, let's just hope he's up to the task. He's got an all-day job just disciplining himself."

"Wilfraed is a better farmer than I'll ever be."

"Not sure that's much of a compliment. Just remember, you still inherit this farm."

His father swaggered away. As soon as he was out of sight, Bertwoin judged it late enough in the morning to escort Flowia to Hebert's farm. They had to bait the master's trap. With luck, he might spend some time alone with Flowia.

Roland was missing from his guard post. No surprise there—it was his mating season. Bertwoin hoped it was also Bertwoin's mating season. When he was seated in the kitchen with ale at his elbow, he pointed at a chess board at the end of the table with the men on it lined up and ready for battle. "Who's winning?"

The alchemist laughed. "No one. The game is changing, and a friend in Bram showed me some new moves. I want to show them to Flowia."

Bertwoin scratched his cheek as he studied the board. The men were all waiting, ready to go into battle just like they were.

The master patted the table to get his attention. "I have something for you, plowman, if you're willing to accept it." He laid a leather thong on the table, its ends tied together to form a large loop. Opposite the knot, a silver figure dangled from it. It looked as if it had been torn off a larger piece.

Bertwoin held it up to examine it. Silver was valuable. Was it a charm to protect him? Flowia watched him with a sly smile.

The alchemist made a dismissive gesture. "It's just a bit of tinkering I did. Still, you might wear it."

Bertwoin slipped the thong over his head and dropped the bit of silver down the neck of his tunic. "Thank you, master. I will keep it safe."

"Flowia will explain it to you later."

Bertwoin cleared his throat. "My uncle says the news of Armendis's arrest spread overnight like water soaking through linen. The crowd at the alehouse has already judged her as guilty."

"Then let's hope that Na Guillema has spread the news that I consider Armendis innocent. And let's hope that it takes hold?"

"My sister," Bertwoin said, "was told that officials in the Church believe these two murders were sacrifices to Satan. Some claim Armendis became one of the Good Folk and now practices devilish blood rites. Everyone knows she was about to marry into Guillema's Good Folk *ostal*."

Frowning, Flowia rubbed a hand over the table's smooth top. "The clergy must have seen the *bayle* bring Armendis into the citadel. If so, they didn't waste more than three breaths before they denounced her."

"It seems the seneschal has a fight on his hands if the Church wants her," the alchemist said. "But then, so do we. I will go to the *château* and try to convince the *visconte* to delay taking action against Armendis. I need time to prove her innocent. Go now, children, and bait the trap. God grant you success."

Raimunda opened the front door a hand's width and peeked out at them as if she expected bandits. Her pinched expression tightened even more when she recognized them, but she did open the door wider.

"Who is it?" Hebert complained.

Bertwoin peered into the shadowy interior behind Raimunda and saw her father sitting at the kitchen table with his back to them. Bertwoin also saw a woman huddled on a bench in the front room, a gray woolen blanket around her. She stared at the floor as if lost in reverie. Was this the cousin Raimunda had mentioned, the one who was more of a hindrance than a help?

"The virgin and the plowman," Raimunda called to her father.

"Can't a man even eat without vermin tormenting him? They're a pox, especially the ox turd. Send them away."

"We bring news of Armendis," Flowia called to him.

"Give me strength," he said. Instead of answering Flowia, he called out to his daughter, "Tell them I'll come out to them."

"He's coming," Raimunda said and shut the door in their faces.

Bertwoin bumped Flowia's shoulder with his arm. "Guess we're not welcome inside his home."

She harrumphed, paused a moment, then said,

"If he allows us to come inside,
he then must act the gracious host.
But in this ostal, it is a duty denied
because Hebert loves hoarding the most."

"So," Flowia said. "No ale for us. Hebert is naught but grumbling thunder that brings no rain. It's a wonder Raimunda isn't hungry all the time?"

Bertwoin leaned sideways and glanced through the front window, its shutters pulled open. No one was listening to them. "If she killed her mother, as the master believes, she deserves to starve to death," he whispered. "He probably feeds himself like a duke, and she gleans off what she needs while cooking. Remember, she made a meat pie for herself when Sibilia came."

Hebert let them wait, probably hoping they would go away. He finally slipped outside, shut the door, and stood in front of it with his arms crossed over his chest. Hebert put up a feisty front, but he didn't look Bertwoin in the eye.

He said to Flowia, "You said you had news."

"May God bless you," Flowia said, her voice flowing with honey. She waited, received no response to her greeting, and said, "We came to tell you the *bayle* arrested Armendis yesterday."

His whole body tensed. "Ach," he said as if clearing his throat.

Bertwoin peered through the open window again and saw Raimunda listening to them. So they hadn't known about the arrest. But how would they? Few people came to see them, and if someone did come, Hebert would discourage their gossiping with Raimunda and distracting her from her work.

Hebert licked his lips. "I wanted Mendy taken at first and punished hard, but then I thought about it. She was bewitched and had no true guilt in this matter. Couldn't control herself. She loved her mother and was a loyal daughter."

Flowia said in a caressing tone, "The master hopes to prove Armendis innocent by All Saints' Day and see her released."

Hebert relaxed. "I should hope so." He sneered at Bertwoin. "Your aunt needs to answer for my wife's death. She laid a charm on my daughter and forced her to kill her mother."

Flowia's eyes narrowed, and she shook her head. "That argument will not save Armendis."

"Why not? Being possessed will slough the guilt off onto Melisende."

Flowia took two deep breaths and let them out slowly. Hebert smiled, enjoying the fact that he had annoyed her.

"The Church has already taken a deadly interest in her case," Flowia said. "They want to be the judges of her, and the Bishop will find Armendis guilty because he believes she follows the ways of the Good Folk."

"That's sheep shit."

"Of course it is. But if you insist Melisende bewitched Armendis, you'll help them turn this into a witch trial. Armendis is now a witch too. Bishop Othon will condemn your daughter as well as Bertwoin's aunt. That will put his name on people's tongues. Even Rome might take notice."

Hebert looked from Flowia to Bertwoin, then back at her again to see if they were lying.

Bertwoin said loud enough for Raimunda to hear, "The master believes Armendis can help name the one who killed your wife. She can also help him prove it."

"I damn well hope so."

"In the meantime," Flowia said, "you have to feed her. She's imprisoned at the citadel."

"I'll go now," Raimunda called through the open window.

"No," Hebert barked. "You've got work to do here. Gather some food. I'll go myself, though I can ill afford the time. I want to be sure those on the hill do her no harm." He pointed a finger at Flowia's face. "And the alchemist needs to put some sweat into this. I don't care if he has to use the black arts. He needs to bring my Mendy home. If she's harmed by either castle or Church, it'll be his fault."

Flowia bit her bottom lip, breathing hard.

Hebert snorted, dismissing her anger, then looked at Bertwoin. "Your family's day is coming, plowman. The Church won't hold its hand forever. I'll see the day when Melisende dances in the fire."

"Well, let's hope your pig-headedness doesn't put your daughter on a pyre beside her."

"Never happen."

"Just remember, farmer, she's going to join my family and be a part of the ones you want to see burn."

"That wedding won't happen, ox ass. I'll see to that."

"Then you'll have to pay back the money you got when you sold her to them."

"What money?" he sneered.

Bertwoin took a step forward, backing the farmer against his door. "Don't forget who my family is, fart sniffer. If you go back on your word and think you'll keep that money, think again. First, Laurence will beat you into a bloody mess. Then if you don't pay up, I'll come when you're back on your feet again. Then we'll let my father come and finish the work by breaking a few bones. He knows how to beat blood out of a leech like you."

Hebert licked his lips.

"Raimunda will have to work full time just tending to your wounds. You'll lose your farm because you can't work."

"God will punish you."

Bertwoin laughed. "Seems like you're the one God's punishing."

"He'll find me steady as Job." Hebert chuckled. "He'll bless me in the end. Won't ever do the same for you and your kind, not for a family with witches in it."

Flowia laid a hand on Bertwoin's forearm. "Enough." She faced Hebert. "The master sent us as friends to inform you of Armendis's plight. We've done that. He will now work to free your daughter and name your wife's murderer."

She turned and glided away. Bertwoin balled his right hand into a fist, breathing hard, and trembled as he fought the urge to smack the farmer. He turned and followed Flowia.

CHAPTER XXXI.

As soon as they had moved beyond Hebert's hearing, Flowia tapped Bertwoin's arm with her knuckle. "The master has gone to the *château*. We have to warn him that Hebert is already bringing food to Armendis—food that is prepared by Raimunda."

Bertwoin and Flowia trudged down the rutted road alongside the Aude River. The citadel gleamed on its hill ahead of them like a golden crown.

The guard leaning against the stone wall of the Narbonne Gate's barbican raised a hand and stopped them. Flowia made a point of noticing a woman in a gray cloak carrying two live ducks and a weaver with a folded cloth thrown over his shoulder—people who marched unhindered into the citadel.

The sentry smirked at her, smug with authority in his square helmet, leather breastplate, and greaves. He jerked his chin at Flowia's hands. "You carry nothing. What's your business here?"

"We have come to visit Na Thea."

Bertwoin looked at her, his eyebrows raised, and quickly changed his expression to show this was true. The guard glanced at Flowia's belly and smiled at Bertwoin. He stepped aside and waved them through the gate with a sarcastic flourish.

"Quick thinking," Bertwoin said when they had gone around a corner and were out of the guard's sight.

Flowia ignored the narrow street leading to Na Thea's shop and hurried straight toward the *Château Comtal's* barbican.

She giggled. "It seemed a good lie until he took it to mean I was pregnant. Na Thea has a reputation for solving that problem for young maidens." She elbowed his arm. "Your surprise amused him. He assumed I had tricked you into coming with me. Na Thea scolds the men who make these problems for maidens. Her tongue, it is said, is a lash that causes marriages to happen or leaves scars if the men don't obey her."

"Pregnant?"

"Yes. So now he may remember me."

Bertwoin shrugged. "I doubt he knows your name."

"No, but I don't want him to notice me at the market or in town and point me out to his friends. There's already enough fallacious gossip circulating about me. Many think an alchemist's virgin must truly be a virgin." She laughed. "Of course, the one who would profit most from this gossip about me is Na Thea. When I don't have a baby within the year, people will believe Na Thea's remedy worked."

They crossed the stone bridge over the *château's* dry moat. A squat soldier guarded the open eastern gate set between two towers with blue-tiled roofs. He nodded to Flowia. "May God look on you with favor, maiden."

"And upon you, Yvain. Is your son well?"

His toothy smile answered her even before he spoke. "Yes, thanks to you. He's almost too lively now for his mother."

"That may well promise a favorable future for him."

From the gate, Bertwoin scanned the château's wide forecourt shaded by a row of elms across its middle. It was alive with noise—the children of the poor people who had gathered for leftover food shouted and squealed as they chased each other, a displeased donkey brayed, and starlings chattered in the elms.

Servants hurried about on errands, people carried produce or poultry, and here and there small groups of peasants talked among themselves. This was the beating heart of the *visconte's* domain. Had all this noise and bustle stopped when Armendis was brought into the courtyard? How had she felt?

"Has the master come?" Flowia asked Yvain.

"Yes, maiden. He's gone to see the seneschal."

"Not the *visconte*?"

The guard shook his head. "The *visconte* is away to Bram this day and night."

Flowia sucked in her lips, and Yvain asked her if anything was amiss.

"Then the master will find his task difficult," she said Yvain. "I think I need to find Hytha."

"Oh, she too is away. She accompanied the *viscontesse* to Bram."

"Then this day brings me ill luck."

"I'm sorry for you, maiden. Is there anything you need?"

"No, Yvain. What will be, will be. Do you know where Armendis is being kept?"

"Yes." He led them farther into the front courtyard and pointed at the Lady's Tower set in the north wall. "The guard is not likely to let you inside to see her."

"Thank you, Yvain," Flowia said. "I think I'll go—"

"Well met," a voice drawled behind them.

They turned to see dapper Sir Reginald de Lastours, a knight hostage, standing behind them. Some joked that Sir Reginald wouldn't go to the privy unless he was so well dressed that everybody would notice him. The cost of his knee-length black tunic over his red-and-white striped hose and pointed felt boots would feed a peasant family of eight for a year.

"Hah!" he said, rubbing his thin hands together as he surveyed Bertwoin. "The peasant knight who unhorses his enemies with a hoe."

Yvain stared at Bertwoin as if noticing him for the first time. "I heard of this. So it was *him*?"

"Indeed, it was he," Sir Reginald said. "So what brings you here, Sir Bertwoin of Montredon?" He bowed to Flowia. "And with a fair *virgin* by his side." He pronounced the word *virgin* with insulting deliberation and darted his eyes from her to Bertwoin, his doubt of her virginity as transparent as sunlight.

Flowia's face looked as if it were cut from limestone.

Amused, Sir Reginald drawled, "I find most women I meet are less like the Virgin Mary and more like Eve after the Fall."

"Perhaps you should keep better company."

The knight brayed laughter. "Well said, maiden. But is it not every woman's heritage to be like Eve? She was not satisfied until Adam was driven out of paradise."

"Pah," Flowia said, matching the knight's disdain. "I find my womanliness worthy of respect, though men do not think it so. I refuse to accept the shame laid on us by eunuchs in the Church."

"Maiden!" Yvain exclaimed.

Sir Reginald arched his eyebrows. "I am intrigued. How do you argue this?"

Her eyes sparkled. "Adam, oh poor Adam. You men speak as if only he was punished. Let us not forget that she too was expelled from the Garden of Eden, which was her birthplace, unlike Adam, who was not born in paradise but outside of it and then brought into the Garden. Eve was fashioned from living bone. Adam was formed from common dirt. And remember that it is a woman named Mary who has magnificent cathedrals named after her, a woman who is the *mother* of God. Show me one cathedral dedicated to your Adam."

"Take care, maiden. Your heresy might see you condemned beside Armendis as a witch and burned."

"Always, when I debate a man, he ignores the truth in my words and attacks me by calling me a heretic."

Bertwoin said quickly to Sir Reginald, "We hoped to visit Armendis in yonder tower. We also must speak with the alchemist. He pleads her innocence with the seneschal."

"The master alchemist's opinion carries weight, of course, but I think it is a burden he must haul up a steep hill if he wishes to change Sir Jean-Luc's judgment. I am told her tunic was slick with the blood of her dead mother."

Bertwoin shrugged. "The master believes she was drugged and then smeared with the blood."

"Ah yes, I heard of his defense. The rumor also flits about that a witch laid a charm on her. These excuses fall on barren soil here and wither rather than thrive."

"Because those in the Church wish to use her," Bertwoin said.

"Exactly so. And if that comes to pass, everyone will start searching their neighbors' houses for witches." Sir Reginald frowned at the Lady's Tower. "Anyway, I would help you if I could, plowman, but I doubt even I could get you inside that tower."

"There is a way," Bertwoin said.

"Well then, I look forward to hearing how you vanquished this obstacle. Good luck to you." He nodded to Flowia and pranced away, whistling.

Yvain glanced at the gate behind them. "I must get back to my duties. God keep you both well."

They thanked him and walked further into the forecourt. "What now?" Flowia asked.

"Eudes. He's the cook in Chef Arundel's excellent kitchen, who is to marry my sister. He may help us get food for Armendis—food we won't have to buy or steal."

CHAPTER XXXII.

The keep formed the forecourt's southern side. Bertwoin and Flowia stepped around a pile of fresh horse droppings as they ambled toward it. A shadowy doorway in the keep's rough-hewn wall led to the kitchen below the ground floor and to the stairs that led upwards to the *visconte's* Great Hall, where the master was probably at this very moment arguing with the seneschal.

Flowia said, "Chef Arundel is not predisposed to let either of us into his kitchen, especially if we come empty-handed. So what do we do if he chases us away?"

"Let's hope luck smiles on us, and Eudes is there. If he sees us, he'll know to come out."

They strolled through the keep's open doorway and stopped outside the kitchen's entrance. Haughty chef Arundel was as jealous of his domain as a duke is of his dukedom. Peasants bringing supplies, servants getting food, and nobles were welcome, but he would pounce on anyone else who dared trespass into his kitchen, anyone who might interrupt his cooks or bellows boys in their duties. So they crept to the doorway and peeked inside.

Activity was subdued at this time of day between meals, especially now that the *visconte* and his retinue were absent. A boy lazily turned cuts of pork skewered on a spit in a soot-blackened alcove built in the left wall, and a young woman ripped feathers from a limp chicken.

Bertwoin sighed with satisfaction at not seeing Arundel and stepped into the kitchen's arched doorway. Eudes stood at a scarred table in the center, dicing onions almost faster than the eye could follow. Bertwoin cleared his throat.

Eudes glanced up, frowning, then broke into a smile when he saw the intruder was his future brother-in-law. He set aside his knife and sauntered to Bertwoin. When he came to the entrance, he saw Flowia in the shadowy hallway. "Health to you, maiden."

"And to you, cook."

Eudes led them into the forecourt without speaking and stopped. He smiled up at the weak sun, enjoying being outside. After asking about the health of Rachel and everyone in Bertwoin's household, he asked. "Is it me you've come to see? The chef is resting."

"Yes," said Bertwoin. "We need to talk to Armendis and tell her the alchemist doesn't want her to eat any food until after we've tested it." Bertwoin looked at the noisy people in the forecourt waiting for handouts. "Maybe we can warn her if we take her a bit of what the kitchen gives to the poor."

Eudes laughed. "There's no need for the food. The day guard is Lothiers, my cousin. Come, I'll take you to him."

"That's great luck," Flowia said.

"Not really. My father worked here at the château for years. Whenever a job came open, he recommended someone from our family. I'm related to eighteen people here."

Lothiers dozed just inside the tower's thick oak door, wearing a leather helmet and a padded jacket that was too short for him. He jumped up and looked pleased when he saw Eudes with visitors. Bertwoin thought that sitting alone all day in a hallway full of silence and shadows would also bore him into falling sleep.

After Eudes introduced them, Lothiers glanced down the hallway at the rows of iron gratings on both sides, as if to make certain all the prison cells were locked. He muttered, "You're the plowman who escapes from dungeons."

"But," Flowia said, "he comes this time to ensure your prisoner doesn't escape. You need not fear us. We've come to help you."

"There's danger of her escaping?"

"Worse," Flowia hissed. "Someone wants to poison her and will do so right under your foot. So the alchemist wants all the food brought to her, even that from her family, to be tested before she eats it." Lothiers glanced at Eudes, who nodded.

"I'm here all day. No one is allowed to visit her."

Flowia said, "Her father is on his way here now with food for her."

"I shall see that she eats nothing before the master examines it."

Bertwoin rubbed his hands together. "Good. Is there anywhere down here where we can keep a piglet?"

Lothiers laughed, then looked interested when he realized Bertwoin wasn't joking. "We've got two empty storage rooms where it might stay. I'll let the night guard know not to bother it." Understanding lit up his face. "Ah, you'll use the pig to taste the food. Smart."

"No one needs to know anything about this," Eudes warned. "Even the night guard only needs to know you're keeping a pig here, not why."

Lothiers looked as if he had been slapped. "You think I can't keep a secret?"

"No, I didn't mean it that way, but it might be an amusing story, and it would be easy to slip and tell the night guard a bit too much."

"I understand. Remember, if she dies, I might be blamed."

"Is it possible to see Armendis?" Flowia asked.

Lothiers hesitated. "My instructions are not to let anyone visit her."

"We don't want to make trouble for you," Flowia said. "Can I just talk to her through the bars?"

"Well, I must get back to the kitchen," Eudes said.

They thanked him. After he had hurried away, Lothiers pointed to an iron grating set into an archway of stone. "Third one on the left. I'll stay here."

They peeked into the cell. Bertwoin swallowed. Except for a straw mattress, the tiny room was as bare as a monk's cell. It made him feel cold and hopeless. Everything around her was made of heartless stone or hard metal, from the flagstone floors to the vaulted ceilings, to the iron gratings used as doors. Even the winter light coming through the cell's iron-barred window had no softness to it.

"Armendis," Flowia called through the bars.

She sat up on the mattress. "Who is it?"

"Flowia and Bertwoin."

She stared at them, bewildered. "Is Jehan with you?"

"He's in St. Vincent, working to help free you."

"No one can help me," she wailed.

Bertwoin remembered how helpless he had felt when he was a prisoner in the bishop's dungeon. Her bed would be alive with lice. He looked in the corners, and yes, there was a large spider web. When she woke in the mornings, there would be scorpions on the walls.

As Armendis came toward them, the noon-day light from the room's small window behind her lit the edges of her hair. As she got closer, they saw her black eye and bruised cheeks.

"They've already begun torturing you?" he asked.

"No. I wouldn't walk, so the men beat me. But I wouldn't give in, so the *bayle* made them drag me." She pointed to her feet. The tops of her toes and lower shins were scraped raw. "Can you bring me some salve?"

"I will if they let me," Flowia said. "We think someone wants to poison you. Only eat what the day guard gives you. Don't eat anything from anyone else. That includes your family."

"My family? But I'm starving."

"Do you remember anything now about the day your mother was killed?" Bertwoin asked.

"No. It's like I was asleep."

Bertwoin almost told her that the alchemist thought her sister had drugged her and killed their mother, but he decided not to. He didn't want to put her into a deeper pit of darkness.

"We will test all the food brought to you," Flowia said. "What Lothiers gives you, you may eat."

Armendis began sobbing. "I don't want to be tortured. Poisoning me might be a mercy."

"I doubt the poisoner will give you a painless death," Bertwoin warned. "We must go."

Flowia reached through the bars and patted her arm. "The master will save you, Armendis. You will marry Jehan."

"Can I see him?"

Bertwoin realized that the hope of seeing his cousin might strengthen her. "If it's possible, we'll sneak him in here."

"Bring him, please."

"We must go now." When they came back to Lothiers, Bertwoin told him, "I'll bring you the piglet. It's waiting for me in St. Vincent."

Flowia said, "Thank you, Lothiers. We are in your debt."

"I do this willingly, maiden."

Bertwoin opened the tower's door and saw Hebert standing a stone's throw away.

CHAPTER XXXIII.

Bertwoin shut the door. "It's Hebert with a reed basket. He's arguing with a shepherd. We can't let him find us here."

Lothiers pointed at the first iron-bar door in the hallway. "It's unlocked."

They ran to it and clanged it shut behind them. The cramped cell, like Armendis's, was cold and bare with only a straw mattress on the stone floor. They shoved their backs against the rough wall and hid where no one coming down the hallway could see them.

They heard the tower door open and shut. "I brought food for my girl," Hebert complained.

"I'll give it to her."

"I want to see her."

"My orders are that no one visits her."

"I've got to make sure she's being treated right." After a moment, Hebert shouted, "Don't you push me!"

"I said no. You can't go down there."

"I'm her father. That gives me the right to see her whenever I like."

"Go tell that to Sir Jean-Luc. I'm sure he'll change his order just for you."

Hebert yelled, "Hell, I might just as well ask for an audience with the Pope."

"You can pick up your basket tomorrow," Lothiers said, "when you bring more food. Now get out of here before I throw you into one of our cells for the night."

Flowia and Bertwoin heard the tower's oak door bang shut and joined Lothiers. After giving Hebert enough time to leave the *château's* forecourt, Lothiers peeked outside. "He's gone. I'll not feed Armendis before you come back with the pig and test the food."

They thanked him and stepped blinking out into the milky winter sunlight. Both of them looked across the courtyard at the brooding keep, hoping to see the master, but he was nowhere in sight.

"What now?" Flowia asked.

"I'll go fetch the piglet Jehan bought for us and bring it here."

Flowia nodded toward the keep. "And I'll go find out if the master is upstairs with the seneschal. I think he'll be pleased with what we've accomplished so far this morning. Then I'll come back here and wait for you."

That sounded promising.

Bertwoin strolled down the citadel's steep hill into St. Vincent and collected the sacrificial pig from Jehan. When he returned with it tucked snuggly under his arm, he found Flowia waiting for him in the forecourt.

"I talked with the master," she said. "He's in a vexed mood. Sir Jean-Luc refuses to believe that Raimunda is the killer. He's adamant that when the *visconte* returns from Bram, Armendis will be examined and persuaded to confess. The master did take heart, though, when I told him that our plan for testing Armendis's food will be firmly in place today."

Bertwoin scratched the piglet's shaggy back. "Maybe the food Hebert brought is poisoned, and we can expose Raimunda before the seneschal questions Armendis. And maybe," he whispered into the boar's hairy ear, "Our piggy only needs to taste a little of the food. He only needs to get sick and doesn't to die."

They returned to the Lady's Tower and let the docile piglet sample some of the stew and bread that Hebert had brought. After Flowia judged that sufficient time had passed for poison symptoms to appear, Bertwoin accompanied her home. They agreed he would escort her to the citadel each afternoon to test the food.

Two days passed without incident. Rather than imprison the little boar, Lothiers kept it with him for company. Few people came into the tower, and those who did ignored his pet. At night, he locked the piglet in a dank storeroom. It ate with appetite and seemed to enjoy all the attention it was getting.

On the third day, the little boar ate and was going from person to person for petting, when it began convulsing. It stood rigid, jerking spasmodically, staring straight ahead. Bertwoin felt like kicking a wall.

Flowia stroked the piglet. "It's blind," she said in a voice husky with sorrow.

"Poison?" Lothiers asked.

"Yes, and a powerful one." Flowia knelt beside piglet, petting it, and whispering, "Poor dear. We're so sorry, piggy."

"So, the master is right," Lothiers said. "Armendis is innocent." He watched Flowia caress the young boar. "I'm going to miss his company."

Bertwoin felt as if a plum were caught in his throat. He had grown to like the little beast, even though he knew he shouldn't have.

CHAPTER XXXIV.

A guard pulled open the small door leading from the forecourt into the *château's* keep and led the alchemist and Bertwoin up two flights of slippery stone steps to a small landing. Bertwoin walked behind the master, his hands held up to catch the old man should he stumble on the steps, which were uneven so enemies would find their footing awkward while fighting their way upward to the Great Hall. Bertwoin had once heard a knight brag that the *Château Comtal* had never been taken by force.

On the landing, the guard knocked on an oak door. After a few breaths, the door swung open on well-oiled hinges, and the guard stepped back to allow them to enter.

Though Bertwoin had been inside the Great Hall before, its magnificence made him gasp. They had entered through a door for servants and unimportant guests. Bertwoin smoothed his tunic to make himself more presentable. He felt humble, as when he entered high-ceilinged cathedrals, but also honored to be allowed inside this room.

A good distance to their right, a raised platform ran across the back wall. On it sat *Visconte* Raimon-Rogièr in regal solitude, enthroned in a high-backed chair. Behind him hung his red-and-white coat of arms with its black fingerling fish.

He waved the alchemist forward. Bertwoin stepped aside to stand along the wall. It was not his place to approach the dais.

As the master hobbled toward young *Visconte* Raimon-Rogièr, Bertwoin stared across the wide room at the row of windows set in the opposite wall, each taller than any man. Between them hung tapestries of men hunting boar, bear, or stags—real animals, unlike the unicorn in the tapestry that hung on the master's cottage wall.

The *visconte* signaled for a servant to set a chair facing the dais for the master alchemist. Bertwoin remembered when he had been on trial here with angry Sir Jean-Luc against him. The wise alchemist had argued for him. At least, this time, he wasn't the one accused of murder.

The *visconte* watched the alchemist with soft pity. "Your lameness afflicts you still, goldsmith?"

"My enemy is ever with me, my lord, and will be so until I finally lie comfortable in my grave." The alchemist seated himself with a sigh.

One of the double doors at the opposite end of the Great Hall opened. The seneschal, Sir Jean-Luc de Béziers, strode inside with studied dignity. Hebert and Raimunda followed him like wary mice nosing out of a shadowy hole into a cat's hunting ground. The *bayle* marched inside last and closed the door. He swaggered to where Bertwoin stood along the wall and joined him, crossing his arms over his burly chest.

The seneschal strode past the alchemist without acknowledging him, stepped up onto the platform, and stood beside the seated *visconte*. Hebert glanced around, trying to know where he and Raimunda should stand, before he stopped beside the seated alchemist. Raimunda wore a dress and Hebert a linen tunic, both probably borrowed.

Visconte Raimon-Rogièr cleared his throat and said to Hebert, "There is a difference of opinion as to who killed your wife. I am told that fresh evidence has come to the alchemist's attention. He will now present it."

The *bayle* winked at Bertwoin as if wishing him and the alchemist luck.

The master rose with dignity, his back straight, and his expression grave. "I found small but disturbing inconsistencies. They contradicted the unthinking assumption that Armendis was guilty."

Hebert nodded. "She was bewitched, my lord."

"Quiet," Sir Jean-Luc shouted. "Speak only when you are spoken to, peasant."

Hebert's posture shrank, but Bertwoin noticed he balled his hands into fists.

"It's clear," the master continued, "that the murderer carried hatred in her heart for Ermessen, something Armendis did not do."

Hebert jerked his head up and stared wide-eyed at the alchemist. "Her?"

Raimunda looked so stricken that Bertwoin thought she might faint. Of the seven people in the vast room, she and her father were the only two who didn't know that the master believed Raimunda had killed her mother.

The seneschal hawed derisively at the idea of Armendis's innocence.

The *visconte* raised his hand. "I wish to hear what the goldsmith has to say without interruption."

Sir Jean-Luc scowled at the master as if he had caused the *visconte* to rebuke him.

"First," the alchemist continued, "a ram had its throat cut. This, I believe, was the killer practicing. Ermessen was murdered in the same manner. Then a young woman, a friend of Armendis, had her throat slit because she had seen Raimunda make three meat pies on the morning Ermessen was killed. Raimunda was the only one who could have drugged her sister's meat pie without tainting the other two."

"Sheepshit," Hebert whispered.

Raimunda put her hands over her mouth and staggered sideways, but didn't fall.

"Also," the alchemist continued, "when Armendis was found, she had bleeding scratches on her face, as if her mother had tried to defend herself. But there was no skin or blood under Ermessen's fingernails. Someone else had scratched Armendis's face.

"When I visited Na Thea, she made me realize that Raimunda knew her mother was dead even before she ran to fetch her father. It was Na Guillema who found the corpse, and she purposely did not tell Raimunda that Ermessen had been murdered. Yet Raimunda told her father at the blacksmith's forge that her mother was dead.

"And so I laid a trap. I tested all the food brought to Armendis while she was in the Lady's Tower. We found poison in her last meal. Only Raimunda, or her father—whom I discount as doing so—could have put it there."

All eyes turned to Raimunda, who was now on her knees, crying.

"It's unnatural for a daughter to kill her mother," Sir Jean-Luc announced. He looked down on Raimunda like an Old Testament prophet filled with God-given power. "Why would you do this?"

When she shook her head, gulping air, Sir Jean-Luc glared at the alchemist, wordlessly demanding an answer.

"Jealousy and shame. Her mother preferred her sister to her, and her father was indifferent to her. She found no love in her family. Only abuse. She also had no suitor. She is the eldest daughter, but no one seeks her hand in marriage. And any proposals that would come after Armendis was wed and living elsewhere would be spurned by her father. Hebert has too much need for her at home."

"Did you kill your mother?" Sir Jean-Luc shouted at her.

"No, no," she wailed. "I did poison Mendy's food, but only what was brought to her while she was a prisoner. Not her meat pie. I did this to spare her from being tortured. She is my sister, my only sister."

The seneschal flicked a hand at her. "Attempting to forestall the *visconte's* justice is a crime." He stared at Raimunda, considering her a moment before saying, "Though I think the punishment will be less than hanging."

The seneschal then smiled at the alchemist. "She tried to kill her sister and failed. Her motive does have a modicum of kindness in it. But trying to subvert the *visconte's* law is serious. Whipping her in public should provide a suitable example. The law must be upheld."

The alchemist grimaced. "But charity, sir, had nothing to do with her motive. She was merely trying to save her own neck by killing her sister."

"Why would she bother to kill her sister if not to spare her pain?" the *visconte* asked. "She had only to wait for Armendis to be hanged for the murder of her mother."

"My lord, Armendis's memory of what happened on the day she was drugged is returning. She might remember something damning to Raimunda."

"Let me not lose all of my daughters?" Hebert cried.

"And what of Sibilia?" the master asked.

The seneschal shrugged. "Was Armendis not free when this girl was killed?"

After a moment of silence, Sir Jean-Luc growled at Hebert, "You, peasant, have failed to manage your womenfolk and household appropriately. Perhaps your holdings should be given to someone who is stronger and more efficient."

"No." Hebert fell to his knees and threw his arms apart, pleading with the *visconte* for mercy.

"I think," the *visconte* said and paused. The room became so quiet Bertwoin could hear the *bayle's* breathing. "That the father bears some responsibility for this girl's impertinence. She shall spend an afternoon in the pillory and be shamed appropriately. The farmer shall pay a fine equal to one gold coin."

The seneschal praised this judgment with a celebratory laugh.

Hebert cried out, "So much?"

Bertwoin understood that the *visconte* not only knew that his Uncle Josse had found the pot of gold coins, but also knew how much money his Aunt Guillema had given to Hebert. His web of spies was as good as, and maybe better, than Na Thea's informants.

"But, my lord," the master protested.

The *visconte* raised his hand. "I appreciate your efforts on maintaining justice in my lands, goldsmith, but I do not find your evidence persuasive."

"And Armendis, my lord?"

"She remains accused of the heinous crime of killing her mother, and if found guilty, will be punished accordingly."

CHAPTER XXXV.

Two days later, while Bertwoin was shoveling mule manure from a handcart onto their dung heap, he realized someone stood behind him. He turned to see wiry Hugon watching him with disapproval. The bearded boatbuilder looked as if he had been sleeping in the woods. Bertwoin could almost feel the lice on him, and Hugon's bare feet—white with cold—made him shiver.

"You're welcome here," he told Hugon.

The boatbuilder ignored his greeting and muttered, "I hear tell the alchemist laid the blame for the killing of my girl on Raimunda. I also hear Raimunda was let go and is now back at home. Is their truth in that?"

"The *visconte* and seneschal don't believe she killed her mother or your daughter. And Raimunda denies doing so."

"But the master still believes it was her doing?"

"He does, but he has no solid evidence against her, nothing that the citadel will accept."

"The master's word is good enough for me." Hugon strode away, but turned back after four slouching steps. "You didn't name the killer for me like we agreed."

"She was *judged* as not guilty."

"But you agree with the alchemist, don't you?"

"My opinion means no more than a puff of wind."

Hugon spat on the ground and walked away.

Bertwoin finished emptying the two-wheeled handcart and stored it along with their wooden shovel in the barn. Did Hugon still believe he and Flowia might have led the killer to his daughter? Feeling uneasy, he went into their kitchen to warm himself and to appease the gnawing emptiness in his stomach. Rachel and his *maman* sat at the table, their heads bent over the cabbage and carrots and turnips they were cutting.

"Who do you think is feeding Armendis?" he asked. "I doubt anyone, not even Hebert, would trust Raimunda to prepare food for her. Not now."

"Guillema," his *maman* answered, her tone letting him know this was not a guess.

Bertwoin settled into the contented warmth of their kitchen and ate a bowl of stew kept hot on the hearth. He wondered what he would do if he lived in Hebert's *ostal*.

"Raimunda!" he said, realizing the boatbuilder might not be on his way home. Deep in the marrow of his bones, he knew what Hugon, half-crazed with grief, would do now.

Did Raimunda deserve whatever punishment came to her? It was still possible she hadn't killed her mother. Maybe she hadn't even drowned her little brother. She was just a girl at the time. Also, Hugon might get himself hung if he killed her.

Bertwoin slammed the front door behind him and began running. If only he had realized earlier where Hugon would go.

When he reached Hebert's farm, the winter sun was well above the horizon's mountain tops. The house looked empty and forlorn. The geese in the poultry yard backed into a corner and huddled there, watching him and making no noise. That was strange. He knocked on the front door, paused for two breaths, then slipped inside the house.

The hearth fire had died out, leaving the long front room and kitchen cold. He left the door open for light. The kitchen table lay on its side, and two clay bowls had fallen on the dirt floor. He then saw Raimunda's head lying on the bare dirt floor with her body hidden behind the table's top.

He touched his knife for reassurance and listened, but heard no one moving about. Was Hugon gone? Where was Hebert?

He crept toward the kitchen, checking the side rooms as he went, and blunted his feelings. Raimunda lay curled on the floor, her woolen tunic stiff with blood. Bertwoin shivered. Hugon had stabbed her over and over again.

He moved away, gulped deep breaths, and relaxed his muscles to calm himself. Had Hugon killed Hebert too?

He lit a candle and checked the side rooms. Nothing. He went up the ladder, but the *solier* was also empty. He went outside, where the geese still huddled in a corner. Somehow, they knew something unsettling had happened.

He searched the barn and farm, including the copse of chestnut trees where Ermessen was murdered, but he didn't find Hebert. Maybe he was with his sheep.

Good. There was luck in the farmer being gone. It allowed Bertwoin to do what he must do. He must hurry. If he was caught, the seneschal, who had little liking for him, might choose to think he was Raimunda's killer.

He ran back to the house. While searching for Hebert, he had seen a crude poppet lying on an oak trunk in Raimunda's bedroom. He brought the doll and the woolen blanket on Raimunda's bed into the kitchen. He spread the blanket on the dirt floor, rolled her cold body onto it, and wrapped the corpse in it to keep blood from getting on his clothes.

Bertwoin lugged her and the wooden poppet to the chestnut copse and laid Raimunda exactly where her mother had been found. He then pulled his knife, took a breath, and cut away her tunic. Hugon, enraged, had done most of the work for him. Seven deep stab wounds covered her chest and belly. Her forearms were slashed. Unlike her mother, she had not been caught unawares and had tried to protect herself.

Gritting his teeth, he slit her throat—a bloodless wound—and laid the doll between her ample breasts.

Hebert would see as soon as he entered his house that someone had fought and bled in his kitchen. He would go looking for Raimunda and find her exactly as Guillema had found Ermessen.

Now to get back home before anyone saw him. Bertwoin ran along a footpath, carrying the blanket and bloody tunic with him. He would bury them in the woods somewhere on the way home. He felt more and more relieved the farther he got from Hebert's accursed farm.

CHAPTER XXXVI.

The next afternoon, a quiet day muffled by mist, Bertwoin sat huddled on an oak stump under the leafless elm that stood halfway between their barn and cottage. He was skinning a squirrel while two magpies, hoping to eat the guts, perched above him. They cawed to encourage him.

When he glanced across their fields, he saw Flowia coming toward him. Joy shivered through him. Then he remembered that her coming meant poor Hebert had discovered Raimunda's body. The man, loathsome as he was, deserved some pity. He had lost all of his women, even Armendis, who was the only one still alive.

Bertwoin hoped he hadn't left any clues behind, and that no one had seen him running away from Hebert's *ostal*.

At least this time, Flowia wouldn't have to endure torment from Laurence. His father, *maman*, and uncle were away at the market in Montredon and had taken Maud with them. They had gone more to talk and laugh with neighbors than to barter goods. Both Rachel and Wilfraed were visiting the families they were going to marry into.

Flowia glided up to him and kissed his cheek. She smiled when he beamed at her. He took her in his arms, and she snuggled against him, but only for a few warm breaths before she pushed him away, her manner abruptly solemn. "Another murder has occurred."

As if surprised, he winced. "Is it like the others?"

"We don't know. The *bayle* sent a boy who knew nothing more than to tell us that there was another body, and we were to come to Hebert's *ostal*. The master is already on his way there. We must hurry."

He held up the dead squirrel. "Let me store this, then I'm at your service, my lady." He raised the carcass higher for the magpies to see. "No guts today, you rascals."

The alchemist stood at the front gate, his face a weathered mask of resignation. "I still await the *bayle's* coming. It's Raimunda this time. She was killed in the house but found in the same place where her mother lay. It seems this killer means to well and truly punish Hebert."

"Was he not here?" Bertwoin asked.

"He was away, courting Widow Cabrol." The master waved at the front door. "She's here now, fully occupied in the house. When Hebert discovered the body, he immediately ran to her for help. She sent one of her sons to notify the *bayle* and has taken command of the body. She reminds me of Na Guillema."

"Is it the same murderer?" Flowia asked.

"It seems so." The alchemist's solemn eyes appraised Bertwoin. "Perhaps I should not have called you out—" He squinted down the main path. "Ah, luck is with us. Here comes the lawman now."

The *bayle* moseyed toward them with two men, one pushing a two-wheeled handcart.

"You intend to transport the body somewhere?" the master asked when the lawman stopped at the gate.

The *bayle* grumbled, "Sir Jean-Luc wants to examine it."

"Well, it awaits you inside the house. Hebert is in there, along with Widow Cabrol and her entire brood."

"Same murderer?"

"That appears to be the situation. Frenzied attack with a knife, a naked corpse, the victim's throat was slit, and a doll placed on the body."

The lawman made the sign of the cross over the crusader's rood stitched on his chest. He sighed and jerked his chin at one of the men. "Gefrei, bring out the body and let's get back to the citadel."

The two men shoved the pushcart into the poultry yard and barged into the house.

"You don't need to examine the body?" the alchemist asked the lawman.

"You've already done that for me, and I take your word to be true."

"Yet the seneschal wishes to see the body himself?"

"It's not us he doubts. He wants to inspect the body for unnatural signs of witchcraft. The bishop is sniffing around these murders. The last thing we want is churchmen interfering in our business." He shook his head in mock despair. "We need all the help we can get, don't we, old man? We each picked one of Hebert's daughters to blame, and both of us got it wrong. His two daughters are innocent."

"Will Armendis now be set free?"

Bertwoin watched the men haul Raimunda's corpse out into the poultry yard and lay it on the cart. It wore a tunic that, no doubt, the widow had put on her.

The *bayle* blew out his breath. "Makes you think, doesn't it? Just five days ago, she was alive and talking with us in the Great Hall. Armendis, on the other hand, is lucky the seneschal hasn't yet found time to make her confess." He smiled at Bertwoin. "My guess is she'll soon be free to marry your cousin. Armendis got lucky twice. Hebert mightn't have let her go if he hadn't gotten the widow's attention."

"If Armendis has any sense," Flowia said, "she'll live with Bertwoin's aunt instead of going home."

"Which one? Oh, you mean Na Guillema." The *bayle* nodded. "Though I'm told the other aunt is also very fond of the girl." He shook his head. "Melisende now has trouble of her own. Artal has taken to his bed. I'm told fire blazes in his belly and bowels. Word is he might not be walking above the ground much longer."

Was his Aunt Meli punishing Artal for kidnapping Armendis and for the great harm he had caused his daughter? Had Meli used some of Na Thea's powerful herbs to cause this sickness? Bertwoin doubted they would be deadly, but his uncle would suffer. He glanced at Flowia and saw she looked pleased.

The lawman asked Gefrei, who stood beside the cart. "Who found her?"

"Hebert. Came home from the widow's place to find an empty house. Went looking for his daughter and found her in the same place where her mother was found. Ran back to Widow Cabrol so she could come and take charge of everything."

"Ah well," the alchemist said. "We're of little help to you here."

The *bayle* asked, "So, are you going to find this killer?"

The alchemist shrugged. "Only if I'm told to do so."

The lawman yawned. When the alchemist understood that the ex-crusader had nothing more to say, he nodded goodbye, and they left. No one spoke until they came out of the woods and turned onto a track along the river.

"You know who did this, don't you?" Flowia asked the master.

"I think I do."

"You do?" Bertwoin asked.

They trudged along in silence as they passed a couple coming back from the market with the woman holding a goose tight under her arm.

"Were there any clues?" Bertwoin asked, keeping his voice calm.

"None that will provide enough proof to satisfy the seneschal. We must look at why she was killed. Revenge? Probably. So Hebert didn't do it. He doesn't believe Raimunda killed her mother. Na Guillema had sufficient reason and anger to kill Raimunda, but unless rage gave her monstrous strength, I think the stab wounds show a man's strength. I hear Hugon is almost insane with grief."

Bertwoin asked him, "Will you bring him to justice?"

"I will decline to do so, though hanging might be kinder than allowing him to live as prey to the demons that now plague him. Perhaps in this case, where the citadel failed to provide justice, this revenge is the only form of justice he and Sibilia will receive."

CHAPTER XXXVII.

Bertwoin's *maman* walked out to him while he was chopping wood. "Maud is lively enough, but she still has diarrhea and a raw throat. I need Flowia's help, and I'm too busy to fetch her. Bring her here."

Bertwoin laid the axe on the stump and stood a moment, trying to figure out how to slip Flowia in and out of their household without his uncle seeing her. If he failed, and Laurence attacked her, he was determined to defend her this time, even if it meant a brawl.

Seeing him hesitate, his *maman* clamped her hands on her hipbones and thrust her head forward as if she would to peck him. "I came to know Flowia a bit while we sat by your sick bed at Guillema's. She cares about you. I *don't* need your father's permission. Get going."

"I'm going, I'm going. I was just paralyzed with shock that you'd changed your opinion." He dodged her slap and trotted toward the woods, laughing.

Flowia decided that another dose of wormwood for Maud's bowels and a throat-soother were needed. So she stuffed leaves and a jar of honey in a small pouch and returned with Bertwoin. He led her into the front room of his home and stopped. Guillema, Meli, and Rachel were combing wool in the kitchen while his *maman* used a drop spindle to turn a long sleever of fibers into yarn.

Meli laughed. "You can close your mouth, Ox."

"It's a pleasant surprise."

An uncut loaf of maslin lay on the kitchen table, a gift no doubt from Guillema. They all smiled at Flowia.

His *maman* said, "Welcome, maiden," and hurried forward to hug her.

Bertwoin stared down at the reeds covering the hard-packed dirt floor so no one would notice his eyes had blurred with sudden tears. His *maman* had just welcomed Flowia into their *ostal* as if she were a dear friend.

When Flowia came into the kitchen, both of his aunts also hugged her, as did Rachel. Meli said, "We just stopped by on our way to Montredon. We need to tend to our mother's gravesite and get her blessing."

Bertwoin remembered he still owed the Church the price of a candle. "Her blessing?"

Meli stared at a wall, lost in reverie, her face radiant.

A little smile played on Guillema's lips. "Meli has something that now steals away her thoughts. You will soon have another cousin."

"What? That's great." So Na Thea's fertility remedy had worked. Would it be a boy or a girl? "Did you drink warm wine or cool water?"

His Aunt Meli chuckled. "I'm not pregnant, Ox. One of Artal's cousins is having a baby she can't keep. We will raise the child as our own."

"That's great."

Meli glowed as if she had seen the face of God. Bertwoin assumed his aunts were going to visit his dead grandmother to get her blessing and protection for the baby's birth. He glanced at Rachel. Soon she would be married. How long before she too visited the grave? The idea of being an uncle pleased him. If it was a boy, he might someday teach his young nephew how to plow a straight furrow.

Bertwoin smiled at the warm thought of his grandmother thwarting his pigheaded father. "Grandmother answered my prayer too."

Guillema nodded. "Mother still watches over us."

Flowia's expression turned somber. "How is Armendis faring?"

His aunts glanced at each other, their gaiety gone. "It will take a long time," Guillema said. "For all of us."

So Armendis was already free. He assumed she was living with Guillema instead of Hebert. Her father probably didn't care now. Widow Cabrol would soon marry him and move in with her children.

"Does Armendis need medicine to dispel her black mood?" Flowia asked.

Guillema shook her head. "Na Thea sees to her, body and spirit. And we see that she's never alone. Jehan keeps her company when we're not there."

Flowia dipped her head. "Then she has the best of care." Her smile turned grave and sly. "You've heard of the outrage at the winery in Pennautier, have you not?"

Bertwoin frowned. Why had Flowia shoved the conversation away from Armendis?

"Outrage?" Meli asked.

"Yes," Flowia said with a knowing smile. "A young man who worked there was attacked and castrated."

"Oh," he said. He felt a pang in his groin. In a backhanded way, Flowia hadn't changed the subject. One of Armendis's rapists had been punished.

Did Flowia think his aunts had set aside their religious beliefs to punish a rapist? He doubted that, though he knew they had the grit to do the gelding and the smarts to not get caught afterwards.

Meli eyed him, expecting him to say something. He shrugged. "Did he deserve castration?"

Guillema wobbled her head. "More so than Armendis deserved to be raped."

Bertwoin felt a sickening twitch in his stomach. Had one of his aunts held the rapist down while the other did the cutting? Had anyone helped them? Jehan? Artal? No, not Artal. He was still laid low with a sick gut.

But how had they known who to attack? He was the only one who had seen the two men enter the hut. But no! No, that was wrong. One other person could identify them—Armendis. She knew much better than he did what they looked like.

So, had she gone with his aunts? Had she watched the rapist writhe under the knife? Was it *her* knife that had cut away the bastard's manhood?

"That vineyard," he announced, "is a dangerous place."

"For everyone," Guillema agreed.

"Do you think this is the end of it?" he asked. "Sometimes one crime leads to another one."

"Who can tell," Meli said.

So they were still looking for the other rapist. "Maybe the master will look into this."

That wiped the smiles off their faces. Why had he spoiled the mood by not keeping his mouth shut? Everyone turned to Flowia, the expert on the alchemist.

She shook her head. "I doubt he'll bother with this crime. He hasn't stepped forward to help the *bayle* solve Raimunda's murder. And, will the rapist even bring this matter to the law?

Does he want everyone to know he is now a eunuch? Does he want people asking why someone would castrate him?"

Guillema patted Flowia's shoulder. They began talking, all of them relaxed in each other's company. Their delight in being together was as clear to Bertwoin as spring water. His presence was tolerated, but it wasn't necessary. He considered going out to the barn but decided instead to sit out of the way in the front room where he could enjoy watching Flowia laugh with the female side of his family.

While they chatted, mainly about Meli's getting a baby, Flowia brewed wormwood tea. She handed his *maman* a mugful of the medicine and told her to have Maud drink all of it. She also gave his *maman* the small jar of honey to coat and heal Maud's raw throat.

"Oh, my throat hurts too," Meli whimpered, then cackled.

Bertwoin watched Flowia, at ease and her eyes shining, sit with part of his family. If only he could make this permanent.

The women discussed the three upcoming weddings in their family—his sister Rachel's to Eudes the cook, his cousin Jehan's to wounded Armendis, and his brother Wilfraed's to shy Maria. He wished they were also talking about his marriage to feisty Flowia.

His father and uncle breezed in through the front door. They stopped and stared at the enclave of smiling women, then both of them aimed their eyes at Flowia. All levity leaked out of the kitchen.

"Maud," his *maman* explained to his father.

He nodded, then scanned the group. "It takes so many?"

"Needs three witches, I guess," Laurence said. He glowered at his sisters and Flowia. Then he scowled at Meli. "Shouldn't you be at home tending to your ailing husband?"

"Ah, he's too ornery to die and too miserable to know he's lying in his own puke."

Laurence stared at her with his mouth open. Meli smiled at him as if he were a cockroach, one she would step on and cripple, but not kill outright. She would let him writhe awhile before she squashed him.

Now all doubts were gone. Bertwoin knew his aunts had somehow caught and castrated one of the rapists. If the other rapist wanted to keep his manhood, he needed to become an outlaw shepherd-in the mountains or a soldier in some far-off place.

If Laurence didn't shut up, his sisters might punish him too. Meli sat as calm as a nun with a little devilish smile on her face.

Bertwoin made the sign of the Holy Cross. *Spare me from those we think are weak.*

Flowia rose. "I need to tend to Maud."

His *maman* followed her into the bedroom. His uncle poured himself a cup of ale, then stood frowning at the bedroom door while sipping his drink.

His father limped into the front room and dropped onto the bench beside Bertwoin. "You look like you've seen a ghost, boy."

"Not yet. But if Laurence doesn't keep his tongue still, he might become one."

"Ah, Meli won't kill him. He's family."

"Shouldn't that go both ways? Shouldn't he treat her better? She *is* his sister. And it'll save him from getting a bellyful of poison."

His father grunted. "I might mention that to him."

"No one knows what she's really capable of doing."

His father leaned away from him, eyeing him. "So you know about Artal's ailment and the boy with no balls?"

"You do?"

"I wasn't in on Artal's coming down sick."

"So *you* took care of the rapist?"

"Partially. Were *you* going to do what needed to be done? And Jehan doesn't have the stomach for it. It's not healthy to abuse any woman in our family or who means to come into our family," he boasted. "We'll cut off body parts if need be."

"And you did this alone?"

His father weighed his thoughts before saying, "Hugon wanted to help. So he held the boy down while I gelded him. He was fond of Armendis. She *was* Sibilia's best friend."

Bertwoin leaned back against the daubed wall, breathing hard, and studied his father's scarred face. No, he wasn't making this up to tease him. He asked, "Do your sisters know you did this?"

Pleased with himself, his father chuckled. "Never think that they're fools."

Bertwoin laughed. He would never do that.

"Jehan was the one who should've done the deed," his *papa* continued, "but he doesn't have the experience or grit to do it properly. I thought about recruiting you at first, but decided to ask Hugon instead. Why pick silver when there's gold to be had? Let me tell you, Hugon is still bloated with black rage. It took work on my part to keep him from killing the bastard." His father rubbed his jaw while eyeing him. "Though you might make a brawler yet. Killed those outlaws."

Bertwoin didn't mention that Flowia had sent one of them to hell. Bringing her name up right now might sour their conversation.

"You look like you don't approve of what I did," his father said.

"Just surprised, is all."

"You don't know me better than that? My sisters hinted that they wanted this done. Also, Jehan is my nephew. Artal is family, and the girl is his daughter and will be my niece. They're family. And family is all the good we have in this world. If I asked my sisters to do the same for me, they'd do it. Don't ever forget that."

When Flowia came out of the bedroom, Laurence hurried to the front door and opened it for her—a clear invitation for her to leave and stay gone.

His *maman* again hugged Flowia, which surprised his father and disgusted his uncle. Bertwoin rose and went out through the doorway ahead of her.

"Where are *you* going?" Laurence called.

He ignored his uncle and fell into step beside Flowia. Behind them, the door slapped shut.

Flowia was crying, so he put an arm around her shoulders and pulled her close to his side. They shuffled along awkwardly together. "Oh, Flo. Just be deaf to what he says."

She laughed, the tears trickling down her cheeks. "Don't be silly. These are halleluiah tears." She ducked out from under his arm and skipped two steps. "Your *maman* accepts me. She accepts *me*."

She pulled a chain out of the top of her dress. A silver piece like the one Bertwoin wore dangled from it. She held it up in front of her. "Are you wearing the piece the master gave you?"

"Of course." He pulled the thong out of the neck of his tunic.

She put the two silver pieces together.

He blew out his breath. "They match. They form a heart?"

She kissed him. He slipped her delicate hand into his and led her into the forest.

The End

Did you enjoy *The Virgin Provoked*? If so, please leave a review or rating (it's like clapping after listening to someone sing) and tell your friends. You might also enjoy Bertwoin and Flowia's earlier adventures: *The Plowman's Plight* and *The Wrathful Cup of Scorn*.

Other books by E. A. Rivière:

Magic and Murder Among the Dwarves
The Dwarf Assassin

E. A. Rivière

The author lives in a magical forest where mice claiming to be cousins move in for the winter then take the towels when they leave in spring. He is a winner in the Writers of the Future contest, a graduate of the six-week Odyssey Fantasy Writing Workshop, and a grand prize winner of the Sidney Lanier Poetry Competition.

His paranormal mysteries *Magic and Murder Among the Dwarves* and *The Dwarf Assassin* are also available.

Unlike many writers, he doesn't keep a cat in deference to his mouse cousins and because he couldn't live up to its expectations.

ACKNOWLEDGEMENTS

Appreciation is due to:

Barbara Campbell for professional editing that turned a flawed manuscript into a one readers might like.

Frances at 100 Covers for creating an exciting cover that fitted nicely into this medieval mysteries series.

Eleanor Bundy, my beta reader, who kept me from embarrassing myself.